PRAISE FOR TI
COLIN CA..ıı ᴅᴇʟʟ

"Very real. And very good." —Lee Child

"There's nothing soft about Campbell's writing. If you enjoy your crime fiction hard-boiled, the Jim Grant series is a must read."
—Bruce Robert Coffin

"A cop with a sharp eye, keen mind, and a lion's heart."
—Reed Farrel Coleman

"Campbell writes smart, rollercoaster tales with unstoppable forward momentum and thrilling authenticity."
—Nick Petrie

"Grim and gritty and packed with action."
—*Kirkus Review*

"The pages fly like the bullets, fistfights and one-liners that make this one of my favorite books of the year. Top stuff!"
—Matt Hilton

"Sets up immediately and maintains a breakneck pace through-out. Its smart structure and unrelenting suspense will please Lee Child fans."
—*Library Journal Review*

"This is police procedural close-up and personal. A strong debut with enough gritty realism to make your eyes water, and a few savage laughs along the way."
—Reginald Hill

SWING GANG

BOOKS BY COLIN CAMPBELL

The Jim Grant Thrillers
Jamaica Plain
Montecito Heights
Adobe Flats
Snake Pass
Beacon Hill
Shelter Cove
Catawba Point

The Vince McNulty Thrillers
Northern Ex
Final Cut
Tracking Shot
Swing Gang

The Grant & McNulty Thrillers
Forced Perspective

Short Stories
Permission Granted

The UK Crime Series
Blue Knight White Cross
Ballad of the One Legged Man
Through the Ruins of Midnight

Children
Gargoyles—Skylights and Roofscapes

Horror
Darkwater Towers

COLIN CAMPBELL

SWING GANG

Down & Out Books
3959 Van Dyke Road, Suite 265
Lutz, FL 33558
DownAndOutBooks.com

Cover design by Colin Campbell

ISBN: 1-64396-268-X
ISBN-13: 978-1-64396-268-9

For The Readers
You've stuck with me so far.
Let's take the next step...

PART ONE
FOUND

"It's not procedures you pay me for. It's attitude."
—Vince McNulty

CHAPTER ONE

"In hindsight, I think we should have stayed in Boston."

"Thought you always wanted to be Mister Hollywood."

Larry Unger looked at his technical adviser. "Do you know how much they charge for location services in Los Angeles?"

Vince McNulty kept quiet. This wasn't the time to give technical advice.

"Not to mention there're more homeless whack jobs than pink poodles."

Unger threw McNulty a sideways glance. "I saw one the other day, had little pink booties and a lace bonnet."

"A homeless guy?"

Unger raised his eyebrows. "A poodle. Pink fucking booties." He let out a lung-emptying sigh. "No. It was better being a big fish in a small pond."

McNulty looked at the man in charge of Titanic Productions. "Larry. You were never a big fish."

Unger looked hurt. "Big enough to hire an ex-cop from the U-K who doesn't have the first clue about police procedures in the U-S."

McNulty shrugged. "It's not procedures you pay me for. It's attitude."

Unger turned to McNulty. Being short and round, he was facing McNulty's chest. "Yeah well, it was teaching Alfonse

3

attitude that made him go find a bigger studio."

McNulty had taught Alfonse Bayard to stop walking like a duck and a few other things, and now the actor who'd starred in Titanic Productions's breakout cop movies had jumped ship. Some of the reason might have been the confident attitude he'd learned from McNulty, but most of it was Larry Unger's trying to keep the actor on the cheap. Cheap was Larry's middle name. McNulty glanced across the street where the arc lights and filters were being angled toward the mouth of an alley. A hulking figure split from the rest of the crew and started across the street.

McNulty nodded in the figure's direction. "Looks like the new fella wants to talk."

Larry watched as his new actor muscled his way toward them. "Vince. You're gonna have to stop this guy walking like a bulldozer."

It was a night shoot, filming in Hollywood but not the glamorous Hollywood you see in the newsreels. They were set up on North Alexandria Avenue just off Hollywood Boulevard. Even Hollywood Boulevard wasn't the one showcased on Oscar night—at least not the part of Hollywood Boulevard where they hosted the red-carpet event. There were homeless people sleeping rough every three blocks alongside artistic graffiti recalling the Armenian genocide. Little Armenia was just across the street. Little Titanic Productions was around the back of the Papillon International Bakery and the Hollywood Collision Center. The alleyway led to the entrance of the body shop. McNulty reckoned that half the cars being chopped and changed were stolen, but he kept reminding himself he wasn't a cop anymore. In this location, Larry Unger didn't have to remind himself that he was the big-shot producer of a tinpot movie company.

"What does the big lug want now?"

McNulty watched Dennis Charles Buchinsky march across the street. "He wants you, not me."

Unger shook his head. "You're the one supposed to make him walk like a cop."

McNulty waved a finger. "And you're the one made his character a fireman who fights crime in his spare time."

Unger's shoulders sagged. "Not in his spare time. He's a fire investigator who gets caught up in crimes as part of his job."

"Then he should call the police and have them deal with it."

Unger shook his head. "But then we'd be a generic cop movie instead of something fresh."

McNulty smiled. "The only thing fresh is the dog shit he just stepped in."

They both watched the muscle-bound hulk as he scraped his shoe on the curb. He was so top-heavy with his broad shoulders and narrow waist that he was having trouble balancing on one leg. He rested a hand on a telephone pole just below a flyer for a missing dog, a poodle that didn't look big enough to have shit the turd currently clogging Buchinsky's footwear.

Unger felt his shoulders sag even more. "You're going to have to do something about his balance, as well."

McNulty shrugged. "Maybe you can employ an ex-firefighter."

Unger pulled himself to his full height, which wasn't much. "I employed you." He turned his palms upward. "You must have been to some fires as a cop. Improvise." He drew his shoulders back and puffed out his chest. "Teach him the attitude."

Buchinsky stopped cleaning his shoe and was about to make his approach when the director called from behind the camera.

"Chuck. Ready for position one."

The actor looked at his producer then back toward his director, comical indecision on his face. At least that meant he could show emotion. Unger shook his head and looked at the sky.

"And please god, don't let them put Chuck Buchinsky on the poster."

McNulty wasn't listening. He wasn't even there. He'd spotted movement out of the corner of his eye and was squeezing between the arc lights and the wall of the alleyway. Half of the Hollywood

Collision Center parking lot was in darkness and the other half was bathed in filtered light. It was the dark half that concerned him. Something had glinted in the shadows then stopped as soon as McNulty looked its way. In addition to his job as technical adviser, McNulty was in charge of set security, which meant not letting visitors sneak onto the set.

He walked slowly toward the dark side of the lot, careful not to trip over the spare auto parts stored in the far corner. He moved a hand to his belt before remembering he didn't carry a flashlight or handcuffs anymore. That life was gone. If this was somebody stripping car parts, McNulty would just have to warn them with a few harsh words.

He stood in the darkness and let his eyes adjust near a stack of boxes covered by a tarpaulin. The edge fluttered, then stopped. He took two steps then reached for the corner and flicked it up. The eyes that blinked back at him weren't those of a car thief or a burglar. They belonged to a scared child, cowering in the shadows.

CHAPTER TWO

Amy Moore coaxed the girl, who looked to be about ten, out from under the tarpaulin with a mug of hot chocolate and a winning smile. The Titanic Productions makeup lady had a very winning smile. It was part of the reason McNulty had fallen for her, despite not wanting to get involved with someone he worked with. The other part was that she had a kind heart and a dry sense of humor. The kind heart came through in the winning smile. The smile had done more than the hot chocolate, but the girl drank it anyway. Amy glanced at McNulty, who was kneeling behind her.

"We need to call the police."

The girl dropped the styrofoam cup and backed into the shadows. Amy held up a calming hand.

"Or maybe not."

In the end the *maybe not* won out. That and the offer of marshmallows with the hot chocolate. Amy enticed the girl away from the makeshift shelter and shielded her from the crew as she crossed Hollywood Boulevard on the way to the makeup trailer. Titanic Productions had set up location services at a strip mall at the intersection of Hollywood and Alexandria. The illuminated sign advertising Thrifty Dry Cleaners and the L.A.

Smoke Shop was dark. Atlantic Services Tax Center and the Hollywood Coin Op Laundry were closed. Nobody was getting a haircut at the Speedy Barber Shop at this time of night. A ten-year-old girl shouldn't have been hiding under a tarpaulin at two in the morning, either, but she was. The world was full of injustices. McNulty had seen too many of them, both as a cop in West Yorkshire, and before that, as a boy at Crag View Children's Home.

"You want me to get some food from Craft Services?"

McNulty was talking to Amy, but it was the girl who nodded her head. Amy smiled down at her, fighting the urge to put an arm around her shoulder. The girl didn't look ready for physical comforting just yet. She'd pulled back with a sharp jerk when Amy draped the blanket over her. Direct conversation wasn't an option, so Amy had kept it light and indirect, talking to McNulty so the girl wouldn't feel pressured to speak.

"Who'd have thought Larry would invest in location catering?"

McNulty knew what she was doing and played along.

"Yeah, he was just complaining about the cost of going Hollywood."

Amy nodded.

"Good thing he did." She smiled at the girl again. "Or you wouldn't have marshmallows with your hot chocolate."

The girl didn't smile back. She sucked a warm soft marshmallow from the top of her drink and chewed. McNulty watched the hard expression melt as the girl sucked another marshmallow. He tried not to think of another girl, who had only stared at him, a long time ago in the headmaster's office. He continued the charade of talking to Amy instead of directing questions to the girl.

"Do you think she'd prefer a pulled pork sandwich…"

The girl shivered and lowered her head.

"…or a burger and onion rings?"

Her head came up and her eyes brightened. Amy noticed the look and spoke to McNulty while watching the girl.

"She'd probably like some ketchup or mayo with that."
The girl couldn't resist a gentle nod of the head. Twice.
"Maybe both."
A more vigorous nod.
"And a Pepsi."
Almost a smile now. Amy turned soft eyes on McNulty and gave him a gentle nod of her own. McNulty let out a sigh.
"Healthy diet like that." He shook his head. "We just lost the vote for Parents of the Year."

Larry Unger was waiting for him outside the makeup trailer, trying to look cool by leaning against a lamppost. With the light shining on him from above he looked like Danny DeVito as *The Exorcist* on the iconic movie poster. He pushed off from the lamppost and blocked McNulty's path.
"What are you doing?"
McNulty didn't try and push past him.
"Getting a burger with onion rings."
All semblance of cool evaporated.
"With the girl."
McNulty jerked a thumb toward the makeup trailer.
"I'm not doing anything. Amy's looking after her."
Unger looked exasperated.
"Amy's the makeup lady."
McNulty stepped around Unger, heading toward the catering truck.
"Maybe she's showing her how to put on makeup."
Unger fell in step beside his technical adviser.
"She's too young to wear makeup."
McNulty stopped and faced the producer.
"She's too young to be living in a cardboard box, as well."
Unger shrugged.
"So? Call the police and let them deal with it."
McNulty tilted his head and gave Unger a blank look.

"Like your firefighter?"

Unger didn't back off.

"That's creative licence."

McNulty started toward the catering truck again.

"Well, *I'm* using creative licence."

Unger tried to keep up, but his stride wasn't as long as McNulty's. It felt like he was always playing catch-up with the Yorkshire ex-cop.

"That's the movies. Doesn't work like that in real life."

McNulty stopped at the bottom of the stairs to the serving hatch.

"I know about real life."

Unger rested a hand on McNulty's forearm and lowered his voice.

"You can't save everyone."

That brought McNulty up short. He remembered Donkey Flowers telling him that back when they were tilting at the Northern X massage chain. A world away and a lifetime ago. His response hadn't changed.

"Saving one is enough."

Unger kept his hand on McNulty's forearm.

"This angry man survivor guilt's got to stop sometime, you know."

McNulty forced a smile.

"I'm not angry."

Unger moved his hand and tapped McNulty's chest.

"In there. At yourself."

He felt McNulty tense, so he stepped back, holding his hands in the air.

"You found your sister. Everything worked out."

McNulty looked down at Unger.

"You reckon?"

Unger let out a sigh. Now he understood. Some things you can put behind you but not the things you carry the blame for. He lowered his hands.

"The thing that happened to Jim Grant." He shook his head. "That wasn't your fault."

CHAPTER THREE

The burger was a treat. The girl was almost as engrossed in the juicy sandwich as she was in the onion rings hanging from her thumb. Classic soundtracks from the James Bond movies and Clint Eastwood's spaghetti westerns played from hidden speakers above the makeup mirror, music intended to take the actors' minds off the boring makeup process. The bulbs around the mirror were turned off but the music played on. It covered the hushed voices as McNulty and Amy discussed what to do with the girl. Whispers always arouse suspicion. McNulty didn't want to scare the girl any more than she already was. The repeating tones of "Ecstasy of Gold" from *The Good, The Bad And The Ugly* soothed the tension. McNulty looked at Amy.

"You sure about this?"

What Amy was sure about didn't happen until Titanic Productions wrapped the night shoot and struck the set. The swing gang removed the signs and set dressing that had turned the Hollywood Collision Center into Valley Repairs, and McNulty made sure the lights and camera equipment were safely loaded onto the location transports. Making sure nothing went missing was another part of his job. Running interference for Amy Moore was something extra.

The trucks rumbled out of the strip mall parking lot and headed toward the production base on Cahuenga Boulevard. McNulty kept Larry Unger talking about tomorrow's location while Amy kept the girl in the makeup trailer as it slipped into the convoy between the camera truck and Craft Services. By the time McNulty jumped onto the last truck the girl was long gone.

"You can have the bed. I'll sleep over here."

Amy turned the lights on and closed the door. Her room at the Pilgrim Motel was the same as everyone else's, big and square with a queen-size bed, a built-in wardrobe and a chest of drawers. It was designated as an executive suite because it had a settee instead of a chair and a more luxurious bathroom. Luxurious wasn't very luxurious but the settee was big enough to sleep on.

"Do you want a shower before bed?"

The girl huddled into the blanket that was still draped over her shoulders. Amy nodded. Not everyone liked showers.

"A bath then?"

The girl shook her head. Amy wondered what had led a ten-year-old girl to be sleeping rough on Hollywood Boulevard and came up with one scenario that sent a shiver down her spine. That would explain why the girl didn't want to get naked in front of a stranger. Even so, after a night spent under canvas in the wrecker's yard a little freshening up was required.

"There's toiletries in the bathroom."

Amy stayed near the front door.

"You can have a wash and clean your teeth. I'll wait here."

The girl looked at the makeup lady then at the bathroom door. Warm water and fresh breath must have worked its magic because she nodded and went inside. The door clicked shut behind her and Amy let out a sigh. She hadn't realized she'd been holding her breath. Turning to the window she peered out through the curtains and wondered what McNulty was doing.

* * *

McNulty was standing in the dark, trying not to look at the upstairs window, three rooms in from the left. The balcony rail was distressed wood, and the roof was designed to look like a frontier cabin, but the long, narrow two-story building was every inch the modern-day motel. It nestled between the parched hills behind it and the Hollywood Freeway out front. Cahuenga Boulevard East ran alongside the I-101, with Cahuenga Boulevard West across the Pilgrimage Bridge leading to Mulholland Drive. Even at four in the morning the Hollywood Freeway traffic hummed just out of sight down the embankment.

Too many memories kept crowding in tonight. The girl in the headmaster's office. The shooting of Jim Grant. McNulty distracted himself with movie trivia and mistaken identities. When they'd selected this as the production base, McNulty thought the John Anson Ford Amphitheatre next door was in memory of John Ford, director of so many John Wayne movies. That got him thinking that Pilgrim Motel was named after the Duke's penchant for calling strangers pilgrim. Of course, that was a different John Ford, and the motel was named after the bridge. It was one of many mistakes McNulty had made in his life. Choosing the wrong John Ford was the least of them.

That brought him back to the girl in Amy Moore's room. Was this going to be another mistake, or could it be redemption for all the things he'd done wrong? Larry Unger was right; this angry-man survivor guilt would have to stop sometime. Maybe the day he didn't survive. Until then he'd have to live with the fact that while others suffered, he kept coming up smelling of roses.

McNulty threw a glance up at Amy's window and thought he saw the curtains twitch. He blew out his cheeks then turned back to the compound. Chain-link fencing and a padlocked gate enclosed the secondary parking lot, up a ramp to the left of the motel. Now that the location vehicles were safely parked in the compound all he had to do was walk the perimeter, then lock the gate. His final job of the night.

Freeway traffic formed deep music to his left. Cicadas chirruped in the hills to his right. The trees behind the compound rustled in a breeze that did nothing to cool the LA night. It was still warm. It was still muggy. McNulty walked the cleared space, first around the fence along the base of the hillside, then around the back of the compound. He could see the left-hand side along Cahuenga Boulevard. There were no breaks in the fence. The compound was secure.

He came back around to the gate and took a final look inside the enclosure. The equipment trailers were parked along the fence beneath the trees, their cabs side by side facing the middle of the compound. Backcloths and scenery stood alongside Cahuenga Boulevard where the swing gang had stacked them. The cameras and other expensive equipment were locked in shipping containers beside the makeup trailer and the Craft Services truck. McNulty could still smell fried onions and cooked meat.

He hefted the padlock in one hand and was about to go out the gate when something banged near the makeup trailer. Keeping his eyes away from the streetlights to preserve his night vision, McNulty walked slowly toward the noise. The bang had sounded metallic. It had rattled then dissipated. Now there was nothing apart from the freeway, the cicadas and the rustling leaves.

He stopped three paces from where the noise had originated. One thing he'd learned from Jim Grant was not to go rushing in just because that's where you heard the noise. How many movies had he seen where somebody threw a stone to distract a guard only to come up behind him and whack him on the head? He stayed where he was and scanned the shadows.

Then somebody came up behind him and whacked him on the head.

CHAPTER FOUR

"Some security guard you turned out to be."

"I'm your technical adviser. Security is a sideline."

"Well, somebody certainly sidelined you last night."

McNulty shifted the bag of frozen peas he was holding against the back of his head and gave Larry Unger a withering look.

"You come up with this stuff on your own? Or does your scriptwriter do it for you?"

Unger took a sip of orange juice the motel had provided as part of his breakfast.

"You've seen my movies. What do you think?"

McNulty put the bag of peas down when the waitress brought his breakfast. The motel dining room was spacious for a pseudo frontier cabin, and since Titanic Productions had taken all the rooms, breakfast was being provided as a courtesy. The courtesy didn't extend very far. It wasn't a big breakfast.

"Did you get a look at him?"

"Who said it was a him?"

Unger took a piece of cremated bacon from McNulty's plate.

"It's always a him."

The bacon crunched as he ate it.

"Unless you think a woman could hit a big strong Yorkshire-man over the head."

McNulty forked some scrambled eggs into his mouth.

"I don't know about strong."

He paused while he swallowed.

"And some of the women in L-A are shit-fuck scary."

Unger swilled the bacon down with another mouthful of orange juice.

"Who cares what sex? Did you see who hit you?"

"No. He came up behind me."

Unger threw up his hands.

"You just said he."

McNulty smiled.

"It's always a he."

Unger went quiet while McNulty ate his breakfast, indicating for the waitress to refill his orange juice. The waitress pointed at the dispenser then continued serving the other tables. Unger muttered under his breath while he refilled his juice. He had no cause to complain. Titanic Productions didn't usually provide breakfast. McNulty had finished by the time he sat back down. They took a sip of orange juice in unison, then Unger got back on track.

"Anything missing?"

McNulty shook his head and immediately wished he hadn't.

"Not that I can tell. I'll take a better look this morning."

"You didn't take a look last night?"

"I was seeing stars last night."

Neither of them made a joke about Hollywood being the land of stars. McNulty had a headache and Unger was too worried about possible losses. He slid his empty glass across the table.

"CCTV?"

McNulty did the same.

"I'll be checking that as well."

Unger looked McNulty in the eye and gave a gentle nod.

"This where you start thinking you're still a cop?"

McNulty didn't shake his head this time.

"This is where I start thinking somebody's gonna wish they

hadn't whacked me on the head."

Unger was right; McNulty did feel like a cop again. It was a feeling that was never far from the surface. House-to-house inquiries or checking CCTV always brought that feeling back. Once a cop, always a cop. It had got him in trouble with the massage parlors back in Yorkshire and hadn't been much better with the missing girls in Boston. Helping Jim Grant with the fake audition sting in Palm Springs had been a mistake, too. In hindsight. Looking back, your vision is always twenty-twenty. Looking forward is the only way to get over the angry-man survivor guilt. Looking forward today meant doing house-to-house inquiries.

"And you didn't hear anything?"

"It was a night shoot. Soon as my head hit the pillow I was out."

McNulty thanked the third member of the swing gang he'd questioned and stepped back to let him close the door. Now he had questioned everyone who was staying in an upstairs room with a view of the compound. Everyone except Amy Moore. McNulty hadn't asked her yet because he didn't want to frighten the girl with talk of his being attacked near the makeup trailer. He wanted her to feel safe, not threatened. He knew what it was like to feel threatened at her age. He knew how vulnerable a ten-year-old could be in a world of men. Men like Mr. Cruickshank, the headmaster of Crag View Children's Home. Bullies and molesters. McNulty didn't want to add to her stress over some petty thief at Craft Services.

He went down the stairs at the end of the balcony and started knocking on doors. The rooms down here didn't have a view of the compound, but when you're making inquiries you ask everyone. For completeness. And you never know; they might have seen somebody going toward the compound or walking away. Maybe running. Maybe carrying the club that had whacked McNulty on the head. After half an hour nobody had seen anyone carrying the club that had whacked McNulty on the head. Inquiries complete. No witnesses. Now it was time to check the physical evidence—CCTV from the motel security system.

The Pilgrim Motel security system was basic and easy to operate; it consisted of a single monitor in the room behind the reception area with a multiplex controller that allowed the screen to split into four images. The four images currently showing were the front desk, the stairwells at either end of the balcony, and the main parking lot out front. McNulty asked about the other cameras and got the answer he was expecting: There weren't any others. At least the hard drive saved recordings for longer than the traditional twenty-four hours. Back in his early days at the West Yorkshire Police, CCTV had been recorded on VHS and most businesses only had one tape for each day of the week. That meant that if the tape you needed was more than a week old, it would have already been recorded over. Here, the recordings were safe for three months. McNulty wasn't looking back three months; he was looking at last night. The way the cameras were positioned, it wouldn't have mattered if he were looking at the live feed because there was no coverage of the production compound. That left only the parking lot out front of the motel.

McNulty selected the time the location vehicles were returning from the night shoot and changed from multiplex to full screen. The parking lot showed in grainy black and white with a digital clock running the time in hours, minutes and seconds. The access road was a shadowy presence in the background, visible only when headlights swept across the driveway. The trucks swung into the parking lot and disappeared off the edge of the screen.

A few deft finger movements and the recording ran at fast-forward. When the Craft Services truck brought up the rear, McNulty switched to normal speed. He watched the crew walk past the camera on their way to their rooms, some just shadows in the bottom right of the screen and others walking right in front of the camera. There was nothing suspicious.

Then a shadowy figure crossed the screen going the other way. McNulty pressed pause and scrutinized the man walking toward the compound. Tall and broad but not a giant. Not as big as Chuck Buchinsky and not as strong as most of the swing gang. Normal speed again. The figure stopped as if he knew he was being filmed and turned toward the camera. McNulty hit pause again and saw his own face looking back at him. He ran the recording on until he saw himself staggering toward the motel, holding the back of his head. There was nobody else. There was no other movement. CCTV had proved as useful as the room-to-room inquiries. No witnesses. It was time to revisit the scene of the crime.

McNulty had always enjoyed examining crime scenes. He'd never been in SOCO, unlike his friend Mick Habergham, the Scenes Of Crime Officer who had been returned to uniform patrol at the tail end of his career. McNulty still enjoyed walking the scene with soft eyes and a steady touch. Soft eyes were needed so you didn't focus too sharply on one thing and miss the overall picture. Steady touch was so you didn't trample the evidence and ruin any footprints. There weren't any footprints on the stained surface of the secondary parking lot, just oil stains and tire tracks and a lot of heavy scraping marks. A movie company on the road has to take everything with it, and that means lots of heavy lifting and a lack of care for the environment.

There wasn't much activity since tonight was another night shoot, just a handful of carpenters doing some woodwork on the backdrops, and the chef, who was cleaning the catering truck. McNulty stood in the middle of the compound and took stock.

The far left corner housed the woodwork shop, the carpenters busy hammering and sawing. The left perimeter was lined with production vehicles and police cars and any other small vehicles that would be used as set dressing or hero cars. The far right corner held mainly tractor units and their low-loader trailers for the heavy equipment, and the right perimeter accommodated the shipping containers for the film stock and cameras. An unlocked container held the lights and reflectors, things too big to steal. The last time Titanic Productions had had a problem with pilfering, it had been theft of the film stock and some unauthorized use of cameras in Boston. That's where McNulty decided to begin.

The shipping container was still locked. First thing he did was examine the heavy-duty padlock for scratch marks and any other signs that it had been forced open and later relocked. There were no scratches other than what you'd get missing the hole with the key. The hasp wasn't dented or bent from being pried open, and it hadn't been hit with a blunt object, unlike McNulty's head. He unlocked the padlock and opened the container. Since the trouble with the snuff-video gang in Boston, the camera equipment had been stored in designated spaces with painted silhouettes on the floor and walls so you could see immediately if anything was missing. Nothing was out of place. The film stock and snap-on cartridges matched the inventory list McNulty had brought with him. If this container had been the target, then the intruder had been scared off before anything was taken.

McNulty felt the lump on the back of his head. He remembered doing the scaring-off. After one last look around the interior, he went back outside and locked the door. He surveyed the compound carefully, then looked at his feet. This was roughly where the noise had come from, if not exactly where he'd been attacked. He retraced his steps, then turned to face the direction he'd been pointed last night when he was hit—his back to the main gate, facing the container. To his right the chef was finishing his preparations in the Craft Services catering truck. Between the catering truck and the shipping container he'd just examined was the makeup trailer.

McNulty angled slightly in that direction. Now he was facing the makeup trailer with Craft Services on his right and the shipping container on his left. He closed his eyes and tried to remember where the noise had come from. It was more left than right and definitely not straight ahead. He opened his eyes and walked to the makeup trailer door. It had a standard lock in the handle. Without thinking, he scrutinized the keyhole for scratches. In all his service, both in Yorkshire and with the Savage P.D. in Maryland, he'd never known anyone to break in to steal makeup. The door handle had seen a lot of use; it was impossible to tell if there were any fresh scratches.

He stepped back and glanced toward the motel. The upstairs balcony. Third window from the end. He thought about the only thing that had been different about last night: A young girl hiding outside the Hollywood Collision Center who had been transported from the location in Amy Moore's makeup trailer.

CHAPTER FIVE

It felt good, waking up with someone else in the room. Amy had all but given up on ever being able to satisfy her maternal instincts, so having a ten-year-old girl sleeping in the queen-size bed gave her a warm feeling. It was different from waking up with McNulty beside her, something that was becoming a more regular occurrence now that he was finally dealing with his broken childhood. Having the girl with her was more responsibility than having a damaged lover. It required more mothering. The first part of that was breakfast.

"What would you like to eat?"

The girl shrugged, sitting up in a bed that made her look like a bump in the desert. She still hadn't said a word. Amy didn't want to push her. She simply nodded and decided to bring the girl a tray of everything. The Pilgrim Motel didn't provide room service, so that meant going down and loading her own tray from the menu.

When she came back to the room, the girl was in the shower, some kind of country music coming from a timid voice. A sad song. Country music songs were always sad, about broken love or losing your dog. Amy couldn't tell what the girl was singing about but at least she was singing.

"Breakfast's ready."

The singing stopped. The shower was turned off. A few

minutes later the girl came out wearing a fluffy white bathrobe with Amy's initials on the breast. The Pilgrim Motel didn't provide bathrobes either. The girl had lost her voice again, refusing to answer questions about what she preferred. Instead, she ate everything on the plate and drank two glasses of orange juice.

Amy sat cross-legged on the edge of the bed and watched the girl eat. There were still shadows under her eyes but the harsh lines down the side of her nose had softened and the haunted look was less pronounced. She didn't look like a girl living on the streets anymore, but she was a long way from being your everyday California child. There was no hint of a smile but at least she wasn't frowning. Amy waited until the tray was empty, then spoke in soft, friendly whispers.

"I know you don't want to talk so I'll do the talking for you."

She let her voice level out into a conversational tone.

"You can stay here as long as you want."

She watched the girl's eyes to gauge her response.

"You won't have to sleep outdoors."

The girl kept her eyes down, staring at the tray. Amy didn't force the issue, keeping her voice calm and even.

"Is there anyone you want to know where you are?"

The girl didn't move, her face set in stone.

"Anyone you'd like to see again?"

A hint of sadness crept across the girl's face. And something else. Amy thought it might be guilt. The makeup lady let out a sigh. What could a ten-year-old girl have done to feel guilty about? Amy eased off on the questions and gave the girl a gentle smile.

"It would be nice to know your name at least."

The girl looked up with sad eyes that broke Amy's heart but still didn't speak.

"I can't keep calling you Little Miss Nobody."

That almost brought a smile, or at least a softening of her expression. Amy was about to try another witty comment when somebody knocked on the door. The girl drew back and hugged herself. Amy held her hands up in a calming gesture. The knock was gentler than his usual copper's knock, but she still recognized McNulty's rhythmic tap.

McNulty stood on the balcony and waited for Amy to answer the door. His mind was running various scenarios about why the girl had been sleeping outdoors in the City Of Angels but he kept coming back to one thing: It didn't matter why, it only mattered that she was. He rationalized that using the only yardstick he had to measure it with—his own experience of growing up in an orphanage. It didn't matter why any of the kids were living at Crag View, just the fact that they were living there was enough. After that it was simply a case of getting on with it. For McNulty that meant protecting the younger ones from the bullies who preyed upon them. One girl in particular. One bully above all others.

When the door opened McNulty jumped. Amy held the door half closed behind her to shield the girl.

"No point knocking on the door if you don't expect it to open."

"Sorry. I was miles away."

"No point standing here if you're miles away."

Amy said it with a smile but there was a hard edge beneath the light tone. Since she'd started seeing McNulty there had been too many times when he had been miles away; too much going on behind those eyes that he wouldn't share with her. Some days it was more of a problem than others. Mostly they ignored it. McNulty motioned for her to step all the way out and spoke in a low voice.

"She said anything yet?"

"No."

"Is she a mute do you think?"

"She's not mute."

McNulty tilted his head.

"So she *has* said something."

Amy kept steady eyes on him.

"She sang something. In the shower."

McNulty nodded.

"Well, singing's good, I guess."

Amy shrugged.

"Depends on what you're singing. Country music isn't exactly joy unbounded."

McNulty kept it light.

"Maybe she lost her dog."

Amy let out a sigh.

"She's lost something."

McNulty peeked through the gap in the door to make sure the girl was out of earshot then leaned closer to Amy.

"Have you looked through her things?"

"She hasn't got any things."

McNulty rubbed his chin.

"No papers? Wallet or purse? Anything with her name on it?"

Amy shook her head.

"Nothing."

McNulty stepped back and rested against the balcony rail. He hadn't expected the girl to be carrying I.D. at her age, and especially not in her situation, sleeping amid a pile of boxes under a canvas. What he was really doing was avoiding the next question. Amy noticed his indecision and creased her brow.

"What?"

McNulty looked at the woman he was growing increasingly fond of.

"Is there anywhere she can stay?"

Amy jerked a thumb behind her.

"She can stay here."

McNulty pushed off from the railing and stood up straight.

"Somewhere away from here."

Amy was about to protest when she noticed McNulty touch the lump on the back of his head. She closed her mouth, thought for a moment, then put two and two together. She still didn't want to believe it.

"I thought that was somebody stealing stuff like last time."

McNulty kept his voice low, so it didn't carry into the room.

"When was the last time somebody broke into the makeup trailer?"

Amy slipped into denial.

"It's expensive makeup."

McNulty tried to sound less worried than he was.

"I might be wrong."

He waved toward the room.

"Just to be on the safe side until I check it out."

"Check what out?"

"Where she came from."

Amy looked him in the eye.

"And you're going to do that how?"

CHAPTER SIX

The golden rule of police investigation is always start with what you know. What McNulty knew was where the girl had been found. He didn't know her name. He didn't know her age. He didn't know if she had an accent or a lisp or an address tattooed on the back of her neck. That last part was a bit fanciful, but Hollywood was a place of fanciful things. They'd already made a TV show about a woman with clues tattooed all over her body.

What McNulty did know was that the girl had been sleeping outdoors amid wrecked cars and auto parts in a grubby parking lot. The body shop probably had more things to hide than just the origins of a missing girl, so, in answer to Amy's question, McNulty was going back to the beginning. The source of what he knew. House-to-house inquiries at the Hollywood Collision Center.

Not everyone wants to answer questions. Especially when you're not a cop anymore. Especially if the business being questioned has secrets they don't want the police to know about. The legitimate face of Hollywood Collision Center was a wide clean forecourt next to Papillon International Bakery on Hollywood Boulevard. Nice clean cars lined the forecourt, a subliminal message about how good their body people were. The business included franchise space for Vibe Auto Spa and S&M Apollo Muffler and Tires. Titanic Productions hadn't been filming in the wide, clean forecourt; they'd been filming in the rear parking lot just off North Alexandria Avenue.

McNulty sat at a table outside the Thrifty Dry Cleaners across the intersection and nursed a milky coffee in a styrofoam cup. The dry cleaners offered free drinks from a vending machine for customers waiting for their cleaning. McNulty wasn't waiting for his cleaning, so he paid for the coffee. It was thick and strong and borderline undrinkable. He wished he'd bought a hot chocolate instead. The view was better than the coffee. From his seat at the strip mall, he could see the main forecourt out front and the side entrance on North Alexandria. The side entrance had an electronic gate that slid open on rollers and closed a few seconds after the car or someone on foot had gone in or come out. It wasn't an open lot where some kid could sneak in and hide under a tarpaulin.

That was the first thing he noticed. The second was that customers also went in and out through the forecourt entrance. The owners of any cars being dropped off for detailing or new tires went in through the front. Any sales reps, business types or people collecting their cars walked straight in off of Hollywood Boulevard. The North Alexandria entrance remained closed ninety percent of the time, and the people entering that way looked very different from those passing through the front. Body repairmen and grease monkeys used the side entrance quickly. At least three other people who entered through the side gate looked more streetwise and cautious, throwing furtive glances over their shoulders before sneaking through the gap as soon as it was wide enough. Those were people on foot. Cars were harder to judge. Bottom line: the back was the place for shady deals. The front was soccer moms getting their cars cleaned.

McNulty took a sip of coffee and screwed up his face. He'd changed his assessment from borderline undrinkable to completely undrinkable. He put the styrofoam cup on the table but kept his hand around it so it looked like he was between sips. He split his attention between the forecourt entrance and the side gate but mainly focused on the side gate. He wasn't sure what he hoped to learn, other than that the side gate was where the action was. There was a reason Larry Unger had chosen it as a location; because the yard in the back looked dark and dangerous, just the place his firefighter-turned-cop would be drawn to. McNulty wondered what was drawing him, but he didn't really need to ask.

The girl had touched a nerve and it didn't take much to set his nerves on edge. Growing up in a children's home was only part of it; lots of kids had grown up in children's homes. Growing up in Crag View Children's Home was a bigger part but, again, lots of kids had grown up there who didn't have the same hang-ups that McNulty had. It all came down to one thing. One incident. An incident that was burned in his memory and had scarred him for life. The girl in the headmaster's office and McNulty breaking Mr. Cruickshank's nose with a Bible. He had protected the girl on that occasion, but the fallout was immediate and all-encompassing. The girl had been sold into adoption in America and the paperwork destroyed in a fire.

Long before McNulty discovered that the girl was his sister.

That was the first thing. The second reason the girl had touched a nerve was even worse. The underage girls used by the Northern X massage parlors and the even younger girls sold into the behind-the-scenes torture porn syndicate run by Telfon Speed. Helping the police bring down Northern X had wrought its own scars, not the least being that that was when he had learned about his sister. The rest was the death and dismemberment of the other girls. Yes, there was a lot to atone for. Maybe finding out about the girl in Amy's room would help clean the slate.

He pushed the coffee across the table and stood up. He'd seen enough. The side entrance was the place to go. He stepped away from the table, then turned back, picked up the cup and dropped it into the trash bin next to the dry cleaners. Cleaning the slate started with the basics. With the table clear but his conscience less so, he crossed Hollywood Boulevard and walked up North Alexandria.

CHAPTER SEVEN

"Titanic Productions?"

"Yes."

"Why you want to come back? You're done here."

"I think we left something behind."

The crackly voice over the intercom didn't sound interested.

"Finders keepers, losers weepers."

McNulty pressed the talk button and leaned close.

"Larry hasn't paid you yet, has he?"

The crackling stopped. There was no reply. McNulty pressed the button again.

"So keep jerking me around and we'll see who's weeping."

The intercom seemed to consider that, then there was a buzz and a hum as the side gate began to open.

The two men leaning against the office door hadn't been there during the night shoot. If they had, Larry Unger would have had a nervous breakdown. The producer was always on the edge of a nervous breakdown anyway—that was his default setting—but the men cradling industrial spanners would have made him shit a brick. McNulty didn't want any trouble but if these guys had anything to do with the runaway then his angry-man survivor guilt would be happy to oblige. The gate slid closed behind him.

There was no room for maneuver. McNulty felt angry already.

"If your boss wants his movie money, I suggest you find something useful to do and fuck off."

The bigger of the two looked puzzled at being threatened in his own backyard. The slightly smaller one pushed off from the door.

"We are being useful."

He nodded toward the closed gate.

"And you're locked in with us."

McNulty scanned the yard for weapons, then stuck his hand in his pocket.

"No. You're locked in with me."

The bulge in his pocket could have been a gun or just his finger. The smaller big guy slapped the heavy spanner into the palm of his hand.

"You've been watching too many movies if you think we're gonna fall for that one."

McNulty pushed the pocket until the bulge was pointing at the talker.

"Do you know why things become clichés in movies?" He raised the angle. "Because they happen so much in real life."

He kept his eyes on both men but spoke to the mouthpiece.

"But what stops them being clichés is putting a fresh spin on an old story."

He took the phone out of his pocket and chose a number at random.

"So unless you want SWAT dropping in…"

He jerked a thumb toward the workshop.

"…go play with your toolkit."

Now both men stepped away from the door and slapped metal in palms. They were about to move forward when a voice shouted from the office.

"Okay you two. Stand down. I got this."

A short, wiry man who was so small he could have been a jockey stood in the doorway. The look in his eyes said he could eat jockeys for breakfast. The two heavies backed off and went inside. Their boss waved McNulty forward.

"Come in. Our coffee's better than across the street."

Vincent D'Aquino was right about the coffee, but to be fair the bar was set pretty low after Thrifty Dry Cleaners. The chop shop owner had a full chrome barista behind his desk that could do everything except sing and dance. He did whistle while he worked though, whipping up a latte to rival Starbucks's. McNulty thanked him after being introduced.

"Small world. Us both having the same name."

D'Aquino slid the latte across the desk and sat down.

"You a D'Aquino too?"

McNulty sat in a low chair opposite the little man. The chair evened things up.

"I'm a Vincent. But they call me Vince. Vince McNulty."

"They call me Vinnie. Those who dare call me anything."

"Like Joe Pesci in that movie where he's a New York lawyer in the Deep South?"

D'Aquino didn't shake his head or blink. He kept steady eyes on McNulty.

"Like Joe Pesci in Goodfellas."

McNulty returned the stare with soft eyes.

"But not as crazy, right?"

D'Aquino still didn't move. He had stillness down to a fine art.

"Crazy doesn't get it done."

He waved a hand toward McNulty.

"You're a big guy. You don't need to act tough. Where I grew up, the size I am, acting tough didn't get it done either. Now? I have my own barista."

McNulty held his mug up in salute.

"And quite a bit more, I'm guessing."

D'Aquino still didn't move.

"More than I want putting out there by nosy ex-cops and movie executives."

McNulty took a sip of coffee and smiled.

"Titanic Productions doesn't have executives."

"It has you."

"You think I'm a nosy ex-cop?"

"I think you speak bullshit through the intercom."

McNulty put the mug down.

"About Larry not paying you?"

D'Aquino moved for the first time. A small move that was barely a shake of the head but was big enough to rattle the earth.

"About leaving something behind."

McNulty let out a sigh and tilted his head.

"I may have exaggerated a bit."

He lowered his voice.

"It's more like we left with more than we came with."

CHAPTER EIGHT

The pallet of boxed car parts looked smaller in daylight but the tarpaulin was just as grubby. D'Aquino whipped the cover off and stepped aside to let McNulty examine the scene. Even in his role as technical adviser for Titanic Productions, the ex-cop still looked like a cop. D'Aquino was impressed, but like everything else about the hard man, he kept it to himself.

The sun was high in a clear blue sky. A typical Los Angeles day, if you discounted the smog haze across downtown. The oil-stained asphalt reflected the heat. The homemade shelter was a haven of darkness amid the battered cardboard boxes. There was just enough room to squeeze into the middle and barely enough space to curl up and sleep. The girl must have spent an uncomfortable night. Being caught by on-site security must have been even worse. McNulty had been that on-site security. He felt guilty about that, as well.

"How long has this been here?"

Not strictly relevant but a way of deflecting the guilt.

"Not long."

McNulty turned to D'Aquino.

"How long is not long?"

D'Aquino still showed minimal body language.

"Came in just before your guys started setting up for the movie."

Now the timing became a bit more important. If the pallet had been here for days, then the girl might have sneaked in and hidden under the canvas. If it had arrived only yesterday, there was a good chance she had already been hiding amid the boxes when they arrived. That put a whole new slant on McNulty's line of questioning.

"Where did it come from?"

D'Aquino gave another of those little movements that were huge for him.

"The guys I deal with. They don't want people knowing where it comes from."

"But you do know?"

"I have an idea."

McNulty turned to the wiry, hard man.

"Just in case I didn't explain. This is a ten-year-old girl we're talking about."

"How do you know she's ten if she isn't talking?"

"Ballpark ten."

McNulty let out a sigh.

"Too young and too scared."

D'Aquino wasn't ready to give up his source.

"The way you dragged her out of there, I'm not surprised."

McNulty was taken aback.

"You were here?"

D'Aquino waved a hand around the compound.

"You're not the only ones with cameras."

McNulty scanned the yard and spotted three cameras high on the perimeter, two pointing in from the boundary fence and one above the office facing out. The field of view covered the entire compound.

"Recording?"

"I wasn't up all night watching the live feed."

McNulty turned his back on the pallet.

"I'd have thought the guys you deal with wouldn't want people knowing you kept tapes of receiving stolen goods."

"It's a hard drive."

"It's evidence."

D'Aquino shook his head, becoming more effusive now that he was comfortable with McNulty.

"It's insurance."

He shrugged.

"And the stuff wasn't stolen here."

McNulty threw one more glance at the pallet, now laid bare without its tarpaulin cover. His shoulders felt heavy. His breathing was labored. The guilt was creeping back in—all the kids he hadn't helped when he was too young to help them anyway. Age didn't preclude you from doing the right thing. By the time the Bible and the broken nose signalled his transition from boy to man, it had been too late for most of them. He didn't want to be too late again.

"So the girl was under surveillance the whole time."

D'Aquino was back to being a quiet, still presence. McNulty nodded.

"Let's take a look."

The recording was about as much use as the CCTV at the Pilgrim Motel. It didn't show anything they didn't already know but it did confirm what they suspected. The girl hadn't climbed over the fence to hide in the backyard of the Hollywood Collision Center.

The multiplex system was set to time-lapse, rather than full video, so the delivery was captured in jerky freeze-frames every few seconds. It was still daylight when the gate slid open and a truck reversed its way in. A forklift unloaded the pallet and set it down in the corner of the yard. The truck left without any paperwork or discussion. The yard was busy for half an hour, then workmen began to clock out and leave. The office was locked up. Still daytime heading toward twilight. A narrow window of opportunity for the girl to escape.

The tarpaulin twitched, hidden from the office camera but

caught on both angles from the fence. A tiny hand drew the canvas back and a pale, frightened face poked out. It looked like she was about to climb out when she darted back undercover. The gate slid open and Titanic Productions's swing gang began to dress the set. Evening turned to night as arc lights and reflectors were set up near the entrance. There was some acting. Some filming. Then a figure crossed the yard, walking like a cop, not a duck, and McNulty whipped the tarpaulin off. Guilt flushed his cheeks even while watching. There was nothing else to see.

McNulty needed some fresh air, so he wandered back out to the pallet. It was still uncovered. D'Aquino showed admirable tact and stayed in the office. McNulty turned his face to the sky and took a deep breath. The sun had moved across the sky but was no less bright. The heat warmed his face but not his heart. When his pulse stopped racing, he rested one hand on the pile of boxes and looked into the makeshift den.

His mind replayed the usual scenarios. He asked himself the same old questions. What makes a ten-year-old girl stowaway on a delivery truck all the way from God-knows-where? What could she be running from that was worse than living in a box? McNulty knew exactly what she could be running from but that was his default setting. Anything to do with kids and he always thought the worst. In his experience the worst is usually what you got.

Something caught his eye in the corner of the girl's hideaway. Not a glint or a scrap of paper, but something else that was out of place on an industrial pallet. A clean patch of wood. Or several clean patches of wood. He squeezed through the gap, shouldering the boxes aside, and dropped to one knee. The words stood out in the gloom. Carved in the wood of the pallet.

LEAVE NO MAN BEHIND

The motto of several military units, written in a childish hand. Not with a rusty nail but something sharper. McNulty jerked upright. One of the things he'd learned about kids under stress is they could be dangerous and unpredictable. He took out his phone and hoped Amy would answer. When she did, he didn't waste time on preamble.

"She's got a knife."

Amy sounded distant.

"I know."

CHAPTER NINE

Amy knew the girl had a knife because she was looking at another example of the girl's handiwork. Carved into the underside of the toilet lid. One of the other benefits of staying in an executive suite was the quality of the bathroom fittings. Everyone else had to make do with a plastic toilet seat. Amy had a wooden one. But the wood wasn't top quality, which made it easy to carve.

LEAVE NO ONE BEHIND

Not quite the same as what McNulty had described, but close enough. Amy knew that political correctness had changed the military slogan to avoid being accused of discrimination against women. The same reason Star Trek no longer went where no man had gone before. She doubted the girl was prompted by political correctness. It was more likely that whoever she'd left behind weren't men. Men would be prime suspects for whatever she was running away from.

Amy flushed the toilet, not because she needed to but to explain why she was taking so long in the bathroom. She washed her hands for the same reason and made sure the phone was back in her pocket. When she came out, she left the bathroom door open and sat beside the girl on the edge of the bed. The girl didn't shuffle away so at least that was some progress. Carving the toilet lid was not. Amy considered how best to broach the subject and thought it would be better to come at it sideways. She put on a pained expression and rubbed her right buttock.

"Trouble with the executive suite in a budget motel is the cheap wood."

She nodded toward the bathroom.

"Toilet seat."

She rubbed her buttock again.

"You get splinters in your butt."

She looked at the girl.

"Or it could be somebody carving their name under the lid."

This time the girl did shuffle away, hugging herself. Amy kept her voice calm and friendly.

"Except I don't think that's your name."

She stopped rubbing her buttock.

"And I didn't really get a splinter in my butt."

The lightness of tone and constant butt reference brought the faintest smile to the girl's lips, but she banished it immediately. The girl didn't have to say, "It wasn't me," because her entire body language denied the accusation. Amy decided to take the confessional route. She crossed her legs on the bed and rocked gently backward and forward.

"When I was at school, I carved my teacher's name on the restroom door."

She tried to put some meat on the lie.

"Stinky Pete for President."

The girl gave Amy a quizzical look.

"Stinky Pete, like in Toy Story?"

Amy didn't know where she'd got Stinky Pete from and wished she'd come up with a different name.

"This was before Toy Story."

She gave the girl a conspiratorial wink.

"We didn't want him for president, either."

The girl relaxed her arms but was stilling hugging herself.

"So why did you carve it?"

Amy uncrossed her legs and turned to face the girl.

42

"Sometimes you've got to voice your greatest fear."

The girl wasn't convinced.

"You were afraid your teacher might become president?"

Amy let out a sigh.

"I'm worried who you might have left behind."

McNulty stood in the midday sun and put his phone away after Amy told him about the carving under the toilet lid. He wanted her to get the knife off the girl, but the makeup lady said she'd handle it her own way. McNulty hadn't known her long enough to guess what way that was but he trusted her instincts. After all, how dangerous could a ten-year-old be?

That thought sent a shiver down his spine. He hadn't been much older than ten when he broke Mr. Cruickshank's nose with the Bible. Given the right incentive a child could do all sorts of damage. The content of the carvings suggested she had plenty of incentive.

He glanced at his watch. It was creeping into early afternoon, and he still had a couple of things to arrange for tonight's shoot. Unfortunately, he hadn't been able to learn much at all about the girl's origins. D'Aquino came out of the office and leaned against the door while McNulty continued to search the area. Somehow, the little man managed to make even *leaning* intimidating.

"You done?"

McNulty threw one last glance at the makeshift den, then crossed the yard.

"Unless you're going to tell me where the pallet came from."

"I don't know where the pallet came from."

"But you can find out."

D'Aquino pushed off from the doorframe and fixed McNulty with a hard stare.

"For the girl."

McNulty shrugged.

"That's all I'm interested in."

D'Aquino nodded.

"Then for the girl I will find out where it came from. And anywhere it stopped along the way that she might have climbed aboard."

McNulty stopped in front of the office.

"And I'll get Larry to put a rush on the payment."

D'Aquino went back to being an immovable object.

"You think I'm interested in the money?"

Now McNulty was curious.

"Why be a movie location then?"

D'Aquino gave the faintest of smiles.

"This is Hollywood. Everyone loves the movies."

"I'm worried who you might have left behind."
The girl looked at Amy with a straight face, but it couldn't hide the emotion bubbling inside. She refused to blink. She refused to cry. But tears welled up and no amount of positive thinking on her part could stop them from spilling down her cheeks. She kept her shoulders tight to stop them from shaking but she was shaking inside. There was nothing else for Amy to do. She put her arms around the girl and gave her a hug.

The girl didn't fight her off, but she did sit bolt upright. Stiff and silent and trembling. After a few moments she relaxed and let the sobs take over. Her chest heaved. Her shoulders shook. Between gasps for breath and deep exhales she cried herself dry. Amy patted her gently on the back. After a while the tears subsided. The girl pushed back and wiped her face. She looked at Amy, then lowered her eyes.

"I'm sorry about the splinters."

Amy was close to tears herself. She wiped a stray one before it spilled.

"What I'm really worried about is the knife. "If you keep carving toilet lids you might cut yourself."

The girl gave a sad little smile.

"It's not a sharp knife."

Amy shrugged.

"Even so."

The girl sat for a moment then nodded. She reached into the bathrobe and took out an imitation Swiss Army knife, the body short and bulky to house the various blades. The white cross on the red frame wasn't quite straight. The girl held it out to Amy.

"It's got a bottle opener and a thing for getting stones out of horses' feet."

Amy reached for the knife but the girl didn't let go.

"You open a lot of bottles?"

The girl patted the knife as if saying goodbye to an old friend.

"There are lots of horses."

"Maybe I should call you Horse Whisperer."

The girl lowered her hands and stared at Amy. The look was disconcerting, as if she were looking right through the makeup lady, then she focused and looked Amy in the eye.

"My name is Tilly."

CHAPTER TEN

McNulty turned off Los Feliz Boulevard and headed up Western Canyon Drive. The slope was gentle at first and wouldn't begin the real climb until it snaked and looped the back way toward Griffith Observatory. Larry Unger couldn't afford to film at Griffith Observatory, but he could make sure it was in the background of the cheaper location. The Trails Café was a much cheaper location.

The car crunched gravel as it pulled into the dirt and stone parking lot, swirling a cloud of dust that obscured the frontier-cabin-style café and the restroom block just up the hill. He waited for the dust to settle before getting out. Sweat prickled his neck as soon as he left the air conditioning. Everything was scorched earth and dry grass, the only greenery coming from the woods up the hill and the shade trees planted around the café. A newly erected shelter with half a dozen picnic tables stood on four legs over a concrete base. The sun baked down. There was no breeze to rustle the leaves. Then a gunshot rang out across the stillness.

"You *are* in the gun capital of America. What do you expect?"

"I thought Texas was the gun capital."

"Texas is a state. Lots of space. Not a lot of people. L-A is crammed full of low-rent dispossessed motherfuckers, with access to more guns than the Alamo."

The old-timer who ran The Trails Café stepped away from McNulty's car while the technical adviser dusted himself down. Diving under the car had seemed like a good idea at the time, but now it felt stupid, now that he knew the gunfire was just from hunters in the woods.

"I didn't think there'd be much to hunt up here."

The old man wafted away the cloud of dust.

"Didn't you see the warning signs? Dangerous animals in these hills. Mountain lions and rattlesnakes."

"They shoot rattlesnakes?"

Carl Robarge shook his head.

"Tin cans and bottles probably."

He waved a hand to the gate and chain-link fence beyond the restroom block.

"Not much hunting up in the hills."

He pointed at the privacy sign on the gate.

"Private land over there. But empty. Anyone who can climb a fence and point a gun can go medieval for target practice."

Robarge started back toward the café.

"Haven't shot any customers though. So the owners aren't too bothered."

"I thought you were the owner."

Robarge smiled, cracking a face as tough as leather.

"I'm the frontier face folks like to have coffee with. Damn. I barely own the boots on my feet."

McNulty followed the old-timer.

"But you are the one who makes decisions about location shooting?"

Robarge stopped and turned to McNulty.

"I got the final say about any kind of shooting you want."

The smile cracked leather again. "So let's go over the fire regulations."

* * *

Going all the way back to the 1930s, Los Angeles had been obsessed with two things: Fire and water. Back in the Jack Nicholson, *Chinatown* days, it had been mainly water. In recent years, in a city that hadn't had significant rainfall in a hundred and twenty-two weeks, it was fire. The hills and canyons to the north and west of Los Angeles were most at risk. Beverly Hills and the privileged few had more protection than the president. Nobody expected South L.A. to burn unless they had another riot. Wildfires were the province of the powder-dry hinterland.

Backpackers and weekend picnickers were the main danger and were constantly being warned to be careful. Lightning strikes and downed power lines were another source of ignition. Movie companies not only needed comprehensive insurance, they had to comply with the fire regulations. The fire regulations at The Trails Café meant doing what Carl Robarge said.

"I hear your main guy's a firefighter. That should help."

"Only between action and cut."

McNulty walked the grounds with Robarge, making a note of clear spaces that wouldn't be in the shot when Larry Unger was filming tonight.

"Beyond that he couldn't act his way out of a barbecue."

Robarge passed the restroom block and checked the gate in the chain-link fence to make sure it was closed. He dipped a hand into the water trough that had been set up for pony-trekkers.

"He's not going to rush in and save the day then?"

McNulty kept pace with the man in charge.

"Have you seen the size of him? He isn't going to rush any-where."

Robarge showed his knowledge.

"Charles Buchinsky. The next big thing."

McNulty stepped under the shade of the picnic shelter.

"He's already big. But the next big thing?"

He shrugged.

"This is Titanic Productions we're talking about."

Robarge joined him in the shade and rubbed his leathery features.

"It worked okay for Alfonse Bayard. He's over at Fox now, isn't he?"

McNulty rested against one of the picnic tables.

"Lightning doesn't strike twice."

Robarge stopped rubbing his chin and leaned against one of the uprights.

"It did last year. Wildfire over by the San Fernando Valley. Two fires in six months. Both lightning strikes. Exactly same spot."

McNulty wasn't going to give up that easily.

"Yes but burn damage from the first one acted as a fire break. Retarded the second. Buchinsky's isn't going to break out. Not as a firefighter playing cops and robbers."

Robarge wiped sweat from his forehead and flicked it to one side.

"And you only want cops playing cops and robbers."

McNulty stood up.

"Firemen put out fires. Cops catch robbers."

Robarge set off back toward the café.

"Well, you could have a Playboy centerfold playing a Park Ranger for all I care. Just make sure you've got fire backup before you start any gunplay."

McNulty caught up with him halfway across the dusty lot.

"There isn't going to be any gunplay."

That's what he told himself. He wasn't always right.

CHAPTER ELEVEN

"Why do we have to move?"

"It's to do with insurance. Since you're not working on the movie."

That wasn't strictly true, but Amy wasn't lying, either. Tilly Nutton wasn't working for Titanic Productions and she wasn't helping make the movie. That being the case, she wasn't entitled to stay at the Pilgrim Motel and wasn't covered by insurance if anything happened to her. Of course, she hadn't been covered by insurance when she was sleeping at the Hollywood Collision Center, either, and Amy reckoned it had been a lot rougher wherever she'd slept before that.

"And my friend's place is nicer."

Amy continued to pack a motel towel and the spare toiletries into a carrier bag. She tried not to look at the girl she was growing increasingly fond of. Tilly didn't make it any easier.

"But I want to stay with you."

Amy finished packing and sat on the edge of the bed.

"Friends are friends for a reason."

She hoped the encouraging smile wasn't too strained.

"Staying with Kim..." she held a hand against her heart and patted it twice, "...means you *are* staying with me."

Tilly wasn't convinced but she didn't argue. She nodded and took the bag from Amy, the shift of weight making them both bounce on the mattress. The girl found it amusing, so she bounced again. Amy feigned surprise and stood up as if Tilly had bounced her right off the bed.

"Now, let's get you over to Montecito Heights."

McNulty confirmed the placement of the location vehicles on a makeshift map, dropped it on the passenger seat, then looked out across Western Canyon Drive. The engine was running to feed the air conditioner, even though he'd moved up the hill to the paved lot marked "Griffith Park Parking." More space and less dust than the gravel and dirt parking lot behind The Trails Café. This would be their base camp and production office. All the heavy vehicles would be parked here. Craft Services and the makeup trailer would be down near the café. Stuff the stars didn't have to walk too far for. Even on a Titanic Productions movie the front-of-camera talent was pampered. For McNulty, being pampered meant keeping the engine running.

The sun had moved all the way to the west, leaving the powder-blue sky clear and unblemished, apart from a stain of dirty mist across the horizon. The trees and foreground were crystal clear all the way to the observatory on the ridge, but downtown was an impressionist painting of chrome and glass towers. Downtown wasn't what McNulty was considering at the moment. To the east of the towers and just beyond the city limits there was an elevated neighborhood that was all but invisible in the distant haze. Montecito Heights. He let out a sigh and folded the map, wondering if it was a good idea, sending the girl half a mile from one of Jim Grant's L.A. shootouts. Thinking about Jim Grant brought its own set of memories, so he let out another sigh and rubbed his face. He stared out across the sprawling city and gave a little nod, as if Amy could see him, then pulled out of the lot and headed downhill toward Los Feliz Boulevard.

* * *

"So, this is the girl who brought out your maternal instincts."

Kimberley Howe ushered Amy and the girl into the caretaker's bungalow behind Glen Alta Elementary, the low, wide concrete building at 3410 Sierra Street. Banners fastened to the porch railings proclaimed it,

"LA's BEST
AFTER-SCHOOL ENRICHMENT PROGRAM"
and advertised,
"Beyond the Bell Branch
YOUTH SERVICES AFTER-SCHOOL PROGRAM"

None of that meant anything to Amy Moore, who had as much knowledge of after-school activities as McNulty had of makeup techniques. The only thing that mattered was seeing her old friend again after years of promising to visit Los Angeles. Kim gave her a warm embrace and offered Tilly a handshake. Working in the school system for ten years had given her an instinct for these things, and right now her instincts were saying, *damaged girl—handle with care.*

"Nice to see you both."

There was no hint of admonishment for not visiting sooner, something else that singled out Kim as special. She was just an all-around good person. It was a shame that the only time Amy came to visit was when she needed an all-around good person. Kim didn't pass judgment on that, either.

"I hear you've hooked up with some English guy." She gave Amy a sly smile. "Glad you broke out of that self-imposed prison."

Amy nodded across the parking lot toward the concrete building surrounded by barbed wire.

"I see you're still in yours."

Kim looked out the door and laughed.

"Does look a bit like Alcatraz doesn't it?"

She closed the door and waved her guests to the kitchen table.

"But I broke out years ago."

She turned her attention to the ten-year-old girl in the kitchen, the reason they were all here. The kitchen was warm and cozy but sparsely furnished, the cabinets and countertops all faded wood and green marble. There was a cup stand and a paper towel dispenser but nothing else on display. You'd be forgiven for thinking nobody ever cooked in here if it weren't for the warm welcome and the four-seat farmhouse table. She indicated the carrier bag under the girl's arm.

"Travel light, travel far. A girl after my own heart."

Kim noted the girl's nervous glances toward the door. Out there, across the parking lot, was a concrete building festooned in barbed wire and warning signs. The only things missing were searchlights and guard towers. Kim pulled out a chair and sat down, making her shorter than the girl standing over her. Less threatening. She kept her tone light as well.

"That's to keep people out, not in."

The girl shivered. Kim shrugged.

"School isn't for everyone."

She pulled out another chair and waved for the girl to sit. Tilly hugged the bag against her chest and remained standing.

"But everyone needs something."

Kim leaned back in her chair and draped one leg over a knee. Relaxed. Friendly. Just a woman in a kitchen. Tilly still didn't sit down. Kim looked around as if checking whether anyone was listening.

"One thing I do know." She cupped her hands into a bowl shape. "You can't eat soup standing up."

Tilly unclenched slightly. She glanced at Amy then back at the woman whose kitchen they were in. "You don't eat soup. You drink it."

Kim smiled at the breakthrough. "You obviously haven't had any of my soup."

Amy sat on the third chair. "That's true."

Kim smiled at Tilly. "Practically have to cut it with a knife."

With the two women smiling and her being the only person standing, Tilly Nutton unwound some more. She looked at Amy, then at Kim, put her bag on the table, and sat down.

CHAPTER TWELVE

"I can't help you with the acting, but we've got to lighten the walk."

"Walking's fine. It's the acting that tightens me up."

"Let's try this then. Don't act unless you've got to say something. Until then, just pick your spot and walk from point A to point B."

They were standing outside the makeup trailer in the dirt and gravel lot behind The Trails Café, Buchinsky towering head and shoulders above McNulty. The shoulders only just fit through the doorway. Amy Moore dusted the big guy's collar as he went down the stairs, then stepped back inside and closed the door. Buchinsky rubbed his face.

"Makeup doesn't help me feel like a cop."

McNulty stood facing the actor.

"You're not playing a cop. You're playing a firefighter doing some police work on the side."

Buchinsky looked uncomfortable.

"Firefighters don't wear makeup, either."

McNulty gave a little shrug.

"Charcoal rub and singed eyebrows don't work for this scene."

Buchinsky let out a sigh.

"Might help me get into character."

"Your character's a fish out of water. Being a cop doesn't come easy. So, you being uneasy? That's in character."

Buchinsky unwound slightly.

"Did you use psychology on the job?"

McNulty shook his head.

"I just lost my temper and got the job done."

Titanic Productions's ground troops descended on The Trails Café long before sunset. Setting up for location filming takes hours of preparation, which means getting all the production vehicles into the parking lot in plenty of time for Larry Unger to use the magic hour for his establishing shots of Buchinsky arriving with Griffith Observatory in the background at twilight. Still enough blue in the sky as a backdrop but dark enough for the observatory to be lit up by its spotlights.

A helicopter thudded across the sky as the swing gang dressed the set with a couple of false walls to hide untidy trash bins, and the camera department laid the dolly track for the tracking shot. The best boy and gaffer set up subdued lighting for Buchinsky's arrival. The crew were like a well-oiled machine. They'd done this so many times it was second nature.

McNulty's nature was to be a cop.

The sun went down, and the sky began to darken. The makeup trailer rocked on its wheels as a succession of background extras had their faces painted. Craft Services began to cook up a feast, the smells drifting across the open ground between the restroom block and the chain-link fence. Everything was going smoothly. So why was McNulty's cop nature telling him something was wrong?

"You figured out what they were after yet?"

"Whatever they were after, they didn't get."

Larry Unger waited until McNulty had given Buchinsky his

final instructions before joining him behind the camera position.

"There's nothing missing?"

McNulty watched Buchinsky's more natural walk then looked at Unger.

"No."

Unger divided his attention between McNulty and the evening sky, which was rapidly deepening to optimum shade.

"What about the girl?"

"What about her?"

Unger turned to McNulty.

"She okay?"

"She's fine."

Unger watched McNulty's face for any signs of a lie.

"Bit of a coincidence, you being smacked on the head the same day."

McNulty shrugged.

"Shit happens. Sometimes twice on the same day."

Unger still watched McNulty's face.

"I thought cops didn't believe in coincidence."

McNulty smiled at his producer.

"Are you trying that lie-detector thing?"

"I'm watching for any reaction."

McNulty lowered his voice.

"Well, here's my reaction. Cops don't believe in conspiracy theories either. The two things are unrelated. Somebody got disturbed breaking into the compound. That's all."

Unger checked his watch. They should be rolling by now. But he wasn't finished with McNulty.

"Where is she now?"

"Safe."

"Safe where?"

McNulty kept a straight face.

"Safe where she isn't going to be a coincidence."

CHAPTER THIRTEEN

The firefighter doing police work on the side pulled into the dirt and gravel parking lot and climbed out of his car. He looked around, then spotted a light in The Trails Café and closed the car door. After a nervous glance over his shoulder, he crossed the open space with the Griffith Observatory perfectly framed in the background.

"Cut. Let's go again."

The car had hit its mark and the walk was fine. Even the nervous glance looked suitably uneasy, but the director wanted Buchinsky to turn his head a bit more, despite it being an unnatural angle. Better for the camera than the reality.

"Reset."

The crew quickly moved the camera to its start position and a stunt driver reversed the car. Time was money, but mainly they were losing the light. The clapperboard clapped on take three.

"Rolling. And, action."

Buchinsky drove into the parking lot and got out of the car. The nervous look over his shoulder was more exaggerated, then he started to walk. He was halfway to the café when he stopped and glanced over his shoulder again. Not as nervous this time, but suspicious. Something was wrong. He set off again, walking backward for the first couple of steps, then faced forward and walked like a firefighter—all strength and purpose and not bothered about looking like a cop. He reached his mark and the director yelled, "Cut. Check the gate." The camera operator confirmed there was no hair in the gate and the director called for the next setup.

"Did you tell him to do that?"

McNulty had forgotten that Larry Unger was standing beside him.

"I just told him not to fall over."

Unger wagged a finger and gave a sly smile.

"You told him more than that. I knew you could do it."

He patted McNulty on the back.

"Welcome back."

McNulty turned away, not wanting Unger to see that he understood where the producer reckoned McNulty had been. Not physically, but in his head. As far as McNulty was concerned, he was never going to be fully back from that place; the snow-covered hills of Colorado with its gunfire and bloodshed and the single flatline of Jim Grant's monitor. The producer had taken a while to get over losing F.K. Parenteau in the same incident but had replaced his Director of Photography for Titanic Productions's first Hollywood feature. Flip Livingston was no F.K., but he kept it in focus and the gate clear. Buchinsky broke away from the huddle congratulating him and headed toward Craft Services while the crew changed the setup to the interior of the café. McNulty fell in step with the big man.

"You forget how to walk from point A to point B?"

Buchinsky seemed more confident crossing for coffee and a doughnut.

"Playing uneasy comes easy."

He slowed down halfway across the dusty lot.

"If it was me? I'd check over my shoulder twice. So I did."

McNulty kept pace with him.

"You sensed something, huh?"

Buchinsky stopped and faced the technical adviser.

"It's funny, but yes." He rubbed the back of his neck. "Hairs bristled up the back of my neck. How crazy is that?"

McNulty felt a shiver of his own. "Not crazy at all. Happens to me all the time."

He looked around in the gloom but couldn't put his finger on what was spooking him. The door to the makeup trailer opened and spilled light across the gravel. Amy waved Buchinsky over for his touch-up, leaving McNulty to ponder his spider senses alone. After a moment the smell of cooking was too much, and he went to Craft Services instead.

"What do you think of the new kid?"

"Buchinsky?"

McNulty shook his head. "No. The Master Chef. Craft Services."

McNulty was sitting at a picnic table under the shelter with a plate of chicken and pasta. Amy had come over after touching up Buchinsky's makeup and was watching the actor ruin it with coffee and a doughnut at the serving hatch of Craft Services. The big guy hardly needed the steps and platform leading to the hatch, but he used them anyway, stooping to accept the cup and plate from the cook, who looked too young to be a cook. Amy concentrated on the cook.

"He seems okay. Bit young. Food's good."

McNulty had been grasping at straws since his hair-bristling moment, earlier. Trying to find anything that felt out of the ordinary. Jacob B. House felt out of the ordinary. Not just because he insisted on being called J.B., even though he was barely out of his teens. There was a shiftiness about him lately, and it wasn't lost on McNulty that Craft Services had been parked next to the makeup trailer the other night. Yes, he was grasping at straws. He stirred his pasta and smelled the aroma.

"I can't argue with that."

Amy stood behind him and placed a hand on his shoulder.

"It does feel strange though, Larry splurging on Craft Services."

McNulty nodded.

"Yeah. Says he's starting to regret going full Hollywood though."

Amy squeezed his shoulder.

"Regrets paying for it, you mean."

"You got that right."

Buchinsky joined them under the shelter. Amy stepped aside to let him sit down then bent to sniff McNulty's food.

"And since you boys are ignoring the, don't eat at night rule, I'm going to grab a bite as well."

Buchinsky feigned hurt feelings. And held up a doughnut.

"Cop food. I'm getting into character."

McNulty ignored the jibe and forked a mouthful of chicken and pasta. He had to admit the food was good, the pasta slathered in a thick creamy sauce that made the chicken even more tender. He wished he'd sprinkled some Parmesan on top but that was his fault not the chef's. Buchinsky washed down a bite of doughnut with a swig of black coffee. McNulty watched Amy climb the steps to the platform. J.B. asked her something and Amy answered. The chef half turned to serve her and caught McNulty watching him. The shifty look returned. He visibly shrank as he ladled chicken and pasta onto a disposable plate.

Amy took the tray and turned away.

J.B. House stepped back from the counter.

Then two gunshots thudded into the side of the mobile kitchen.

CHAPTER FOURTEEN

It was the third shot that did the damage. The first two thudded harmlessly into the metal siding but the third hit the propane tank that fed the stove. Sparks and hot metal ignited the gas and Craft Services disappeared in a ball of flame.

"Amy."

The deafening explosion drowned McNulty's cry and the heat knocked him off his bench. Pieces of aluminium siding rained down as hot food and shrapnel sprayed the parking lot. The light from the explosion ruined McNulty's night vision and he couldn't see Amy or the front steps or the serving hatch. The parched ground surrounding the mobile kitchen caught fire and the shade trees it was parked under began to steam. The last pieces of debris peppered the ground, then McNulty saw the most terrifying thing he'd ever seen—Amy Moore, struggling to get off the floor, the back of her clothes on fire and her face contorted in a silent scream.

That thing happened that always happens in traumatic situations. Time. Slowed. Down. While at the same time seeming to stretch to infinity. Everything happened at once but so slowly that McNulty could see each individual part as a separate entity.

Amy got to her feet and started flapping at the flames on

her back.

Two more pieces of debris crashed to the ground around her.

Blue lights flashed along Western Canyon Road.

McNulty pushed himself up using the picnic table.

He was rooted to the spot, unable to move. In shock.

Then Chuck Buchinsky broke the spell and proved why he was perfectly cast as a firefighter. He whipped off his coat, plunged it into the water trough then dashed through burning debris to the stricken makeup lady. He knocked her to the ground and smothered the flames on her back with the wet coat. He wrapped the cold damp cloth around her head and patted it gently. McNulty ran over to them as Buchinsky lifted Amy and placed her in McNulty's arms.

"Dump her in the trough."

He carefully removed the coat and looked at McNulty.

"Anybody else in there, apart from J.B?"

McNulty took the weight and braced his legs.

"Just him."

The actor nodded toward the water trough.

"Go."

McNulty shouted over his shoulder as he went.

"There's another propane tank out back."

Buchinsky was already running toward the blazing wreckage of Craft Services, the damp coat draped across his head and shoulders. Blue lights flashed as the fire crew pulled into the gravel lot, fast enough to get there quickly but not so fast they'd spit gravel. Rule of thumb with emergency response: If your tires are skidding you're not in control and if you're not in control you can't help anyone. Buchinsky was helping everyone.

McNulty lowered Amy into the trough, keeping her head out of the water. Her eyes were wide with shock, but she still managed a smile. He didn't think she knew who she was smiling at. He made soothing noises and rocked her gently, letting the water cool her down. Steam rose all around her.

Buchinsky kicked debris out of the way and climbed the

steps to the serving hatch. The basic structure of the mobile kitchen was still intact, but the roof was gone and the interior was a raging inferno. Several different shades of smoke plumed around the flames. Burning plastic, burning wood and something altogether sweeter smelling. The actor ignored the smoke and shouted the junior chef's name. There was no response. He shouted again, craning his neck to see inside the kitchen. Still no response.

There was no way for Buchinsky to get inside and look for J.B. The walls were buckled and melting. The stove had been thrust into the serving hatch by the force of the explosion and the back door had ripped off. Something started to hiss around the back of the trailer, but adrenaline kept the actor calm. In fact, he was feeling decidedly mellow. Almost happy. The sweet aroma overrode the cooking smells and burning plastic. He found himself smiling.

The hissing grew louder.

The second propane tank began to rupture.

The blue lights were bright now, flashing from a safe distance but close enough to pour water onto the fire. Craft Services began to steam as the flames were beaten back but not fast enough to stop the tank from exploding. It went up with a crumpling thud and ball of fire. Buchinsky watched with gentle amusement as the flames rushed toward him. Then McNulty rugby-tackled the actor off the raised platform and dived them both to the ground.

The second explosion demolished the rest of the mobile kitchen and water from the fire hose kept both men from burning up. Steam replaced the smoke as the fire blinked out. The fire crew dowsed everything within striking distance to ensure there were no hotspots. Buchinsky and McNulty patted each other like a frenetic play fight then rolled onto their backs to look at the wreckage.

Buchinsky was laughing.

McNulty was thinking, *I know what that smell is.*

CHAPTER FIFTEEN

"And you were going to tell me when?"

"There was no need to tell you. I hire the best man for the job."

McNulty adjusted the blanket that had been draped around his shoulders.

"The best man to play a firefighter being an ex-firefighter?"

"And the best man to teach him to walk like a cop being an ex-cop."

Larry Unger couldn't understand what McNulty was getting worked up about. Buchinsky had saved Amy Moore and McNulty had saved Buchinsky. Apart from losing the mobile kitchen to the fire, that felt like a win-win situation. McNulty didn't see it that way.

"What about the marijuana stashed in Craft Services?"

Unger threw up his arms in surprise.

"We don't know it was marijuana. Kitchen burnt to the ground."

McNulty snorted a laugh.

"Chuck's gonna be high for a week. Of course it was weed."

Unger shrugged and feigned innocence.

"When they find J.B., we can ask him. Maybe he has a medical condition."

He looked toward the singed actor being treated in the back of an ambulance.

"And stop calling him Chuck. It's Dennis. Christ, I'm still working on changing Buchinsky."

The reason they couldn't ask Jacob B. House right now was because there had been no sign of him once the fire had been put out. Just a tarnished watch with the strap melted off and a scorched chef's hat that the young cook insisted on wearing to increase his street cred as a chef to the stars. Working for Titanic Productions dented that street cred, a Z-list studio that wasn't exactly packed with stars.

The fire marshals had been on the scene almost immediately, having been parked along Western Canyon Road between the location and the bigger parking lot farther up the hill. The mobile kitchen fire had been extinguished and the flames restricted to the parched grass surrounding it and the trees it was parked under. Any danger of a wildfire spreading across Los Angeles had been averted and the damage kept to a minimum. The bottom line was that the safest place to start a fire was on a movie set. The experts knew what they were doing, and insurance premiums assured that the production company hired the right experts. The L.A. Fire Department didn't even attend; their faith in the Hollywood system was that strong.

LAPD did attend. Cops have less tolerance about guns setting off explosions. Two marked units from Hollywood Station blue-lighted to the fire and deployed a skirmish line behind Craft Services once they got the story from witnesses. The main witnesses were Amy Moore and Chuck Buchinsky as the individuals nearest the blast when the gunshots rang out. The night detective conducted the interviews in the back of an ambulance, Amy first, then Buchinsky twenty minutes later. Separately. So their stories were not influenced by the each other's version of events. Good practice.

The other witness was Vince McNulty. Larry Unger took him to one side before the detective could speak to him. Having a trailer full of marijuana on set during filming was something he wanted to keep out of the police report.

"You're an ex-cop, right?"

McNulty nodded. "Eighteen years in the U.K." He kept his tone non-committal.

"A bit less in Savage, Maryland."

The detective gave a little frown and a nod.

"Yeah, I heard about that. Shit happens. There isn't a cop on the force doesn't know how that plays."

McNulty felt the need to explain.

"He hit her. Right in front of me."

The detective held his hands up in understanding.

"Hey, I get it."

He lowered his hands.

"Good thing you're English. L-A-P-D would have shot him."

They were sitting at a table inside The Trails Café, the picnic area being too open for serious questioning. Not too cold—to McNulty it never seemed to get cold in L.A. The swing gang and the lighting crew had been released on coffee break, Unger arguing that filming would resume once the police had finished. The uniformed cops were searching the woods above the location. The detective was finalizing how he was going to record this.

"Okay, being an ex-cop, you know what I'm after. Lay it out for me."

McNulty laid it out for the detective. He explained about sitting under the picnic shelter with Buchinsky while Amy crossed to Craft Services for something to eat. The first two shots that punched holes in the metal siding then the third that set off the explosion.

"Was there a pause between the second and third?"

McNulty considered that. "Maybe a bit. Not much." He tried to put it into words. "The rhythm wasn't bang-bang-bang." He slowed down his words. "More like, bang-bang. Bang."

"So, enough to change targets."

McNulty shook his head. "I'm not sure there was any targeting involved."

The detective consulted his notes. "There must have been some. First two in the side of the trailer, you said. Third around the back."

McNulty shifted in his seat.

"Only because I heard the first two hit on the left and the propane tanks are around the back."

"Two distinctive places."

"But still the same general direction. Just because people own guns doesn't mean they can aim."

"Good enough to hit a mobile kitchen."

McNulty laid his hands on the table. "I don't think they were aiming at the mobile kitchen."

The detective toyed with his notepad. "Even after dark. Easy to see a big silver trailer."

"Bullets don't always go where they're supposed to. And they don't stop if you miss."

"Line of fire, you're saying."

"I'm saying if you miss a tin can, the shot won't stop until something stops it."

McNulty turned his hands palms up. "That's what they were shooting at this afternoon."

Again, the detective consulted his notes. "According to Carl Robarge."

McNulty gave a little shrug. "Target practice. Don't know if it was tin cans."

The detective looked at the technical adviser.

"They didn't improve much by tonight then."

McNulty shrugged again. "If it was the same people."

The detective pounced on that. "There was more than one?"

"Figuratively speaking. People. Person."

The detective changed tack. "Buchinsky says he felt light-headed. A sweet smell, he said."

McNulty had been waiting for this.

"The chicken and pasta had coconut in it. Like a korma sauce."

"Korma makes you lightheaded?"

"Being blown up makes you lightheaded." McNulty raised his eyebrows. "Surviving makes you pretty fucking happy."

The detective closed his notepad. "He was laughing."

McNulty kept his hands flat on the table.

"Shock."

The detective scrutinized McNulty's face.

"He's an ex-firefighter."

McNulty kept it blank.

"I'm an ex-cop. We can all go into shock."

"You didn't."

McNulty felt a shiver run down his spine. He took a deep breath and lowered his eyes. When he raised them, the detective could see a world of hurt that went way beyond what McNulty had seen tonight.

"Seeing Amy like that. That shocked me."

The detective softened his tone. "I'm sure it did. Sorry."

He looked at McNulty a few seconds longer then swept the notepad off the table, pushed back his chair and stood up.

"I'll call off the search for the gunman and close the file."

He put the notepad into his pocket.

"I'm sure the chef is in shock as well. He might be injured somewhere out there. We'll keep looking for him."

He held out a hand for McNulty to shake. The two cops exchanged a silent farewell then the detective walked out the door. McNulty watched him go. He didn't think they'd be finding the chef anytime soon. That left McNulty wondering just how much marijuana had been stored in the mobile kitchen. And who else knew it was there. He was starting to think the intruder in the compound last night had nothing to do with the girl sleeping in the yard at the Hollywood Collision Center.

CHAPTER SIXTEEN

Tilly Nutton didn't learn about the explosion until the following morning. It was part of breakfast television while she was eating Honey Nut Cheerios in the kitchen and watching Kimberley Howe make waffles. The news reporter made light of the fire on Western Canyon Road because that's what breakfast television was. Light and fluffy. The injuries were described as minor and not requiring hospital treatment but the accompanying photos chilled Tilly to the bone.

Amy Moore looked younger in the archive headshot. The actor who used to be a firefighter looked bigger and stronger. Tilly dropped the spoon in her bowl of cereal and hugged herself. Partly it was because the woman who'd been so kind to her had been injured, but mostly it was something else. Her mind raced through a variety of scenarios but the one that made her shiver was, *they've found me.*

Stowing away amid the spare car parts at the truck stop had been the easy part. Getting to the truck stop had been much harder, not only physically but emotionally. The horses had made Rancho Verde feel idyllic, despite the danger. Horses are sweet and innocent and just want to live a simple life. No drama. No pain. They don't want to hurt anyone and always seem to be smiling. She wasn't sure about the smiling part, but they certainly never looked unhappy. Tilly was unhappy when she left.

The hike across parched hills and dry riverbeds took three days, traveling mostly at night to avoid detection. A child alone in the wilderness would draw attention. Tilly had had too much attention already. She was eight years old, but life added a couple of years, making her appear older and much more mature. A hard skin that nobody could penetrate. That's how you survive when you're on your own. Except she wasn't on her own, that was the problem. Until now. She felt guilty about that.

You shouldn't need to feel guilty at eight.

Coming out of the hills, she'd found the truck stop at Sulphur Springs around midday. Just north of the Six Flags Theme Park on the I-5. The final half-mile had been the dangerous part because the foothills ran alongside the Hillcrest Parkway housing estate and a bedraggled eight-year-old was always going to stand out at that time on a school day. Her food had run out the day before and she'd just finished the last of the water. The truck stop stood out like a beacon on a stormy night. Truck stops always have a diner next to the gas station and diners always have leftovers.

She reached the back of the diner in the early afternoon. The sun had dried her skin and made her scalp itch. She felt lightheaded and dizzy. She'd heard about people in the desert seeing mirages and oases before dropping to their knees, babbling like a crazy person. Tilly was beginning to feel like a crazy person. She wouldn't believe the diner was real until she actually tasted some food. She found the food in a trash can around the back and drank water from an outside faucet.

Stowing away had been an accident. She'd seen a truck driver bring pizza and bottled water from the diner and put the box on the footplate when he was caught short and had to dash to the restroom. Tilly snuck between the other trucks and opened the box. Hawaiian with extra cheese. The smell of ham and pineapple lulled her into a false sense of security, and she hadn't heard the restroom door close until it was almost too late. She left the pizza but took the water and scrambled onto the back of the truck. A tarpaulin covered the pallet of spare car parts and she hid under the tarpaulin, waiting for the driver to leave.

Except the driver didn't leave; the truck did, and it didn't stop again until it pulled into an enclosed yard at the Hollywood Collision Center. As if that weren't bad enough, just when the yard grew quiet so she could sneak out, a bunch of movie people started setting up for the night shoot and she was trapped until a big man with a quiet voice whipped off the tarpaulin.

"You want anything else with that?"

Kimberley Howe didn't think the girl could possibly eat anything else. She had never seen a child eat so much in such a short time. You'd think she'd been starved for a week to be able to fit it all in. The girl shook her head and continued to eat. Kim glanced at the TV but the breakfast show had moved on to the weather. This was Los Angeles, so she knew what the weather was going to be: hot and sunny with a U.V. factor through the roof.

"I've got a couple of things to do over at the school."

She looked at the spread of food the girl still had to eat.

"Will you be okay for a while?"

The girl nodded, either unwilling to speak or not wanting to talk with her mouth full. Kim reckoned it was the former. The girl hadn't said two words since Amy had dropped her off yesterday. That wasn't a problem. She knew about damaged kids. She'd been one herself. Time and understanding were great healers. Kim and Amy had plenty of understanding. Time would take care of itself.

"Okay. I won't be long. Help yourself in the refrigerator."

She went to the door and looked back at the girl, still engrossed with her food. Like Amy had said, it was nice to have someone to look after. She nodded once then crossed the parking lot to Glen Alta Elementary.

Tilly watched Kim shut the door and disappear. People disappearing was something she'd grown used to. People with shared experience living in the prison the grownups called a school. She looked across the parking lot at the concrete building with barbed wire that Amy and Kim had called a school. Tilly didn't know what Alcatraz was, but she knew about prisons. Places where you were locked in and bad things happened. Places you break out of to leave the bad things behind.

She put her knife and fork down and pushed the plate away. She'd eaten enough to keep her going, and there was plenty in the fridge to last the journey back. She looked around the kitchen and felt a moment of sadness. This was the nicest house she'd ever stayed in. She couldn't remember where she'd lived before the bad place, but she knew where she'd lived after. After the breakout. The place with horses and running water. The second place she had run away from. Running away wasn't what made her feel guilty. It was the kids she'd left behind. The other kids with shared experience. The ones she'd brought with her when she escaped, then abandoned when she ran again.

CHAPTER SEVENTEEN

McNulty was working from a different angle. Not a missing girl being hunted by unknown parties but a missing chef who'd been dealing marijuana from the location kitchen. Finding the missing chef was less important than discovering who wanted to put him out of business. The best way to find out whose turf J.B. had been treading on was to ask the police. McNulty couldn't ask the police, but he could do the next best thing—ask someone who used to be a police officer. Once a cop always a cop.

He remembered Jim Grant talking about the technical adviser he'd met during the L.A. bank robbery and porn investigation. Around the same time as the Montecito Heights gunfight and the showdown with the Dominguez Cartel. Chuck Tanburro had been filming *CSI: New York* on the streets of Los Angeles. Ex-cops always have contacts that are still on the job and technical advisers always have contact with other technical advisers. McNulty found Tanburro's number and gave him a call.

"It's a shame, what happened to Grant. But I'm not surprised."

McNulty gave Tanburro a steady look.

"You're not?"

Tanburro returned the stare. Two ex-cops chewing the fat.

"Same thing nearly happened here. At the bank heist."

He shrugged.

"Nobody's fault."

He softened the stare.

"What happened in Drake. That was nobody's fault, either."

They were sitting outside The Terrace Café on West Washington Boulevard at Venice Beach. Tanburro was consulting on a new cop show, having previously worked on *CSI: New York* and *Southland*. McNulty thought *Southland* was the most authentic cop show after *The Sweeney* but dismissed *CSI: New York* as a piece of TV nonsense. They were filming at the Venice Canals around the back, a location that had featured in everything from *Chinatown* to *Hollywood Homicide*, including a brief scene in *Southland*. After getting the call he'd agreed to meet McNulty during a break in filming. Blue sky. Hot sun. Brightly colored café. The atmosphere didn't feel brightly colored. Tanburro took a swig of fresh orange juice.

"He survived."

"He was dead for five minutes."

"But he survived. I'm sure he told you himself. It wasn't your fault."

McNulty sighed and looked out across the beach. Women in next-to-nothing jiggled past and surfers rode their boards. Two girls on rollerblades proved what exercise could do for toning your buttocks. They stopped outside the T-Shirt Shop next door, flexing their butt cheeks until they did a little jiggle dance. Even the display of naked flesh couldn't distract McNulty.

"We kind of lost touch."

Tanburro put his glass on the table.

"You haven't been to see him?"

McNulty shrugged and didn't answer. Tanburro folded his arms.

"Survivor guilt."

"Larry Unger, my producer. He reckons I'm an angry man."

Tanburro laughed.

"We're all angry men. That's what makes us good cops."

McNulty smiled at something Grant once said.

"Good cop, bad cop."

Tanburro nodded.

"Bad cop being a good cop. Good cops always run toward the danger, not away from it. Jim did that here. I'm sure that's what he did in Colorado, as well. End of story."

He leaned back in his chair and took another swig of orange juice.

"So, now I've given absolution. What can I help you with?"

People had been lobbying for the legalization of marijuana for years, but they'd had no more success in America than they had in England. The authorities saw it as a stepping-stone to hard drugs and didn't want to be accused of helping promote addiction. The fact that more people were addicted to cigarettes than weed did nothing to dissuade the powers-that-be. Bottom line was the government was making too much money from tobacco and nothing from marijuana. That strengthened the argument to legalize and tax it but the Bible belt was a powerful force in America.

"Corporate hospitality is mainly responsible."

McNulty frowned.

"Business types?"

Tanburro held his glass up for a refill.

"Show-business types."

The waitress nodded and went inside. Tanburro put the glass down and turned in his chair so he could stretch his legs. He looked the epitome of the laid-back California dude—if you didn't know he'd been a hard-as-nails cop.

"TV. Movies. Hollywood in general. They all want to keep the talent happy. Getting a little high keeps them happy. They can afford to. Legality doesn't come into it."

McNulty shifted his position but didn't stretch out his legs.

"Marijuana not being considered hard drugs."

Tanburro nodded.

"Everything has consequences. The consequences are just different for the haves than they are for the have-nots."

McNulty let out a sigh. It was the same story the world over.

"The rich go into rehab. The poor go to jail."

"That's about the size of it."

McNulty looked at the Californian.

"The police turn a blind eye?"

Tanburro shook his head.

"The police don't have a blind eye. They just have priorities. Things that get people killed come first. Most drug wars are over the hard stuff. Nobody gets killed over weed."

McNulty toyed with his empty glass.

"Somebody got pissed off over ours."

The waitress brought two refills even though McNulty hadn't asked for one and took the empties. Tanburro nodded his thanks and took a drink.

"I know somebody in the D-E-A. Local guy. I'll reach out."

McNulty wiped the condensation off his glass and used it to cool his brow.

"DEA work marijuana?"

"Not so much. But he's got his finger on the pulse. When he can."

He finished his drink in two big gulps and let out a satisfied breath.

"They've been stripped out. Like everything, more work, less staff. Diverted for terrorism first. Now it's people trafficking."

McNulty pushed his glass toward Tanburro and waved for him to take it.

"They still do that? I'd have thought they'd be smuggling people out of the states these days."

Tanburro chuckled.

"Building a wall works both ways."

He held the glass up in thanks and took another drink. He could certainly knock back his orange juice. A rollerblader skated past in a high-cut swimsuit and nothing else. Both cops watched the toned thighs and perfect buttocks glide along the Ocean Front Walk then turned back to the table. McNulty looked at Tanburro.

"Has he still got it in for the Mexicans?"

Tanburro finished his third orange juice.

"It's not just Mexicans. It's East Europeans. Even middle America."

"Why smuggle Americans?"

"Not smuggling. Trafficking. Moving around the country. It's modern-day slavery. Sex workers mainly."

His tone became serious.

"Kids groomed from birth. Like battery hens."

McNulty shivered. The last place he'd seen young girls groomed for the sex trade had been the Northern X massage chain. It seemed some things never leave you alone.

CHAPTER EIGHTEEN

Amy Moore wasn't the type to sit in bed and be nursed. She was dressed and ready for some fresh air when McNulty got back to the Pilgrim Motel. It was mid-morning, and the sun was already blazing out of a clear blue sky. The rest of the production team was taking it easy and waiting for the revised shooting schedule. Larry Unger was being optimistic when he'd suggested filming would continue after the fire was put out. The night shoot had been abandoned and was due to catch up tonight. That meant trying to cram three nights' filming into two. Amy was climbing the walls. McNulty tried being diplomatic.

"Your hair looks good cut short."

Amy gave him a hard stare.

"It's not cut short. It's burned-the-fuck off."

Considering how close she'd been to the explosion, Amy's injuries were superficial at best and life-changing at worst. It was only life-changing if you considered that having a new hairdo forced upon you was life-changing. There were no major burns and hardly any discomfort caused by the slight reddening from the heat. The leather coat she'd been wearing after touching up Buchinsky's makeup had taken most of the blast and McNulty's dumping her in the water trough had reduced the heat. There was no pain, so superficial sounded about right. But it didn't feel very superficial to Amy.

"I haven't had my hair this short since convent school."
"You were in a convent?"
"Convent school. The nuns were in a convent."
McNulty sat beside her on the bed.
"How are you feeling?"
Amy wasn't ready for sympathy.
"Like I was slow roasted then dropped in a cold bath."
"You remember that?"
Amy's shoulders sagged.
"I remember a lot of things."
McNulty wanted to put his arms around her but was afraid the inflammation would still be sore. It seemed like every time somebody got hurt, he felt guilty that it wasn't him. Angry-man survivor guilt was a heavy cross to bear and he wished he didn't have to bear it for everyone. He wasn't the one who'd been selling weed out of Craft Services.

"Take it easy for a couple of days."
Amy let out a sigh.
"Taking it easy gives me too much time to think. What I need to do is keep busy."
She turned sad eyes on McNulty and he could see she was struggling with her own version of survivor guilt.
"Have they found J.B. yet?"
At least he could help ease that for her.
"Master Chef was selling weed from the kitchen. My guess is we won't be seeing him any time soon."
"He survived?"
"Apart from his watch and his chef's hat."
This time she sighed in relief. She leaned against McNulty and rested her head on his chest. McNulty risked putting a gentle arm around her waist and they both sat in silence for a moment. He could feel the heat through her clothes, so he kissed the top of her head. After a few minutes she jerked upright and looked at McNulty.
"What about Tilly?"

McNulty nodded. This was something else he could ease for her.

"I spoke to Kim this morning. Looks like the girl doesn't know about the fire. Eating like a horse apparently."

Amy's face softened.

"Horse Whisperer."

She remembered the imitation Swiss Army knife with its bottle opener and that thing for getting stones out of horses' shoes. She relaxed against McNulty.

"This wasn't about her then?"

McNulty shook his head.

"It's about corporate hospitality."

Amy proved she had her finger on the pulse.

"And somebody not wanting J.B. to be so hospitable."

McNulty gave her a gentle squeeze.

"You step on somebody's toes, sometimes they step back."

He kissed her head again then stood up. Now that he'd checked on Amy and knew she was okay, it was time to get back to police work. He took the master key he'd borrowed from the receptionist, tossed it into the air and caught it.

"So it's time I found out who's doing the stepping."

CHAPTER NINETEEN

Jacob B. House was a single guy living the Hollywood dream, if that dream was being a chef and selling weed to the stars. Befitting his station in life, he had a downstairs room at the opposite end to the motel reception. The room was the farthest from the compound and his supply of marijuana, giving McNulty hope that he might not have left all of his stash in the Craft Services trailer. If there was any in his room the packaging might give a clue about who had been supplying him.

McNulty stood at the door and felt a shiver run down his spine. There was a reason that deja vu and cliché were so closely linked. Because cops searching a suspect's room is something that cops do, and the feeling of having lived something before was because McNulty had done this before. Back in Boston, Brad Semenoff had been the second assistant cameraman on a movie, and McNulty had suspected him of making pornographic snuff movies, using Titanic Productions's equipment and film. While searching Semeoff's room, McNulty had been hit on the head. He didn't want to be hit on the head again.

Now, standing outside J.B.'s room, he couldn't see through the window because the draperies were drawn. All he could see was the reflection of Cahuenga Boulevard East and the Pilgrimage Bridge, which were behind him, and his own face. He listened as traffic hummed below the bridge on the Hollywood Freeway and studied his reflection, a shadowy figure who looked tired. McNulty knew it was more than simply fatigue. It was the weight of history. Apart from all the shit he'd grown up with, he'd had to witness Semenoff's being mown down while running across the parking lot. Semenoff was disfigured and dead, but worse, he'd lasted long enough to know he was disfigured and to feel the pain. McNulty didn't want any more pain today.

He hesitated, glanced over his shoulder then slipped the key into the lock. Fuck the pain. He opened the door.

Amy Moore pushed back from leaning over the balcony rail once she'd seen McNulty disappear into the downstairs room. It felt like she was watching a cop movie, the detective checking around him before breaking into the suspect's room. McNulty wasn't a cop, but he sure acted like one. He walked the walk and talked the talk. That's why he made such a good technical adviser. Even so, breaking into somebody's room was more than Larry Unger was paying him for. Amy hoped he wasn't overstepping the mark.

She took a deep breath, glad to be out in the fresh air at last, and flexed her back and shoulders, careful not to aggravate the inflamed skin. Like she'd said to McNulty, she needed to keep busy, so she went back into her room and started packing some things for Tilly.

McNulty was doing the opposite—he was unpacking, and not being very tidy about it. J.B.'s room had the same layout as Amy's, except it wasn't an executive suite. That meant it had a chair instead of a settee and a more basic bathroom. The narrow desk and wardrobe were identical to Amy's. It was the wardrobe he was emptying first.

J.B. House must have been the tidiest single white male McNulty had ever known. Half a dozen coat hangers hung straight and tidy on the left, mainly shirts and a spare jacket. Two shelves on the right had neatly folded T-shirts and sweaters, and the three drawers below them held underwear and socks. There were no handkerchiefs but there was a six-pack of paper tissues on the bedside table. McNulty bunched the coat hangers together and threw them on the bed before patting each shirt and the jacket for hidden items. He did the same with the T-shirts and sweaters before emptying the drawers. He pulled the drawers all the way out and checked behind them for Scotch-taped envelopes, a favorite place to hide things. There was nothing taped behind the drawers.

Next, he checked the desk. There wasn't much to check. The desk was small and narrow, fastened to the wall and barely protruding far enough to get your knees under. There was a thin drawer above the leg space that was just thick enough for the Gideon Bible and a notepad. There was nothing written on the notepad. McNulty held it sideways to the light, looking for indentations. He had never seen that work outside of the movies. When he'd finished, he stepped back and surveyed the damage. The room was a mess and he'd found nothing.

Now it was time to inspect the bathroom.

Again, the bathroom was the same layout as Amy's just not as luxurious. The Pilgrim Motel didn't do luxurious so J.B.'s bathroom was downright basic. There was a bathtub with a shower curtain, a toilet with the cistern hidden in the wall and a single sink with a boxed-in cupboard underneath for storage. An empty wastebasket sat next to the sink. There was no bathroom cabinet, just a mirror and a glass shelf with J.B.'s soap and toothbrush on it.

The most popular hiding places in a bathroom are the toilet cistern and the bath panel. The cistern was inaccessible without plumbing tools and the bath rested on the floor with no room under the bathtub. He took the panel off anyway for completeness but there was no space inside. That just left the boxed-in sink. He sat on the edge of the bathtub and looked at the cupboard door.

The motel room was quiet. Double windowpanes and the bathroom door muted the freeway traffic. The only sound was a car door closing in the parking lot and McNulty's breath in his own ears. He leaned forward, resting folded arms on his knees, and took a deep breath. So far, there had been no sign of illegal activity. The cupboard beneath the sink was his last hope. He let out a sigh and opened the cupboard door. It was empty.

McNulty stood up and kicked the wastebasket next to the sink. He gave J.B.'s toiletries a cursory examination but the chef wasn't going to be hiding weed in his toothpaste. He dropped the tube on the shelf and leaned against the washbasin. He closed his eyes and tilted his head to the ceiling. He took a deep breath and let out another sigh, then opened his eyes.

One of the ceiling tiles above the bath wasn't straight.

Archimedes reportedly exclaimed "Eureka!" twice when he stepped into the bathtub and discovered that the water level rose. McNulty had his eureka moment in the bathroom as well, except it wasn't the water level rising, it was the ceiling tile falling—together with a cascade of pretty little baggies of happiness.

McNulty reached up and tilted the ceiling tile.

Happiness rained on his parade.

The tile fell out of its frame and dropped to the floor. McNulty stepped back to avoid being hit on the head, something he was specifically keen to avoid. The little plastic dealer bags showered his head and shoulders, coming out of the hole at an angle, like somebody taking a piss. When the pissing stopped, he was standing ankle deep in a pile of individually wrapped marijuana portions.

"Eureka!"

He didn't say it twice. He dropped to one knee and riffled through J.B.'s backup stash. There were different shades of leaf and several blocks of concentrated dope. His fingers unearthed a plain white business card. McNulty thought he was going to have a second eureka moment but the card was blank, apart from a rubber-stamped pink poodle. He checked the bags. They had the pink poodle stamp as well, each with a number denoting whatever the bag contained.

McNulty made sure the toilet lid was down and sat on the toilet. He shifted the bags with his foot then looked at the ceiling. The hole was dark, exposing plumbing and wiring that no doubt stretched the length of the motel. It appeared to be empty, but he couldn't be sure. Just because one ceiling tile was out of place didn't mean it was the only access point. He stood up and tilted the neighboring tiles.

More plastic bags fell out.

"Yippee ki eureka!"

He got up onto the edge of the bathtub, and using the flashlight on his phone, looked into the darkness. Now the roof space was empty. There were no more surprises. He jumped down, avoiding squashing any baggies, and stood in the doorway looking at the haul. He leaned against the doorframe and let out a long slow whistle. No more surprises? He was wrong. The front door burst open and two cops came in. The uniforms were intimidating enough, but it was the guns that got his attention.

CHAPTER TWENTY

They took him to Hollywood Station on Wilcox Avenue, a plain, red brick building that reminded McNulty of an outside restroom block. There were no windows. There was only one entrance. There had been no attempt to beautify the building. The letters on the front read:

LOS ANGELES POLICE DEPARTMENT
HOLLYWOOD STATION
1358

The only other markings were a blue sign on one wall, advertising a "Twenty-Four Hour ATM Inside" and a sagging banner asking people to "Help Keep Our City Safe—Join LAPD Reserves." There were eight Hollywood Walk-of-Fame stars on the sidewalk in front. McNulty couldn't tell if they were real or fake as the patrol car drove past the entrance and swung into the loading bay for the custody suite in the rear of the building.

A rundown single-story building opposite was the home of SOS Bail Bonds, Central Jail Bail Bonds and Potter Bail Bonds ("Collateral Not Always Necessary"). McNulty reckoned he'd have more use for the ATM than the Bail Bonds. He'd keep quiet until he needed to speak. He didn't need to speak until they processed him, took his property and sat him in an interview room.

***

"My producer said he saw a poodle once, wearing little pink booties."

"Your producer being the guy whose location catering truck blew up at Griffith Observatory."

"It wasn't at the observatory."

"I'll bet the observatory was in the background though, wasn't it?"

McNulty couldn't argue with that, since the decision to use The Trails Café was based entirely on having Griffith Observatory in the background. Almost entirely. The cost was dramatically reduced while still looking like they were filming at the iconic location. McNulty nodded.

"If you got the angle right. And the light."

The interview room got the light right. They always did. There were no windows and no mirrors, just fluorescent tubes in a white ceiling and absorbent wall tiles for soundproofing. It could have been morning, noon or night. The idea was that, in the absence of a wall clock or a personal watch, the prisoner would be disorientated if the police kept him waiting long enough. The detective hadn't left McNulty long enough. He knew exactly what time it was. It was time to choose Bail Bonds or the ATM.

"Why would anyone need an ATM in a police station?"

Miguel Guerrero leaned back in the chair and crossed his legs, ankle of one leg resting casually on the knee of the other. Relaxed. Informal. Guerrero wasn't the same detective who had interviewed McNulty the night before, but he obviously had been in touch with the night detective. They both agreed it was never a good situation, interviewing an ex-cop. Even an ex-cop from the U.K. There was always an assumption of professional courtesy toward a fellow officer, even when that officer was retired. McNulty wasn't retired; he'd been sacked—twice. The night detective and Guerrero had discussed a lot more than the awkwardness of having to interview an ex-cop.

"So prisoners can pay the bail."

McNulty sat sideways, drumming the fingers of one hand on the interview table. He reckoned that the professional courtesy was that the interview wasn't being recorded. Yet.

"I thought collateral wasn't always necessary."

Guerrero laid a hand on the manila folder as if swearing on the Bible.

"You don't need to worry about bail. Standing in a roomful of industrial-grade recreational drugs."

"Not my drugs."

"Somebody's. And you're the nearest."

McNulty stopped drumming his fingers.

"It wasn't my room."

Guerrero tapped the folder.

"You were in it."

"I can explain."

"I wish you would."

McNulty swivelled in his chair to face the detective, his legs under the table. He took a deep breath and arranged his thoughts. He wasn't sure he could explain so he decided to tell the truth. Or at least a version of the truth. He knew from interviewing countless felons that the best lie was the one that was almost true. McNulty went with almost true.

"Jacob House has been missing since the explosion last night. He's our location chef. I was checking to see if he'd come back to his room."

Guerrero kept his tone non-judgmental.

"And you had to break in to do that?"

McNulty kept his tone matter of fact.

"I didn't break in."

Guerrero kept soft eyes on McNulty, not exactly staring at him but watching for any small movement that would give away the lie. It was good interview technique, not provoking a response but not being soft, either.

"You didn't knock and get let in."

McNulty dressed the lie.

"I did knock, but there was no answer."

"So you broke in."

McNulty wouldn't be drawn.

"I used the master key from reception."

Guerrero wasn't going to let McNulty off the hook that easily.

"And used it to gain entry to a room that wasn't yours and that you had no legal right to enter. That's entering as a trespasser. That's burglary."

McNulty didn't know the wording in America, so he quoted the U.K. law.

"Enter premises or part of a premises belonging to another and steal property or commit criminal damage. Or enter with intent to steal property or commit damage. I didn't steal anything."

Guerrero put his leg down and crossed the other one.

"You trashed his room."

McNulty kept a straight face.

"That was done before I got there."

Guerrero turned the folder sideways, then straightened it again.

"You're saying someone else burgled his room?"

McNulty didn't nod or shake his head. He knew he was being maneuvered into giving a yes or no answer that would tie him to the lie. There was no way out of giving an answer, so he fudged it.

"Somebody did."

Guerrero uncrossed his legs and rested his arms on the table.

"And left three hundred dealers' bags on the bathroom floor."

McNulty knew there was no way of getting around that one, so he took it head-on.

"No. That was me."

Guerrero was taken aback, getting a confession so early in the interview.

"Your drugs?"

McNulty shook his head.

"My action that brought the ceiling down."

Guerrero sat back in his chair.

"Did you think you'd find him in the ceiling?"

McNulty twisted the knife in the lie.

"I was shocked at the mess in the room so I went to rinse my face in the bathroom. When I looked in the mirror I saw the ceiling tile had been dislodged. When I pushed it, the whole thing came down."

"And you found yourself ankle deep in Pink Poodle dealer bags."

McNulty shrugged.

"I know it looks bad."

Guerrero turned the manila folder on the table once again and rested his hands on either side.

"Oh, it's worse than bad. They found the dealer's body two hours ago."

CHAPTER TWENTY-ONE

There are many upsides to being an ex-cop. There's the self-confidence and body language that single you out when you walk into a room. The shoulders-back-straight-walking approach. The steady look and no-blink stare that tells people you're not someone to mess with. It doesn't hurt your resume either, being able to say you spent X number of years as a serving police officer in X place, and X number of years in X. It helps if you're ex-military, too, something that applied to Jim Grant but not Vince McNulty.

The downsides are fewer but significantly steeper. Self-confidence and body language can get you into trouble without the badge to back you up. And you always feel you're safe if you didn't do the thing you're being accused of. You assume the truth will out. Bottom line, McNulty should have kept quiet after the body was mentioned. But he didn't.

"So let me get this straight. Finding me in a roomful of dealer bags somehow makes me a suspect for killing the dealer?"

"I didn't say you were a suspect."

"But you're talking to me about it in an L-A-P-D interview room."

"I'm talking to you about a man being dead, and the Pink

Poodle dealer bags probably being the reason he was killed."

"Maybe you should talk to the Pink Poodle guy."

Guerrero turned the manila folder slightly so McNulty couldn't see and opened it. He appeared to be reading something then closed the folder. He gave McNulty the steady no-blink stare.

"What happened at The Trails Café?"

McNulty no-blinked back.

"You know what happened. You talked to the night detective."

Guerrero smiled a gentle humor-me smile.

"You tell me."

McNulty wasn't fooled by the smile but still felt safe in the knowledge that he'd done nothing wrong. Instead of clamming up and asking for a lawyer he settled back and folded his arms.

"We were taking a break from filming on location. Buchinsky, me and Amy. Amy went over to the Craft Services truck to get something to eat; then there were gunshots and the kitchen exploded."

Guerrero wasn't writing anything down.

"How many shots?"

"Two in the side and one in the back."

"So, three?"

"Yes, three. The third must have hit the propane tank. That's when the whole thing went up."

Guerrero still wasn't writing.

"Targeted shooting."

McNulty shrugged.

"The side was a long way from the propane tanks."

"Not a very good shot then."

"Depends on what he was aiming at."

Guerrero tilted his head in inquiry.

"You saw it was a he?"

McNulty shook his head.

"Figure of speech."

Guerrero drummed a little paradiddle on the folder.

"And you didn't see the daytime shooter either?"

"I didn't see anything. I was under the car."

"He shot at you?"

McNulty shook his head again.

"Somewhere up in the hills. I don't know what he shot at. Could have been random, like the night shooter."

Guerrero signed off the paradiddle with a double-tap.

"Except the night shooter blew up a catering truck full of weed."

McNulty kept steady eyes on the detective.

"It burned to the ground. It was certainly full of chicken and pasta."

"Chicken and pasta didn't get Buchinsky high."

Guerrero leaned forward.

"And you weren't ankle deep in dried chicken baggies at the motel." He lowered his voice. "But you were caught in possession of dealer weight narcotics."

McNulty was beginning to doubt his I'm-safe-because-I-didn't-do-anything stance. The other downside of being an ex-cop is you think you can talk your way out of anything. McNulty continued to try.

"Standing in the same room isn't possession. It's standing."

Guerrero confirmed that the same was true in the U.S.

"Possession is…"

He held up a finger and tapped it with a finger of his other hand.

"Having it on your person."

He held a second finger up and tapped that.

"Having it in a building or part of a building in your control."

He held up a third finger.

"Control being the room was locked and you had the key."

He turned the hand into a fist.

"And you were caught in the room. That's possession."

McNulty's confidence took another hit, but two things made him carry on. One, he wasn't guilty of anything. And two, the interview wasn't being recorded. If he were truly a suspect, he'd be sitting in front of a microphone wearing handcuffs. The detective wasn't even taking notes. This was bullshit aimed at shaking things loose. McNulty had nothing to shake loose.

"You seem like a good detective. I'm sure you've worked the timeline."

It was McNulty's turn to use his fingers.

One finger.

"I was interviewed most of the night after the explosion."

Two fingers.

"I've been at the motel all morning."

Three fingers.

"And I got the key from reception half an hour before your boys found me in the room."

He turned his hand into a fist.

"Meaning I didn't store the drugs in the ceiling and had no time to kill the poor bastard who'd been selling them. Check your time of death. Watch the C-C-T-V."

He leaned back in his chair, looking more confident than he felt.

"I'm accounted for the whole time."

Guerrero watched the show of confidence and drummed another paradiddle. No particular tune. No particular tempo. Just a thoughtful little rhythm to give him time to think. He stopped the drumming and rested both hands flat on the manila folder. He'd been right earlier—it was always awkward interviewing an ex-cop. He'd extended professional courtesy by not having McNulty in handcuffs and by not formally recording the interview. He'd had enough leeway to do that because he didn't think the Englishman had killed the drug dealer or stored the narcotics. He took a deep breath and let it out slowly. Not so much a sigh as a statement of intent—that he was giving this due consideration but that he didn't consider McNulty a serious suspect in either crime. He wasn't letting him completely off the hook, either.

"Something you might want to consider."

He put his hands together and interlaced the fingers.

"Jacob B. House worked for Titanic Productions."

He turned his hands inside out and flexed them till the joints cracked.

"Your producer has a thing for poodles in little pink booties."

He stood and picked up the manila folder.

"And House was supplying bags of Pink Poodle before he was blown up on a Titanic Productions location shoot."

He went to the door, knocked to be let out, then turned back to McNulty.

"Professional courtesy ends here. Think about that in your cell."

McNulty swiveled in his seat to watch the detective.

"What about bail?"

The door opened but Guerrero didn't go out. He stood in the doorway and looked back into the interview room.

"You only get bail if you're charged and going to court."

"So, release me without charge."

Guerrero shook his head.

"I told you. Professional courtesy ends here. There's something you're not telling me. I'm keeping you while I make further inquiries."

He went out and shut the windowless door. It sounded heavy and final in the soundproof room.

CHAPTER TWENTY-TWO

The something McNulty wasn't telling the detective was currently buying a ticket north at Union Station. Tilly Nutton felt guilty about stealing money from the woman at Montecito Heights, but rationalized it by weighing it against the guilt of leaving the other kids behind. If there was good and the greater good, then the opposite was also true. Tilly reckoned taking the money wasn't for the greater bad.

Mid-afternoon in Downtown Los Angeles was hot and busy but at least an eight-year-old girl didn't stand out as much as she had while crossing the parched hills adjacent to the Hillcrest Parkway housing development. Union Station was more welcoming than the truck stop at Sulphur Springs, but it also was more confusing.

Tilly sat in a small park across the street from the main entrance for half an hour while she considered her options. She sat beneath a statue of some Mexican on a horse whose name was Antonio Aguilar. She didn't know who Antonio Aguilar was, but she felt comforted by the horse. It reminded her of Rancho Verde, the place she was trying to get back to. It would have been easier to steal a horse and ride there than figure out how to use Union Station.

The approach was lined with tall, thin palm trees and multiple pathways. The building itself looked like a Mexican church with its high windows and red tiled roof. The clock tower was imposing and looked down on the constant stream of humanity flowing in and out of the main entrance. There were bus stops out front and a walled garden beside the clock tower. The station housed a metro stop for the subway and eleven aboveground train lines, including Amtrak and Metro Link trains. Some had exotic names like Sunset Limited or Pacific Surfliner, along with more traditional routes like Ventura County Line and Antelope Valley Line. All the way through the other side was the Megabus Station. Tilly had never been on a bus or a train. She preferred being at the Sulphur Springs truck stop, hopping a truck.

She leaned back on the park bench and opened the backpack she'd brought from the house at Montecito Heights. There was bread and cheese and sliced meat, but she hadn't wasted time making sandwiches. There was also fruit and chocolate and three cans of soda, but it was the bottled water that made her lick her lips. Sugar rush she didn't need but she knew from past experience that water was the lifesaver. The sun was hot and she checked the shadows to gauge the position of the sun. Mid-afternoon. Sun heading west. That meant north was to her left. Now all she had to do was find a train that went that direction.

The departure hall was even more impressive than the exterior. Tilly felt the strength go out of her legs at the sight of it and knelt to fasten an imaginary shoelace to cover her dizziness. She didn't want some do-gooder coming over to help the poor little eight-year-old. The poor little eight-year-old scanned the room for likely predators, the kind of men who'd been preying on the kids at Rancho Verde long before they'd escaped to Rancho Verde. Everyone seemed to be intent on getting wherever they were going. Nobody paid any attention to the girl fastening her shoelace.

Tilly stood up and adjusted the backpack on her shoulder. The hall was high, wide and handsome with heavy wooden beams supporting the ornate wood ceiling. Comfortable leather chairs lined either side of the central walkway, which was lit by low-hanging chandeliers and tall, narrow windows. The Arrivals and Departures boards were on the far wall, Arrivals on the left of the walkway and Departures on the right. A sign above the central plaza read, "TO TRAINS & BUS PLAZA." Tilly didn't know which she needed so she went to the Departures board.

She looked up at the list of trains going to a variety of places, most of which she'd never heard of and certainly never been to. There were listings for the Orange County Line, the Pacific Surfliner and Southwest Chief, but she didn't know which line went north. The listings named the final destinations but not the stops along the way. She knew her final destination but not the nearest town with a train station. She doubted Sulphur Springs was on the main line. People milled around, checking their departures then followed the signs to whichever track they were leaving from. Tilly just stood there.

This was taking too long. She was acutely aware that some of the passengers were giving her sidelong looks. Pretty soon somebody would ask if she was lost and then the game would be up. The best way to not look lost was to make up your mind and get moving. Coming in from North Alameda out front there was only one direction to go and that was through the arch to the central plaza.

The central hub was a crossroads for the tiled walkway. You could go back the way you'd come, turn left to Starbucks and the Food Court, or go right to the restrooms and Trimana Fresh Foods Market. Straight ahead was the sign, TO TRAINS & BUS PLAZA. Tilly still didn't know which train she needed so she looked around for a route map on the wall. There was no map of the routes leaving Union Station but there was a ticket office for Amtrak and Other Inquiries. Tilly went to Other Inquiries. The woman behind the ticket window looked bored and worn out.

Tilly plucked a name she'd seen from the back of the truck.

"Santa Clarita please."

The woman spoke without looking up.

"Train or bus?"

Tilly looked at the stairs to the underpass beneath the tracks. The enclosed space felt claustrophobic even standing here. That thought translated to a worry about being stuck on a train with only one way off. End of the line.

"Bus."

The woman looked up and had to raise herself to see the face at the window. The bored look became a furrowed brow.

"You old enough to travel alone?"

Tilly had thought about that before setting off and pulled out the note she'd written in her best handwriting on Kimberley Howe's notepad. The note giving permission for her daughter to travel alone to meet her aunt. The woman read the note twice then looked at Tilly.

"She meeting you at McBean Transit Center?"

Tilly kept her answers short to avoid further explanation.

"Yes."

The woman considered whether to believe the girl, then considered whether worrying was part of her job. The bored expression returned. They didn't pay her enough to look out for waifs and strays. She passed the note back.

"You want the 799."

She waved toward the departures hall.

"Out front. Up the hill then right. Stops at Main and East Chavez."

Tilly took the note and the ticket and was about to thank her, but the woman had already lowered bored eyes to her desk. The eight-year-old girl mingled with the crowd again, just one more person intent on getting wherever she was going.

CHAPTER TWENTY-THREE

McNulty wasn't intent on getting where he was going. He wasn't going anywhere. He sat among a handful of shitbags and lowlifes in the central holding cell and wondered how long Miguel Guerrero was going to play this game. They both knew the detective had nothing to hold McNulty on, but Guerrero was right about one thing. There was something McNulty wasn't telling.

The bars echoed as the gate opened and another sad loser was ushered through. The gate clanged shut and there was a murmur among the inmates as they considered whether the fresh meat was worth pursuing. McNulty looked at the teenager and thought he was going to be very popular. Nobody wanted sex with a grizzled old Yorkshireman so at least McNulty's ass was safe. That thought sent a shiver down his spine. He reckoned that the girl he wasn't telling Guerrero about had been anything but safe. At least she was being looked after now.

Kimberley Howe took longer than she'd planned to get back to the caretaker's bungalow. Glen Alta Elementary might have been a modern concrete and barbed-wire school, but it still had its share of problems for the caretaker to sort out. This morning it was the plumbing in the gymnasium changing rooms, then just when she'd gotten that fixed, there was a damaged section of carpet tile on the headmaster's stairs that needed attention. The tile had been scuffed and was sticking up at one corner. Kim used yellow tape to cordon off the danger zone while she glued down the offending tile. Before the headmaster could give her something else to do, she'd excused herself and headed back across the playground.

At first she thought the girl was hiding. Troubled kids often act out with strangers and Kim knew she was still a stranger to the girl. After a quick search of the bungalow, she realized the girl had left. She didn't notice that food had been taken from the fridge or that the backpack was missing. If she had, it would have influenced the decision she had to make. Tell Amy now or give Tilly time to return?

She picked up the phone three times before deciding to leave it until later. Amy was still recovering from the explosion from the night before. The burns weren't too bad, but shock could mess with your head. Kim didn't want to mess with Amy's head any more than it had already been messed with. She rationalized her decision by arguing that the girl might have gone for a walk, tired of being cooped up in the narrow bungalow. Troubled kids didn't like being cooped up. Kim reckoned the girl had been held in worse places. Getting some fresh air was essential. So, she put the phone down and had a cup of coffee instead.

Amy distracted her messed-up head by packing a bag with toiletries and snacks for Tilly. She got the snacks from the motel cafeteria and the toiletries from the housekeeping trolley when the maid came to refresh the room. She added a couple of towels and the bathrobe the girl had been wearing the previous night. Satisfied, she sat on the bed. It didn't feel right, sitting on the bed alone. She was already missing the girl.

She checked her watch. McNulty had been gone a long time. She didn't expect him back anytime soon. She glanced around the room. There was nothing else to do until McNulty got back. She put her hands together and fiddled with her fingers. She stopped that and folded her arms. She unfolded her arms and checked her watch again. Then she had another idea. Maybe she could teach the girl about cosmetics. Being the Titanic Productions makeup lady made her uniquely qualified. That put a smile on her face. She stood, picked up her room key and went to the door. The best place to get cosmetics was the makeup trailer. With a final glance around the room, she walked out onto the balcony, hurried down the stairs and headed toward the production compound.

Tilly Nutton watched the world go by through the window as the bus passed the Chinatown Metro Station heading out of Los Angeles. She had chosen a window seat on the right side so she wasn't in the sun as the 799 headed north. It felt strange, having such a good view instead of being cooped up in the back of a truck.

Her eyes darted from left to right, from top to bottom, taking in everything. Dodger Stadium stood out on the left. Los Angeles Historic State Park drifted by on the right. She was sitting toward the back so she wouldn't have to talk to anyone, an eight-year-old girl heading to Santa Clarita to meet her aunt. She hugged herself to cover the shiver of anticipation and the fear—how would the other kids react to her running out on them? Mainly though, she was thinking about the woman who could have been her aunt in a different life. The movie makeup lady who had taken her in. Somebody else she was running out on.

McNulty looked through the bars at the clock above the charge desk. The sergeant was busy completing custody records and noting the hourly welfare checks. The hourly welfare check in general holding meant looking through the bars to make sure nobody was dead or injured. Nobody was dead or injured so he was writing that in each individual custody record. Time, location, result. In order. McNulty didn't feel that everything was in order.

He checked the clock. Almost five o'clock. He'd been cooling his heels for two hours since Guerrero had left. Cool isn't how he was feeling. Hot would be nearer his temperature. Hot approaching boiling point. He glanced around the holding cell. For once the rest of the natives weren't restless. Just McNulty. As a cop he knew guilty men sat calmly as they awaited the inevitable. The man pacing up and down was usually innocent.

McNulty wasn't pacing.

A door opened at the far end of the custody suite and the sergeant looked up from his paperwork. A detective that McNulty didn't know had a few words with the sergeant and the sergeant nodded toward the holding cell. The detective followed the nod and looked directly at McNulty.

Amy crossed the main parking lot and climbed the slope to the compound. The sun had crawled all the way to the west but hadn't started setting yet. The night shoot was still a long way off, leaving plenty of time for the crew to prepare the transports and load the equipment. The trailers were parked in exactly the same places they'd been parked before. Each department had its own spot, including camera, sound and the set decorator. Carpenters hammered away in the corner. The swing gang loaded scenery.

The only thing missing was Craft Services.

Amy said hello to the grips as she walked toward the storage container. The camera would be the last thing they loaded, but there were plenty of other items that needed attending to. The carpenters stopped hammering when they saw the makeup lady enter the compound. The swing gang stopped loading. Everyone knew how close Amy had come to disaster and they nodded their understanding. Amy nodded back and gave a little wave. Nobody mentioned the fire and the explosion. Nobody looked at the empty parking space where Craft Services had been.

Amy didn't cut the corner but walked the square as if the mobile kitchen were still there. It would have felt somehow disrespectful, like walking on somebody's grave. For all she knew J.B. House might be in a grave somewhere.

She slipped the key into the lock, but it wouldn't turn. She checked to make sure she had the right key then tried again. It still wouldn't turn. Backing down the three steps from the door, she scanned the length of the trailer to give her time to think. She shook her head, then went up the stairs again. This time the key turned halfway but jammed. Now she couldn't turn it back or remove the key. She slapped the door with an open hand.

The door bounced open on the rebound, the keys dangling from the lock. There were two dents in the doorframe and corresponding lever marks on the edge of the door. The tongue of the lock was twisted and bent inward.

Amy took a deep breath and pulled the door open. Her mind immediately went back to McNulty's being hit on the head by an intruder he thought had been trying to break into the makeup trailer. But who would want to steal makeup? Unless it hadn't been about what was inside so much as who had been transported in it. She looked inside. The devastation was total. She let out her breath and started to tremble.

CHAPTER TWENTY-FOUR

Chuck Tanburro was leaning against the SOS Bail Bonds sign when McNulty came out. Detective Bob Snow from Rampart Station left McNulty putting his property back into his pockets and crossed to Tanburro.

"You moonlighting as a bail bondsman now?"

Tanburro pushed off from the sign and shook Snow's hand.

"Thanks for this, Bob."

Snow waited for McNulty to join them before expressing his displeasure.

"Got to say, I'm not happy interfering with another detective's case."

Tanburro held up a placating hand.

"You did check with him though, right?"

Snow nodded, then turned to include McNulty.

"He wasn't too upset. Just making a point, is all."

Snow looked at McNulty.

"What is it with you Yorkshiremen? Can't keep out of trouble?"

McNulty slipped the wallet in his back pocket and finished putting his watch on. He glanced at Tanburro then looked at the detective who'd just signed him out of custody. Released without charge. That didn't make them friends, though.

"Do you know a lot of Yorkshiremen?"

Snow kept steady eyes on McNulty.

"Just the two."

Tanburro stepped between the pissing contest.

"Jim Grant. That Montecito Heights thing. The Dominguez Cartel, and the bank robbery at Pershing Square. He couldn't keep out of trouble either." He nodded at the detective. "Bob was *his* get out of jail card as well."

McNulty checked his watch then shook the sleeve of his jacket down. Being locked up for the last few hours had done nothing for his temperament but since he'd been lying to the police he couldn't hold that against them. The way this was shaping up he'd probably need their help soon anyway. The best way to accomplish that was to play nice.

"Thanks."

He didn't offer to shake hands. He wasn't playing that nice.

"I'm still in shock about J.B."

Tanburro and Snow spoke in unison.

"Who?"

McNulty twirled a hand as if that explained.

"J.B. House. The location chef who was dealing Pink Poodle marijuana. Guerrero said they found his body a few hours ago."

Snow glanced at Tanburro to give him time while he considered how much to tell the Yorkshireman. In the end it Guerrero nodded, giving Snow the go-ahead. He turned to McNulty.

"It wasn't the chef they found. It was the Pink Poodle guy, the dealer who was supplying the chef. Shot in his house on Colfax, over in Studio City."

McNulty was quiet on the ride back to the Pilgrim Motel. There was a lot to think about while Tanburro drove, the most obvious being that whoever had shot up Craft Services had also killed the dealer who had been supplying the location chef. That put suspicion firmly in the turf-war camp. He'd never heard of a turf war over marijuana. Maybe weed was a bigger market than he thought. Tanburro threw McNulty an occasional glance but didn't speak until they crossed the Hollywood Freeway.

"I hope you're not thinking what I think you're thinking."

McNulty kept his eyes front.

"What's that?"

Tanburro came out of the underpass on Odin Street and stopped at the junction with Cahuenga Boulevard. The lights were red. The intersection was busy as nine-to-fivers took the surface roads home instead of the freeway. He kept McNulty in his peripheral vision while watching the traffic crawl past on Cahuenga.

"That whoever killed the Pink Poodle guy also put your girlfriend in the hospital."

"She didn't go to hospital."

"Her burns must be pretty sore, though."

"They're sore."

The lights changed but traffic was so jammed that Tanburro simply exchanged being stationary at the stoplight for being stationary in the queue. At least it gave him time to concentrate on McNulty.

"Revenge only works in the movies. We're both ex-cops." The car inched forward half a length. "Leave police work to police who aren't ex."

McNulty didn't answer. He stared out of the window and tried to marshal his thoughts. He didn't know what he planned to do and since he didn't know who killed the Pink Poodle dealer or who shot at Craft Services, there was no obvious line of inquiry. Tanburro was right; the police had the resources and the connections to do whatever needed to be done to arrest the culprit or culprits. They had access to all the forensic evidence, and street CCTV and the authority use it. What they didn't have was the motivation. McNulty had always been easy to motivate. Just slap a girl in your office and you'd get a Bible across the nose. Sometimes what needed to be done wasn't what could legally be done.

The car inched forward. Traffic stretched past the John Anson Ford Amphitheatre to the Pilgrimage Bridge. That was the holdup, cars waiting to turn across the bridge and traffic coming across the freeway to join the queue on this side. Beyond the bridge the traffic thinned out. They'd just have to be patient. McNulty wasn't a patient man. Glancing at Tanburro he could see the ex-LAPD cop wasn't patient either. McNulty let out a sigh.

"Do you ever miss being on the job?"

Tanburro kept his eyes on the road.

"Every damn day."

McNulty nodded.

"Then you know as well as I do. We don't feel like we're ex."

He indicated an entrance on the right.

"Pull in here. You can cut through the Ford Theatre parking lot."

Tanburro turned right into the lot, navigated three wooden sawhorses blocking the access road and snaked past the box office and souvenir stand. The driveway offered two routes: one took a sharp turn up the hill to the amphitheatre and the other continued back down toward Cahuenga Boulevard. Just before reaching Cahuenga, Tanburro pulled into the Pilgrim Motel lot. Tanburro was wondering what to say about the rundown motel. McNulty was wondering why Amy Moore was sitting on the makeup-trailer steps.

CHAPTER TWENTY-FIVE

Amy watched from the top step of the makeup trailer as the car pulled into the parking lot. Early-evening sun glinted off the windshield so she couldn't see who was inside, but she knew instinctively that it was McNulty. She sat up from resting her head in her hands and leaned against the trailer door, keeping it closed behind her. There were no tears to wipe away, but she flexed her mouth to soften the worry lines that had etched themselves into her face. She didn't want him to worry until there was something to worry about. Once she'd shown him what was inside, there'd be plenty to worry about.

McNulty thanked Tanburro and promised to keep in touch. He meant it, too, knowing he'd need Tanburro's contacts sooner rather than later. He just didn't yet know what he'd need them for. Tanburro gave him a hard look but *he* couldn't see the future either. They exchanged pleasantries then Tanburro turned the car around and headed for the bridge. McNulty waited until the car was entangled in traffic, then turned his back on the sun. The compound gates were open. Preparations were well underway for the second night shoot at The Trails Café. The place was a hive of activity, apart from an oasis amid the chaos—Amy Moore sitting alone on the steps of her trailer.

McNulty paused at the gate, reluctant to go through because he sensed that something bad was coming. It was the feeling he'd had outside the headmaster's office at Crag View Children's Home. Amy reminded him of the girl sitting on the window seat who had turned out to be his sister, slapped and abused by Mr. Cruickshank. A broken girl. He wasn't sure he wanted to go through that again, but even as he thought it he knew it was too late. He'd already taken responsibility for another broken girl and it wasn't Amy Moore.

He glanced around the compound to delay the inevitable. The swing gang was loading scenic backdrops. The carpenters helped. Trucks were being maneuvered into position to form the convoy of location transport. Camera and lighting equipment were waiting outside the relevant containers. Dolly tracks and reflectors too. The only thing missing was the location caterer. And the makeup trailer. The makeup trailer looked a long way from ready to join the convoy.

McNulty turned to Amy and their eyes locked. Hers were wide open and staring. His were steady and calm. He felt anything but steady and calm. His heart was racing, and his mouth felt dry. He feared the worst but hoped for the best. He knew from experience that the best never won. He took a deep breath and let it out slowly, then crossed the compound. He stopped in front of Amy.

"What's up?"

Amy looked up at him from the steps but couldn't speak. She sat there, forcing her hands not to tremble, and blinked several times. The blinking did the trick and broke the deadlock. She stood up and opened the door.

"Take a look for yourself."

McNulty wasn't sure what to expect as he climbed the steps, but he recognized the signs straight away. He'd been to enough burglaries when he was in uniform. He scanned the doorframe as a matter of routine and saw the dents in the frame and the lever marks on the door. The twisted lock spoke for itself. This was the break-in he'd expected on the night somebody hit him across the head. It had to be the work of the same person, the one he'd at first thought was targeting the makeup trailer but later reckoned was after the drugs in the Craft Services trailer.

He stopped on the top step and examined the door. Location trailers didn't have solid doors or strong locks but this one had been destroyed with two swift jerks of the crowbar. That could denote extreme strength or a very big crowbar. Like Archimedes said, "Give me a fulcrum and I will move the world." The intruder had moved the world.

McNulty pulled the door all the way open and went inside. The lights were on. The place was a mess. The drawers and cabinets had been ransacked and the contents strewn across the floor. The makeup chair had been slashed and the stuffing pulled out. Face paint and lipstick had been daubed on the walls like graffiti from a drunken artist. All irregular shapes and sharp edges. Nothing decipherable.

"Over there."

Amy was standing behind him. Close enough that he could feel the heat from her body. She put a hand on his shoulder, angled him toward the mirror and gave a gentle push. McNulty picked his way across the floor and straightened the gutted chair. Twenty-four light bulbs surrounded the mirror, providing even light on the faces requiring makeup. It gave the workspace a golden glow that banished shadows. The mirror was cracked, shards emanating from an impact just left of center, halfway up. Several pieces of glass had fallen into the makeup tray. A single lipstick stood on the worktop, the waxy finger fully exposed. Dark red. The writing on the mirror was big and angry. A single word.

WHERE?

McNulty didn't need to be told what the question was about. He turned to Amy, who was still standing in the doorway, and tried to keep his voice calm.

"Phone Kimberley Howe. Now."

CHAPTER TWENTY-SIX

The red, white and blue panel van pulled up outside the care-taker's bungalow just above Glen Alta Elementary. The real estate slogan on the driver's side was partly obscured by a terrible paint job that was meant to obliterate a previous owner's adver-tisement but hadn't quite hidden the smiling face asking, Do You Need Help NOW!, without even a mark: The front quarter was overloaded with advertising that read, 333-KEY-CURE and underneath, Si Habla Espanol and a telephone number. The man who got out didn't Habla Espanol. He didn't fix keys, either.

Kimberley Howe finished washing the dinner plates and saw the van through the kitchen window. It was parked outside her house but that didn't mean anything. Sierra Street was so tightly packed with parked cars that sometimes you had to go three houses up to find a space. The first half-dozen bungalows after the school had driveways and off-street parking around the back, but none of them had For Sale signs outside, so Kim figured the driver must be looking for a house farther up the street.

Kim dried the plates with a tea towel and stacked them in the cabinet. Her mind was only half on the job at hand, the other half was wondering when to call Amy and tell her that Tilly had gone missing. She was pretty sure by now that the girl wasn't coming back and she felt guilty for delaying the call. It was still only early evening and she had made dinner for two but ended up eating on her own. She had been surprised at how nice it felt to prepare a meal for company. Washing the dishes alone felt lonelier than usual.

She stacked the last of the dishes and looked out the window again. The man wasn't looking for a house farther up the street; he was coming up Kim's front walk. His brightly colored clothes put her off her guard.

The man climbed the steps to the front porch and smiled at the figure in the window. Sun on the yellow Hawaiian shirt and bright red trousers reflected a warm glow onto the shady porch, but the smile couldn't hide the man's eyes: They were as cold and dead as a busted keyhole. As soon as he stepped into the shade, the warm glow disappeared, along with the smile. The brightly colored clothes and the stolen van were part of the plan. When the neighbors were questioned later it would be the colors they remembered—not the face.

This was the part of the job the man didn't particularly like—interrogation and torture to find out what the subject knew or didn't know. The kid at the truck-stop diner hadn't really known much, but the man had to be sure. Broken fingers had been enough to make him talk. The broken toes and severed ear were insurance to make sure he told everything he knew. The girl had stowed away on a truck of car parts heading for Los Angeles. The kid remembered the hauler but not the licence-plate number. The name of the hauler had been enough to lead to the Hollywood Collision Center. The body of the kid who'd been tortured wasn't found until the following day. Inquiries at the crime scene would reveal a man wearing darker clothes. Work-wear. Not the bright colors the killer was wearing today.

The man pressed the doorbell. Knocking would be too harsh and might provoke a defensive reaction. A musical chime sounded inside the house—much more civilized. The figure in the window moved toward the hallway, her shadow approaching the door when the telephone began to ring.

Kim flicked the tea towel over her shoulder and went to the front door. Maybe the guy was lost, looking for an address somewhere else in Montecito Heights. She passed the telephone table in the hall and was about to open the door when the phone began ringing. She glanced over her shoulder with one hand halfway to the door handle.

Amy? It was the only person she could think of who might be calling at this hour. Guilt resurfaced at not having phoned her earlier. She felt the tug of answering the phone against opening the door. The doorbell chimed again. The phone continued to ring. Red and yellow stood out through the windowpanes in the door. Kim was trying to think of how to break the news to Amy while her hand turned the doorknob.

She opened the door.

The man smiled.

Kim held up a hand.

"Hang on, I've got to answer this."

She was turning toward the phone when the man pushed into the hallway and slammed the door. He grabbed the outstretched hand and twisted it around her throat, forming a neck lock with her own arm. She couldn't scream. The man jabbed his knee into the back of her knees and she dropped to the floor. The man ignored the ringing phone as he knelt beside her.

"No. You've got to answer *this*."

CHAPTER TWENTY-SEVEN

Amy Moore let the phone ring until it went to voicemail. At first she was going to simply hang up but decided to leave a message instead. Amy was a makeup artist for Titanic Productions, not a cop or a soldier or a Special Forces operative. She put makeup on neurotic actors, she didn't have to make life or death decisions or think on her feet. She wasn't sure what to say so she said the first thing that came into her head.

"Kim. It's Amy."

So far, so obvious. She fumbled trying to balance calm with urgency.

"Just checking that Tilly's okay."

Then calm went out the window.

"Some bad shit's happened. I need you to call me back."

The girl at the center of the bad shit was at that moment dealing with moderately good shit at the McBean Transit Center in Santa Clarita. The coach arrived at the bus station off Valencia Boulevard and pulled into the bay marked 799. The hydraulics sighed as the suspension lowered the front for wheelchair access and the door hissed open. Nobody needed wheelchair access, so the passengers started to disembark, using both the front and halfway exits. Tilly used the exit halfway along.

That was the good shit part. Passengers mingled on the platform or drifted toward the parking lot around the back. Sunshine
glinted off hundreds of cars left there by commuters into Los
Angeles. The platform cleared, leaving a handful of stragglers
who appeared to be calling for Ubers or taxis. Tilly stood beside
the bus and considered what to do next. That was a mistake.

"You okay there, Girl?"

The driver paused in his changeover routine and spoke
through the open door. Tilly couldn't read his expression,
which was somewhere between concern and suspicion. She
didn't want either one. She noticed a pedestrian exit for the
Westfield Valencia Mall across the Parkway.

"Yes thanks. I'm meeting my aunt at the mall."

Without waiting for a reply, she followed the signs for the
footbridge over McBean Parkway. As she crossed the bridge,
she could see that the mall was a busy place, signs on the access
road advertising Macy's, JCPenney, and Lucille's Smokehouse
Bar-B-Que. Hiding in plain sight seemed like the best plan until
she figured out a better one.

Amy hung up after leaving the message. She slumped into the
makeup chair with the cell phone still in her hand. McNulty
leaned against the workstation with his back to the mirror.

"Bad shit? I thought you were going to play it cool."

Amy held the phone as if warming her hands on it.

"I don't feel cool."

McNulty leaned forward and put a hand on her shoulder.

"Sorry. I know."

He wanted to fold her in his arms but the desire for intimacy
receded until he could barely touch her. That was the legacy of
Crag View Children's Home. You can't comfort the ones you love
because comfort is an alien concept. He patted her shoulder then
withdrew his hand. He didn't want to dwell on the importance
of the missed call but couldn't ignore it. He tried to steer Amy

toward other possibilities.

"Does Kim do any after-school work?"

Amy stopped cuddling the phone and dropped it into her pocket.

"There's sometimes maintenance she can't do during school hours."

McNulty played along.

"And the girl wouldn't answer if she was there alone?"

Amy hugged herself.

"She hardly speaks when she's not alone."

McNulty nodded. He'd never been much of a talker himself, back in the days of the headmaster's office and the Bible. None of the inmates at Crag View talked much. It was a way of keeping your thoughts to yourself. Having some privacy in a place where nothing was private. The home purported to help disadvantaged children, but "inmates" was how the kids saw themselves. Prisoners of the system. He wondered where Tilly Nutton had been a prisoner. He was beginning to understand the girl's mindset. He checked his watch.

"The show'll be heading out to location soon."

He waved a hand at the mess.

"Let's clean this up. No point giving Larry something else to worry about."

Amy stood up.

"Apart from losing his location caterer, you mean?"

McNulty started sweeping broken cosmetics across the workstation.

"He never wanted a location caterer. Losing his makeup lady. That's a different matter."

Amy opened a plastic bin liner and swept the broken cosmetics into the bag. It felt good to keep busy, but it couldn't stop her worrying. McNulty straightened the furniture and used a damp cloth to wipe the mirror. Location preparations would start long before sunset, but he had no intention of being there once the night shoot began. As soon as he got Buchinsky in character, he planned to drive over to Montecito Heights. His hands worked on autopilot. His mind was thinking about the girl who didn't talk much.

The girl who didn't talk much still wasn't talking. She was watching the world go by in the open-air courtyard between Macy's and Lucille's Smokehouse Bar-B-Que. The sun was beginning its descent in the west, but half of the courtyard was still bathed in warm evening sunshine. It glinted off storefront windows and shoppers' mirrored sunglasses. There was happy chatter and the occasional squealing baby but mainly it was an oasis of anonymity for the eight-year-old girl who didn't want to be noticed.

She opened the backpack and took inventory. Bread and cheese and ham. Yes. Chocolate bars and fruit. Yes. Bottled water. Yes. Three cans of soda. Everything she had taken from the kitchen in Montecito Heights. None of it touched yet. She still had a long way to go. She looked at the happy faces milling around the shopping center, some of them eating pizza from the food court. She wondered if it was Hawaiian pizza with extra cheese, like the one she'd left on the truck at the Sulphur Springs truck stop. Her mouth began to water but she wasn't hungry yet. Staying hydrated was more important than eating for fun. Travel light, travel far was good advice only if you had the strength to travel. She compromised and popped the ring pull on a can of Pepsi. Sugar rush and fluids.

Sitting in the shade of a clutch of palm trees she drank the soda. The bubbles tickled her nose, and she stifled a burp. Burping was fun but would draw attention to her. Stealth and secrecy were her friends. Burping in public was not. That thought brought to mind her other friends and her quest to return to them. It had taken three days to cross the parched countryside. It would no doubt take the same going back. Tonight wasn't an option, tomorrow neither, so she'd have to find somewhere to sleep.

Shifting on the bench she felt the banknotes crease in her pocket. Something that was different from her previous journey. This time she had money. That wouldn't help the closer she got to Rancho Verde, but at least tonight she wouldn't have to sleep outdoors. She consulted the mall map she'd collected on her way in. The layout of the shopping center was big and yellow on one side. An inset in one corner showed the mall location in relation to the surrounding area. The reverse side was what interested her. The street guide of Santa Clarita was large-scale and colorful. Countryside was shaded green, even though in reality it was dry and brown. Urban areas were yellow and orange, the buildings showing white against the background. An index down one side broke it down into categories.

Entertainment.

Food.

Shopping.

Hotels.

She wasn't planning on staying at a hotel but there was a subcategory listing bed and breakfast establishments. Checking the locations on the map she found a little cluster of houses on the outskirts of town. Not a built-up area. Not big premises. Individual houses. She fingered the note she'd used at Union Station. That should do if anyone asked her why she was traveling alone.

Feeling the note made her think of something else. Her fingers slipped into her back pocket to look for it. Her hand came out empty. She stood up and searched all her pockets then rummaged in the backpack. It wasn't there. Tears welled up but she forced them back. She tried to remember when she'd last seen it and remembered looking at the photo in the motel bathroom. When the makeup lady had called through the door, she'd put it in her pocket. In the bathrobe she'd left in the room when they drove to Montecito Heights.

PART TWO
LOST

"Larry. Tell me again about the pink poodle."
—Vince McNulty

CHAPTER TWENTY-EIGHT

Nobody heard Kimberley Howe scream because the school caretaker hadn't been able to scream. If there was one thing the man in the Hawaiian shirt and red trousers prided himself on, it was not leaving loose ends. A screaming woman would get noticed. Being noticed was a loose end. Cramming a tea towel in her mouth while he broke her fingers meant no screaming. Taking it out between questions was the risky part. Kimberley Howe didn't scream then either. She was too exhausted from tensing against the pain.

The questions had been answered but the pain hadn't stopped. That felt like he was cheating on the bargain, the inferred promise of relief if she told what she knew. The trouble was she didn't know much. So her only relief from the pain came when he broke her neck before eating pizza from the fridge. Warmed in the oven. Hawaiian.

They finished cleaning the makeup trailer with twenty minutes to spare. Amy replenished the cosmetics and McNulty Scotchtaped the shards back in the mirror. The mirror was still cracked but at least the place didn't look like a war zone anymore. He fixed the door so it would at least latch shut, even if it wouldn't lock. The makeup chair was the hardest to disguise but he managed to refill the stuffing and tape it shut. Amy covered the chair with a fancy towel that she could argue was there to protect from spillage. The overall effect wasn't much worse than a busy day on set. That busy day was about to start in twenty minutes.

Tilly Nutton thanked the landlady and closed the door. The bedroom was small but cozy with an en suite bathroom that didn't have a bathtub. The shower cubicle barely had elbow room for an eight-year-old and she wondered how adults could shower in there, but at least she wouldn't have to leave the room if she needed to use the toilet in the night.

The landlady was a kindly old woman who fussed over the girl who was traveling to visit her aunt. Tilly had adjusted the story but being tall for eight meant she could claim to be small for twelve. A twelve-year-old traveling alone was less conspicuous. Tilly needed to be inconspicuous. She put the backpack on the chair in the corner and went to the bathroom. She brushed her teeth with her fingers. Despite this not being a hotel there was still a selection of toiletries in a little basket tied up with a bow. Being in the bathroom brought its own memories.

The photograph.

She splashed water over her face, but thoughts of the photograph wouldn't recede. She stood in front of the mirror and didn't recognize the face looking back at her. Water dripped from her nose and chin. The eyes were hard and flat, and showed no emotion whatsoever. Bruises crept across her shoulders, but she couldn't see the ones on her back. That was a good thing. The bruises on her back were the worst because the things that caused them had been the worst. The photograph was the only thing that had allowed her to look back on something with pride and a smile. The smile had deserted her, but she tried to remember the warmth the photo had provided.

The photograph was a battered Polaroid taken on a borrowed camera. She remembered how the others had gathered to watch with awe as it developed in front of their eyes. High up on the Dough Flat Trailhead overlooking Lake Piru. Not far from Rancho Verde and the last place they had all been safe. She rubbed the water from her face with an angry swish of the hands. Safe? When had they ever been safe? In that respect the photo was a lie because it gave the impression of a happy childhood with six friends grinning at the camera. Five, because Tilly had taken the picture. The hills were humpbacked silhouettes in the background and the hanging tree formed a frame in the foreground. Five children stood with arms linked across each other's shoulders and dust settling on their shoes. The horseman had let them use his camera, then ridden off into the sunset. Not long after that Tilly had ridden off as well. Walked off, because the horses were as unreachable as freedom.

Tilly dried her face and got dressed. The B&B on the outskirts of Santa Clarita felt clean and safe, but she'd sleep in her clothes just in case. Leaving in the middle of the night was always a possibility for the runaway with nowhere to run.

The red white and blue panel van did a U-turn outside the caretaker's bungalow and drove down the hill toward North Broadway. The driver was surprised to see that his hands were shaking on the steering wheel. No matter how many times he did this, the torture and interrogation, he always had the same delayed reaction. He'd thought that taking time to warm the pizza would negate the usual after-effects but no, he got the old trembling-hand thing again.

The assignment had gone smoothly from the point of origin to the truck stop and all the way to the Hollywood Collision Center. Management had connections and resources that amazed even him, one of those resources being himself, the hired tracker and interrogator. Mr. Incognito. Red trousers and Hawaiian shirt. The collision center was where things had gotten complicated, but by process of elimination, and the aforementioned connections, he had managed to track the girl to the movie company that had been filming at the repair shop. Blowing up the location caterer had flushed the girl out. Killing the Pink Poodle dealer had added misdirection. Moving the girl had been the desired effect. Tracking her to a friend of the makeup lady had been easy. Those connections again. Having the girl run away was a fly in the ointment. Where would she go? Where *could* she go? The girl had no friends or family. There was no trail she could retrace to uncover her past.

He paused at the junction with North Broadway, then turned right toward downtown. Traffic was heavy coming out of town but not so bad going in. He crossed the I-5 and passed Dodger Stadium as he headed back toward Hollywood. The answer to his question hadn't come from the dying words of Kimberley Howe, but from the message left on her answering machine.

"Just checking that Tilly's okay."

More importantly the next part.

"Some bad shit's happened. I need you to call me back."

The first bit emphasized the makeup lady's affection for the girl. The second showed her grasp of the situation. More importantly, it suggested a connection that the tracker could exploit. If the makeup lady liked the missing girl then the girl might like the makeup lady. The woman was certainly the girl's only connection in Los Angeles so it made sense that's the place she would run to.

The driver's hands stopped shaking. Resources and connections. He knew exactly where Titanic Productions was filming tonight, and he knew the best place to find the makeup lady. He cut across from Stadium Way and joined Sunset Boulevard, headed west, and followed the setting sun.

CHAPTER TWENTY-NINE

McNulty watched the movie convoy take over the parking lot on Western Canyon Road. It never ceased to amaze him just how much effort went into capturing a few short minutes on film. Titanic Productions set off early to make up for lost time the previous night and the location army set up camp two hundred yards up the hill from The Trails Café. McNulty supervised the placement of the makeup trailer behind the café even though it wasn't his job. Keeping Amy safe was his priority tonight. After that it was checking on the girl and Amy's friend Kim.

"Do you think you can stop anything blowing up tonight?"

Larry Unger crossed the dusty lot. He was putting on a brave face, but McNulty could tell he was rattled. That was hardly surprising after losing his location caterer and the corporate hospitality. McNulty looked at his producer.

"Larry. Tell me again about the pink poodle."

The producer and his technical adviser sat on the patio around the front of the café as the sun set in the west and Griffith Observatory caught the last of the light in the east. The iconic image wasn't important tonight because they'd captured the establishing shots last night, before gunfire and explosions called an early halt to the night shoot. McNulty had his hands around a one-shot latte. Larry Unger had something stronger.

"I told you we should have stayed in Boston."

"This shit isn't because we're in L-A."

"This shit is exactly because we're in L-A. We didn't have to provide location catering in Massachusetts."

"It's not location catering they blew up, and you know it."

"We didn't need corporate hospitality, either."

McNulty took his hands from around the cup and leaned forward.

"There's always been corporate hospitality. But in Boston it was coffee and doughnuts, not mind-altering substances."

Unger took a drink of strong black coffee.

"Coffee and doughnuts are mind-altering substances."

McNulty picked up his cup and slammed it on the table. The noise snapped Unger's head up. Frothy latte splashed over the table.

"Was the poodle in pink booties a Freudian slip?"

Unger threw his hands up in surprise.

"Hell no. I saw it at a coffee shop off Hollywood Boulevard. Big hairy biker type with this tiny poodle. Pink booties and a fucking bonnet."

"But you knew about the Pink Poodle marijuana."

Unger looked at McNulty then deflated in his seat.

"I'd seen a baggy or two."

"And you knew the supplier."

Unger shrugged. "This is the movie industry. Suppliers are like assholes. Everybody's got one."

"That's opinions."

"What?"

"Opinions are like assholes. Everybody's got one."

Unger let out a sigh.

"Well, every corporate hospitality has a supplier."

McNulty pushed his cup to one side.

"Except Pink Poodle has one less supplier than yesterday."

Unger blinked and shifted in his seat.

"J-B?"

McNulty kept steady eyes on his producer.

"The guy supplying J-B."

Unger straightened his back and sat bolt upright. His eyes were wide, but he tried to stay cool. His body language was anything but cool. He clenched his hands in his lap to stop them shaking. Sounds of the crew dressing the set drifted over from the café. They were shooting interiors tonight. Nobody was dressing the patio. The ex-cop and his producer were alone. Unger swallowed then licked his lips. His mouth was so dry he didn't think he could speak. When McNulty didn't expand on his statement Unger had no choice.

"Meaning?"

McNulty didn't have to swallow.

"Meaning somebody blew up your corporate hospitality trailer and killed the guy supplying your chef. And the only person who knew where to find the supplier was J-B House." He lowered his voice.

"And you."

They danced around the subject and came right back where they'd started. McNulty had his suspicions. Larry Unger denied them. Evidence pointed one way but didn't make sense of the overall picture. The bottom line was that the only person who knew why the dealers had been targeted was the person who had targeted them. It was just speculation that it was the same person who had trashed the makeup trailer and written on the mirror. That could have been bad timing and coincidence. Cops don't believe in coincidence, and McNulty still thought of himself as a cop.

The producer finished his coffee and went inside to check on the swing gang. The technical adviser stayed outside and thought about being a cop. More accurately, he thought about not being a cop anymore and no longer having the resources he needed at his disposal. But somebody had access to those resources, or resources with the same information, like who the local drug dealer was and where he lived. He also knew where Titanic Productions had been filming and which motel they were staying at. Some of that information was readily available. This was Hollywood. There are lists and directories that anyone with a computer can check. You don't need to be a Hollywood insider to know which movie company is shooting where, and it wouldn't take much phoning around to find its production base.

McNulty did what he'd always done as a cop, broke the investigation down to its component parts, individual crime scenes, each with its own unique set of circumstances. He started with the one that wasn't a crime scene. The place where he'd found the runaway girl hiding amid the auto parts.

Hollywood Collision Center was a location that Titanic Productions had registered with its requests and permissions. Every movie shooting anywhere has to comply with local ordinances and register the location on the database. It was one of the things the accountants considered when finalizing the budget. So, anyone who was interested could have found out where they were filming. None of that became relevant until the chance discovery of a girl under the tarpaulin. So, if that was the starting point for McNulty, whoever was after her had started further back. Wherever she had come from.

Next was the production compound at the Pilgrim Motel, when McNulty had disturbed the intruder and gotten hit across the head. That had followed pretty quickly from the discovery at Hollywood Collision Center and could therefore be considered the connective tissue between the first location and the movie company. If the intruder had been looking for the girl and not the marijuana stored in Craft Services. Was it a coincidence the two trailers were parked next to each other in the compound? Again, McNulty didn't believe in coincidence.

The third incident was definitely a crime scene, the gunfire and explosion at The Trails Café on Western Canyon Road. The fact that the location catering trailer had been targeted suggested a link between the intruder in the production compound and the drugs being supplied to the corporate hospitality chef, and therefore, may have had nothing to do with the girl. That theory was strengthened by the fact that nobody really knew about the girl except McNulty and Amy Moore. Larry Unger only suspected.

The fourth incident was also a crime scene, the Pink Poodle supplier killed in his home on Colfax at Studio City. This was the scene McNulty hadn't visited, so he didn't know the details other than the supplier's connection to J.B. House and possibly Larry Unger. The murder of the supplier muddied the water because now it looked like a turf war over who had the right to sell marijuana in that area. It also tied Pink Poodle to the production compound and the supply McNulty had found in J.B.'s room. So, once again, was the intruder after the drugs or the girl? That was the question.

Until the most recent incident—a crime scene that hadn't been reported—the break-in and trashing of the makeup trailer in the production compound. The graffiti on the mirror was brief and ambiguous. *Where?* If you were leaning one way, you could read it as *where are the drugs?* If you leaned the other way, it could mean *where is the girl?* McNulty was leaning the other way.

He checked his watch as the light faded. The sun had set and Buchinsky would soon need his technical adviser. McNulty toyed with his empty cup then stood up. After running all the scenarios he'd gotten exactly nowhere. The only thing he knew was that his next move was to check on the girl at Montecito Heights. He left his cup on the table and rounded the corner toward the makeup trailer. He was halfway there when the phone buzzed in his pocket. It was Vincent D'Aquino at the Hollywood Collision Center.

"I know where the truck came from."

CHAPTER THIRTY

Vincent D'Aquino leaned back in the chair with his feet up on the desk. He even managed to look hard as nails leaning back in his chair. Hollywood Collision Center had closed for the night and the yard was empty. The sliding gate was closed. Music played quietly from the radio, disguising the harsh ticking of the clock. The phone was wedged between his shoulder and his ear while he traced a finger across the page of the roadmap he was looking at.

"Hundred and twenty miles north."

McNulty's voice came down the line.

"You steal auto parts from that far?"

D'Aquino lowered the map book.

"I don't steal auto parts."

McNulty tried to sound apologetic. It wasn't easy over the phone.

"That's still a long way."

D'Aquino gave a thin hard smile.

"You don't shit where you eat."

McNulty didn't have a roadmap so he had to conjure up a rough layout of Southern California in his head, although he couldn't picture anything away from the coastal belt. He knew

Malibu and Santa Monica and Ventura were toward the west, San Diego was all the way south, and he remembered Palm Springs being inland somewhere northeast of that but he drew a blank when it came to Bakersfield, which was one-hundred-twenty miles northwest of Los Angeles.

"Run that by me again."

D'Aquino painted a word picture over the phone.

"North on the I-5 out past San Fernando."

McNulty didn't know where San Fernando was either but remembered that the Golden State Freeway ran past the Autry Museum of The American West and the Los Angeles Zoo. He let D'Aquino continue.

"Santa Clarita, past Six Flags, then through the mountains."

There was a pause while D'Aquino consulted the roadmap.

"Nothing much else until you take the 99 into Bakersfield."

McNulty stood in the dark beyond the picnic shelter.

"Through the mountains? You really don't shit where you eat."

D'Aquino ignored the comment and continued.

"The girl could have climbed aboard in Bakersfield or any number of stops on the way south. I don't know the driver's route."

There was another pause while his finger retraced the route.

"Roadside cafés and truck stops all the way down."

"Can you find out where he stopped?"

McNulty could picture D'Aquino giving the phone a cold hard stare. The voice was hard enough.

"This isn't U-P-S. It's not the kind of delivery that keeps records."

McNulty kept an eye on the makeup trailer, waiting for Buchinsky to come out.

"But he'll remember where he took a break."

"This is America. A hundred and twenty miles doesn't need a break."

"Then we'll know she climbed aboard in Bakersfield.

Wherever she came from, that'll be the intersection. A starting point."

D'Aquino's voice softened.

"You don't think she shits where she eats?"

McNulty let out a sigh.

"Back when she set off, I don't think she was eating at all."

The man switched vehicles on Winona Boulevard, leaving the red, white and blue panel van behind the Kruang Tedd Thai Restaurant. The parking lot of the Hollywood Inn Express across the street was full, meaning the overspill guests had to park farther up the street. The man changed out of his yellow shirt and red pants in the back of the van, becoming the man in black as he stole a car from the motel. Boosting cars was another skill his employers valued. That and the fact that nobody ever connected his activities to them.

The man in black put his equipment in the trunk and opened the driver's door. He paused with one foot inside the car. Winona ran between Hollywood Boulevard and Franklin Avenue. The long, straight road had a perfect view of the hills beyond, silhouetted against the darkening sky. Griffith Observatory stood out on a shoulder of land, lit up like the Hollywood star it was. He shifted his gaze slightly lower and to the left. The Trails Café was hidden from view, but he knew it was there. He nodded and got in the car. He knew the person he was looking for was there as well.

"Don't forget. Walk straight and keep your eyes on the target."

"I'm just questioning the café owner. He's not a target."

"Until you know different, everyone's a target."

They were walking side by side across the hardscrabble lot. Even after dark little puffs of dust exploded with every footstep. Buchinsky was the taller by six inches, so McNulty had to crane his neck or talk to the actor's chest. Now he knew what Larry Unger felt like with practically everybody. Buchinsky stopped at the hitching rail that was designed to make The Trails Café feel more frontier-like.

"Is this where you tell me that when a cop knocks on a door, he doesn't know what's on the other side until it opens?"

McNulty rested a hand on the hitching rail.

"A cop doesn't know what's on the other side of anything until he's on the other side. Witnesses can cut up rough if you press the wrong button. Secret is not to press any buttons until you know what you're dealing with."

Buchinsky nodded.

"And keep your eyes on the target until then."

McNulty looked at the big man who was beginning to slip into character.

"You've got it."

Buchinsky straightened his jacket and turned his neck one way and then the other. He took a deep breath and let it out slowly, relaxing before the stress of going in front of the camera. That was something he was still uncomfortable with.

"Same applies on a shout. Keep your eyes on the fire or it can flash in a second. Temperature gets up and you reach crossover. Anything that hot—*whoosh*. Trick is to keep the temperature down."

McNulty stepped away from the railing.

"Same deal for a cop. Keep it cool. Avoid flashpoint."

He patted Buchinsky on the back and turned away.

"Go get 'em."

Buchinsky watched McNulty go.

"You're not staying?"

McNulty shook his head and spoke over his shoulder.

"Welfare check. I'll be back soon."

Then he saw Amy sitting in the makeup trailer doorway.

* * *

The man in black moved into position, keeping to the shadows and avoiding the light. There was no rush. He knew how long a night shoot could take. He wouldn't be making his move until the activity died down and there were fewer people around. The sky was clear but light from the city dulled the star field.

The stolen car was parked near enough for a quick getaway, his bag of equipment nestled between his feet. His work required quiet and privacy. Gags and restraints provided the quiet. Privacy was something he'd have to work on, but not yet. He settled into the darkness and waited.

Amy stood as McNulty approached. Standing on the top step made her taller than the technical adviser so McNulty climbed the steps and swept her inside. He closed the door and held her in his arms. She didn't resist, hugging him in return until he stepped back.

"Wow. Where'd that come from?"

McNulty didn't know where that had come from. Maybe he'd been holding back too much since the explosion, unable to comfort her when she needed comforting. Sometimes his past restrained him and sometimes he just broke loose. It wasn't an exact science. He simply went with the flow. The flow tonight felt like he should give her a hug. Now that the rush had elapsed, he held her at arm's length and confessed.

"I don't know. It just felt right."

Amy twisted her back and flexed her shoulders.

"Unless you were slow-roasted the night before."

He stepped back and raised his hands.

"I'm sorry. Are you all right?"

Amy nodded, then shook her head.

"It doesn't hurt."

She looked McNulty in the eye.

"But something isn't all right." She leaned against the makeup table.

"What's wrong?"

McNulty leaned beside her and let out a sigh. They both knew what was wrong but neither wanted to admit it. McNulty spoke first.

"Did you call her back?"

Amy lowered her eyes.

"No reply."

"Did you leave another message?"

"No."

She hadn't said, *"No point,"* but it's what they were both thinking. It was dark outside. Any after-school maintenance would have been long finished. Amy was thinking maybe the girl had run away again. McNulty was thinking something worse. He kept that to himself.

"I'm going to take a ride over there. I won't be long."

He pushed off from the makeup table and went to the door. He was back in his *unable to comfort her* mode. It was amazing how quickly Crag View could slam the door on his feelings. He threw her one last glance and left.

CHAPTER THIRTY-ONE

McNulty crossed the I-5 on Los Feliz Boulevard and took the surface roads to North Broadway, going under the interstate twice more before hitting the bottom of Montecito Heights. Traffic was light, apart from the Golden State Freeway. Seeing the constant flow of taillights heading north reminded him of where the girl had come from. It reminded him of where he'd come from as well—nowhere as exotic as Southern California but the gothic architecture of Crag View Children's Home. No matter how hard he tried, it always came back to Crag View. He could teach actors how to walk like a cop, but he couldn't escape the swing of the Bible as it slammed against the headmaster's nose. Every time something came up that involved troubled kids, he flashed over quicker than a hotspot in a wildfire. He slowed and took a left onto Lincoln Park Avenue, heading up into the Heights, trying to do what Buchinsky had suggested: Keep the temperature down.

The first sign that something was wrong at the caretaker's bungalow was the darkened house. Back in his days on patrol in West Yorkshire, any routine visit where the lights were out was filed as *house in darkness—rebook for tomorrow*. This wasn't a routine visit. This was more of a concern-for-neighbor visit. You never rebooked a concern-for-neighbor visit because the house was in darkness; you rebooked it because a house being in darkness simply cranked up the concern. McNulty was already concerned as he passed Glen Alta Elementary and swung the car around to face downhill. That was another holdover from his days in the West Yorkshire Police. Facing downhill for a fast exit in case the shit hit the fan. He parked two doors up on the opposite side of the street. He had a feeling the shit was about to hit the fan.

The engine ticked as it cooled but McNulty didn't get out. He watched the house through the driver's window, scanning up and down the street for any strange or unusual activity. There was no activity, just lights on in every house except for Kim's. Next he checked for strange vehicles, but since he didn't live here and had never visited before there was no way of knowing which vehicles belonged here. There was nothing obvious. There were no junkers or rust buckets—nothing that looked like it was stolen or abandoned.

He opened the door and got out. Standing beside the car gave him a new angle. The house was still in darkness but standing up meant he could see through the living room window. The curtains were closed but not drawn all the way across. An orange light blinked at the back of the room. He crossed the street and stood at the foot of the porch steps. The porch had a swing bench and a vase of dried flowers. There was a light above the door but, like the house, it was dark.

He stepped back and scanned the windows. There were two facing the front and a dormer in the roof, indicating an upstairs bedroom. All the curtains were open except for the ones in the living room. That sent another warning signal. At this time of night, he'd expect the upstairs curtains to be closed, especially with the living room shades being partly drawn. There was no movement apart from the steady blinking of the orange light. It lit the edge of the curtains and bled into the hallway. In fact, the light looked brightest through the front door.

This wasn't good. He went up the wooden steps, one at a time, pausing after each footstep to check the windows again. Still no movement. The porch creaked under his weight as he approached the front door. He paused again. Checked again. Still no movement inside. He listened at the door. No sound there, either. He didn't try the door. He didn't knock.

The house appeared to be holding its breath. McNulty went down the steps and around the side. The bungalow overlooked the school playground and parking lot, but the school was closed. He checked windows all the way to the back. An exhaust fan identified the kitchen and lace curtains suggested the master bedroom. There was a rear window in the dormer, presumably the guest bedroom. Tilly Nutton was the guest. There was no light in the guest room.

He went back around to the front and climbed the porch steps. This was where he'd use his truncheon to break a window after getting no reply to his copper's knock. He wasn't a cop anymore, but he still had the knock. Using the knuckles of one fist he knocked loud and hard.

He stepped back in surprise.

The door swung open.

Radio for backup. Call the police. Don't go inside. The warnings flashed through his mind as fast as he dismissed them. He wasn't a cop so he couldn't radio for backup. There was no point in calling the police until he had something to report, and he couldn't see if there was anything to report without going inside. There was also the concern-for-neighbor scenario, where the policeman's first priority is to protect life and property. That came way before *prevent and detect crime and arrest offenders.*

McNulty went inside to protect life. Then stopped.

The hall carpet was scuffed and pushed to one side. The telephone table had been knocked over, the message-waiting signal providing the blinking orange light. Signs of a struggle.

Evidence of a violent crime. The priority shifted because part of protect life and property was protecting your own life. A cop can't help anybody if he doesn't stay safe himself. The first responder to any crime scene has to make sure the scene is secure. That means making sure the offender isn't still on the premises. The orange light showed him where to go. He reached for the wall switch and turned on the lights.

Criminals don't like the light. They don't like being seen. The hallway was suddenly very bright. McNulty could see the scuffmarks on the carpet and blood splatters on the wall. Not a lot. Not an arterial bleed or a stab wound. More like a smack-across-the-mouth or bang-your-head kind of bleed. The orange light wasn't so bright now, but it was still a distraction. McNulty scanned the hallway all the way to the end. The far door led to the kitchen. He'd recognized that from the exhaust fan in the side window. The other door was to the living room.

He took two steps along the hallway, keeping to the side away from the blood. Preserving evidence was also a concern now. He didn't touch the telephone. He took two more steps, moving into the middle of the hallway so he could see into the living room. There were more signs of a struggle but no more blood. A throw rug in front of the TV was bunched up in the corner. A chair was on its side. A glass-topped coffee table was cracked and upended.

McNulty approached the doorway, knowing what he would find. He braced himself for the shock that even cops experience at the sight of death. He stepped to one side to preserve the common pathway into the crime scene, then gasped.

Kimberley Howe was lying on the floor in front of the settee. Her head was turned backward. Every finger on both hands had been broken, all of them sticking out at impossible angles. There was a slice of pizza next to the body.

CHAPTER THIRTY-TWO

"Kim. It's Amy." The familiar voice played on the answer machine. *"Just checking that Tilly's okay."* It made McNulty's skin crawl. *"Some bad shit's happened. I need you to call me back."* He knew he shouldn't have touched the telephone, but it was important to know who had called. Listening to Amy's message sent a shiver down his spine. Despite what had happened at the makeup trailer it was obvious now that this is where the bad shit had happened.

The orange light blinked off. He didn't touch anything else. He took a few moments to gather himself then took a deep breath. When he let out the sigh his heart rate slowed to normal and he took out his phone. He considered calling Chuck Tanburro but quickly dismissed that thought. This was beyond using the old-boys' network. He opened the dialling screen and called 9-1-1.

Life is full of forks in the road. Decisions you make on the spur of the moment and choices that take longer when you've got the time. Turn left or turn right. Climb up or climb down. Swing the Bible or go back to your room. McNulty had a lifetime of bad choices. As he waited for the police, he felt another one coming and he didn't know why.

Tell them about the girl or keep quiet?

His first consideration of withholding evidence came from having too much time to think. McNulty was much better acting on instinct. Thinking gave him too many options. Too many unanswered questions. The main one being, how had the killer known to look here for the girl? That question expanded to how had he known about the drugs in the Craft Services trailer and the location of the night shoot? These were things he'd considered before but came into focus with the death of Kimberley Howe.

The only people with access to all the databases were the police. Details about drug dealers and the ability to trace known associates. Everybody had connections, and most of that information was available somewhere. Social media. Financial records. Emails and phone calls. The Hollywood grapevine. All of those things were separate but intertwined. It wouldn't have been difficult to find out that Titanic Productions was the company filming at Hollywood Collision Center and even the likely suspects for hiding the girl. But linking the movie company to the drug supplier and tracing Amy Moore to Kimberley Howe would have been a lot more difficult. That information required more than a Hollywood insider.

But the police?

McNulty shook his head. He didn't believe in conspiracies and knew that bent cops only existed in books and films. Cops watched each other's backs because when you're on the front line the only person you can trust is the man fighting beside you. That went all the way up the chain of command until you reached the political hierarchy. But the political hierarchy didn't have their ears to the ground, so this information had to come from the grass roots. Cops don't trample on the grass roots.

So why was he considering not telling them about the girl?

He stood on the porch and looked down the hallway. The signs of violence were enough without being in the room with the twisted corpse. He hadn't covered her up because that might destroy vital evidence, so he stood outside instead. He could

145

hear sirens coming from the bottom of the Heights as he continued to ponder the question of how the killer knew so much.

Cops were the ground troops, but the police infrastructure included personnel in all kinds of supporting roles. There were radio operators and filing clerks and canteen staff. Canteen staff wouldn't have access to the databases but people in headquarters would. Telling them about the missing girl would spread that information across the country. Whoever was tracking her only needed access in one place to plug into that information.

McNulty nodded and made his decision. Keep the girl out of it. He looked again at the disruption in the hallway and caught his breath. Dropping to one knee, he lowered his angle and confirmed that there was a notepad under the telephone table. It was the type with tear-off pages and a pencil in an elastic loop, only here the loop was empty, and the pencil lay on the floor halfway down the hall.

The sirens were getting closer and he could see flashing lights on Lincoln Park Avenue. He quickly moved inside and retrieved the notepad and the pencil. The top pages were creased from the fall, but he could see indentations in the paper. Using the pencil, he shaded the top page.

He barked a laugh. It actually worked! He tore off the page and dropped the notepad onto the floor. Blue lights flashed outside, and the sirens fell quiet. McNulty moved outside with his hands in the air. First officers on the scene were always jumpy; he didn't want to get shot coming out of the crime scene. Two guns pointed at him across the roof of the patrol car. McNulty identified himself as the person who had called 9-1-1 and walked down the porch steps. He'd just added another to his lifetime of bad choices but in the back of his mind he was wondering about the girl visiting her aunt in Santa Clarita.

CHAPTER THIRTY-THREE

Tilly Nutton turned over in bed and stared at the ceiling. It wasn't that something had awakened her because she hadn't been able to sleep, but something sharpened her focus—a feeling that wasn't dissimilar to indigestion, or hunger pangs. She knew all about hunger pangs, but this wasn't that. Her chest felt tight and she wondered if she was having a premonition. If she was, she didn't know what it was about, just that she had a bad feeling about something.

She swung her legs out of bed and went into the bathroom. The light above the mirror etched shadows on her face. Her eyes looked deep-set and hard. She was used to her face looking hard; that's how she survived life on The Farm. That's what the grownups had called it: The Farm. A shiver ran down her spine. The only animals had been the grownups and their guests. It was a long way from the lakeside splendour of Rancho Verde. That was a place the kids had named themselves. Tilly wondered if the bad feeling was about Rancho Verde.

She splashed water on her face, but it didn't soften her expression. Then the hard knot in her stomach eased off and she wondered again if it was indigestion. She thought about the person who had shown her great kindness, the makeup lady, and hoped the bad feeling wasn't about her.

* * *

Amy Moore's bad feeling was all about indecision. Should she call McNulty or wait for him to call her? She checked her watch but couldn't remember what time he'd left to check on Kim and the girl. It felt like a long time ago, but she knew from past experience that life on a movie set shortened time or stretched it out, depending on whether you were busy. Since Buchinsky had walked onto the set Amy's job had been slow, just an occasional touch-up and a basic makeup job on the café owner Buchinsky was interviewing in the scene. There were no extras or day players. Tonight was a tight shoot.

She checked her watch again. The five minutes since the last time she'd checked felt like an hour. The only thing she knew for certain was that McNulty was late. If everything was okay at Montecito Heights, he'd have called right away. That meant the sinking feeling she'd had since leaving the message for Kim was justified. Bad shit had happened over there as well.

She sat on the steps of the makeup trailer and stared into the darkness, the arc lights not spilling beyond the café interior. The trees seemed to huddle close on the hillside behind the trailer. There was a faint swishing of leaves as the branches shifted in the gentle breeze. Dust clouds kicked up with the occasional gust. The crew stood outside the café doors, ready to go in and change the setup for reverse angles. Amy was alone at the top of the dirt and gravel lot.

She checked her watch for the umpteenth time, then took out her phone. The thing about indecision is, once you've made your mind up the indecision fades away. Amy couldn't make her mind up. If things were okay, McNulty would have called. If they weren't, then he'd be busy sorting out whatever wasn't okay. That was the kind of guy McNulty was. She hoped he hadn't got himself arrested again.

* * *

McNulty hadn't been arrested but he was at the police station. First responders had been joined by the night detective and the shift supervisor, who had quickly put a rush on CSI and the coroner. Back in England, CSI used to be SOCO, but even West Yorkshire Police had had to fall in line with policy when they changed Scenes Of Crime Officer to Crime Scene Investigator. The job was the same though, photograph the scene and collect forensic evidence. There was plenty of evidence to collect. Hair. Fibers. Blood. Nobody expected there to be any fingerprints, but the CSI dusted all suitable surfaces after swabbing the blood and saliva. The blood and saliva, like the fingerprints, were unlikely to belong to the attacker, but if they ever caught anybody, having the samples might link him to the scene; there is always blowback whenever blood splatters the wall.

Scene preservation was down to the uniformed cops, who were busy taping off the street and securing the premises. But first they had done what McNulty had already done—checked that the perpetrator wasn't on-site, then started a scene log of anyone who attended the scene. Vince McNulty was the first name on the list. That's why he was sitting in an interview room at Hollenbeck Station on East 1st Street.

"Just write it in your own words."

This was after two hours of telling it in his own words, the night detective playing the sympathetic observer while knowing all the while what all cops know: the first person on the scene is the prime suspect. In ninety percent of domestic cases the husband or wife did it. In seventy-five percent of murders the person who called it in is knee-deep in shit. McNulty was knee-deep in shit and he knew it, so he told the truth in every respect, apart from not mentioning the girl. The Hollenbeck detective pushed the yellow legal pad across the table.

"Including why you were there. I'm still not clear on that."

McNulty took the pad and straightened it in front of him.

The pencil was sharp but not sharp enough that he could stab anyone with it. He lined the pencil up next to the pad and rested his hands on either side of it. He looked at the detective's name badge. Keith Samson.

"Back in Yorkshire, we used to write it up ourselves. Dictation. Tidying up any grammatical errors and timelines and stuff."

Samson leaned back in his chair. He had all night.

"Isn't that a bit like putting words in someone's mouth?"

McNulty twirled his finger across the pad.

"We'd make copious notes, which we kept for evidence. With space in between the lines for anything they remembered halfway through. Signed and initialled with any changes. Telling the story with a beginning, a middle, and an end."

The detective shrugged.

"That's where defense attorneys weigh in." He stared at McNulty. "Telling a story instead of the truth."

McNulty rested his hands on the pad and tented his fingers.

"Oh, it's the truth. Just in the right order. So a jury can understand."

Samson kept quiet. McNulty waved at the door.

"I don't know about here, but back home there were people who couldn't string a sentence together, let alone give detailed evidence."

The detective pointed at the pad.

"In your own words." Then he folded his arms. "But again. Why were you there?"

McNulty drummed his fingers on the pad. He knew what the detective was doing. He'd done it plenty of times himself. Not letting the suspect get too comfortable with the story he was telling. Keeping him off balance and repeating himself in case he slipped up on some of the details—the little things that suspects make up to sound convincing. McNulty had gotten the details straight before the cops arrived.

"Kim's a friend of our makeup lady."

Samson nodded.

"Amy Moore?"

McNulty shifted in his seat.

"Yes. And Amy was worried when she didn't answer the phone."

The detective unfolded his arms, removing the barrier that often closed off the dialogue. He leaned back and crossed one leg over the knee of the other. Relaxed. Friendly. Conversational.

"So this was a routine welfare check."

It was McNulty's turn to nod.

"That's right."

The detective looked at McNulty and waited a beat.

"So, what was the bad shit that happened?"

CHAPTER THIRTY-FOUR

Amy Moore touched up Buchinsky's makeup one last time before the final round of setups. Most of the dialogue had been filmed and there was only coverage left to shoot. Over-the-shoulder shots and reverse angles. Some close-ups. Larry Unger was having his director of photography copy those spaghetti westerns where Sergio Leone shoved the camera right between the actors' eyes. Flip Livingston didn't like copying anyone, but Unger was the producer, and at Titanic Productions the producer trumped the DoP. Buchinsky shifted in the makeup chair, trying to straighten the towel that had bunched up under his backside.

"You two have a fight in here?"

Amy paused with the blusher.

"Who two?"

Buchinsky gave a cheeky sideways smile.

"You know who two."

Amy applied the blusher, forcing Buchinsky to close his eyes.

"What makes you say that?" Amy worried that the actor might have sensed the atmosphere earlier, when McNulty had left. Buchinsky waited until he could open his eyes again. He nodded at the cracked mirror.

"I know we don't have anyone ugly enough to break mirrors."

Amy put the brush down and blended the makeup with her fingers.

"One woman's ugly is another woman's firefighter."

Buchinsky took the jibe with a laugh.

"Ugly don't matter so long as I can carry you out of a fire."

Amy wiped her hands and looked at the man who had carried her out of the fire. Buchinsky might not be a great actor but he wasn't stupid. McNulty had taught him how to walk like a cop, but he was beginning to think like one as well. He removed the tissues protecting his collar and screwed them into a ball.

"Gunshots. Explosion." He indicated the mirror. "This."

He threw the balled tissue into the wastebasket. It rattled around the edge and dropped to the bottom.

"What's going on?"

Amy let out a sigh and looked at the man who had saved her. She paused while she decided how much to say and leaned her back against the makeup table. Her shoulders sagged.

"Bad shit. That's what."

"Oh, you mean the message on the answering machine?"

Samson nodded.

"*Some bad shit's happened. I need you to call me back.*" He hadn't tried to sound like Amy, just stared at McNulty as he spoke.

"What bad shit?"

McNulty was ready for that one.

"Somebody partied in the makeup trailer. Messed it up. Broke the mirror. Shit like that."

The detective uncrossed his legs.

"Seven years bad luck then."

McNulty shrugged.

"For somebody."

Samson raised his eyebrows and gave a sad little smile. The one where it's clear you already know the answer.

"But you don't know who."

McNulty returned the stare with a steady gaze of his own.

"It's a big crew."

Samson tilted his head to one side, maintaining the smile.

"One less since the gunfire and explosion."

McNulty kept quiet. The detective pressed on.

"More bad shit." He straightened in his chair. "Along with you getting arrested for breaking into the motel room." He leaned forward. "The room with the stash of Pink Poodle."

He sat up straight again. "Even more bad shit."

McNulty twirled a hand in the air.

"More like an extension of the first bad shit. Looking for the missing chef."

The detective mimicked using an abacus on his fingers.

"The second bad shit."

McNulty ignored the fingers.

"Not if you work the timeline. Mirror came last."

Samson placed his hands in his lap.

"None of which had anything to do with the makeup lady's friend."

Now they were getting down to it.

"No."

The detective's smile vanished.

"Did Kimberley Howe have anything from the location shoot?"

McNulty kept a straight face.

"No."

Samson was ticking off questions from an invisible list.

"Anyone staying with her from the location shoot?"

Not a flicker from McNulty.

"No."

Samson paused for a moment, watching the technical adviser's eyes. He let the moment stretch into an awkward silence, but McNulty didn't fill the void. He knew all about interview technique, leaving space for the suspect to fill the quiet with lies.

"So there was no reason for Amy Moore to go visit yesterday."

It wasn't a question, but McNulty answered anyway.

"She's not in LA a lot. They go way back."

The detective wouldn't be swayed.

"No bad shit to warn her about? On the phone?"

McNulty shrugged again.

"It's been a bad couple of days. She needed to vent."

Samson's voice was cold and hard.

"And now the ventee is dead."

McNulty let out a sigh. They'd been going around and around for hours. This was not only getting tedious, but McNulty was anxious to tell Amy about Kim and start tracking the girl.

"If you want to make a connection, knock yourself out. As for me, I'm telling it the way I see it."

Samson sat motionless.

"You sure about that?"

McNulty reached forward and picked up the pencil.

"Are you trying to influence my '*in my own words*?'"

The detective pushed back his chair and stood up. McNulty was a witness, not a suspect. He hadn't been arrested and wasn't being interviewed under Miranda. Samson had pushed the technical adviser as far as he could without slapping the cuffs on. He went to the door and turned back to the table.

"Write."

He opened the door.

"The sooner you finish, the sooner you'll be on your way."

The night shoot wrapped shortly after four o'clock. The swing gang struck the set and loaded the scenic flats onto the trailers. The sound department dismantled the boom mikes and recording equipment. The camera and lighting were stowed once the scenery was removed. For twenty minutes the location was a hive of activity. Amy Moore had to wait until the café was cleared before reversing the makeup trailer and pointing it at the exit. Next there was a lull while the convoy lined up all the way down Western Canyon Drive.

The night sky was still dark. The trees surrounding the location were still shadows in a sea of blackness. Amy sat on the trailer steps and leaned against the door. Branches creaked and leaves swished in the gentle breeze. The woods sounded like they were alive. Amy wasn't thinking about the woods, she was wondering why McNulty hadn't called.

The man in black glanced at the night sky then checked his watch. It was almost four-thirty. Night shoots were fickle things. There was no definite end time, unless the location demanded it, so they could finish early or late. The sky was a long way from dawn, with no hint of blue yet, but he knew there wasn't long to wait. A gentle breeze rustled the leaves and something groaned nearby. He quickly checked that his preparations were complete, glanced at his watch one more time, then moved into position.

"The sooner you finish the sooner you'll be on your way."

Keeping it brief and to the point, McNulty wrote as fast as he could but he still didn't finish soon enough. Samson checked his statement, asked for a couple of amendments, then handed it over for signing. McNulty didn't have to wait for his property because he hadn't been under arrest. There was no love lost between the cop and the ex-cop, but Samson did arrange for a lift back to McNulty's car, which was still parked at the crime scene.

McNulty considered calling Amy but this wasn't news to be given over the phone. He wasn't looking forward to the face-to-face but knew it was the only way. He wondered if the night shoot had wrapped yet and whether he should head for the location or the motel. He decided to swing by The Trails Café on his way to the Pilgrim Motel. It wasn't far out of his way. He started the car and glanced at the dash clock. It was a quarter till five.

* * *

The movie circus trailed across Hollywood, avoiding the freeway, and turned north on Highland, taking the same route McNulty had driven the day before. The convoy snaked under the 101 on Odin Street then hung a left onto Cahuenga Boulevard. Some of the trailers had trouble with the sharp corner but the drivers had been doing it for two weeks now and knew how wide to swing for the turn.

The trucks rumbled into the motel parking lot and slowly took up their positions in the compound. The gates swung open and the wrangler guided the trailers. The tractor units were unhooked, and equipment secured. The crew worked hard but quietly at the end of a long night. Everyone was ready for bed. Nobody wanted to waste time talking. The makeup trailer was second to last in the convoy. It slowly eased into its usual spot next to the empty space where Craft Services had been. Amy didn't give missing chef J.B. House a second thought. She had other things on her mind.

The crew thinned out, everyone going to their rooms. Amy had a head start since she didn't have anything to unload. She went up the stairs like an old woman, her body still aching from the blast two nights before and her mind dulled from worry. The first hint of blue was lifting the sky from full night toward dawn but it was still a long way from being light. She trudged along the balcony to her room and unlocked the door. Her shoulders sagged and she let out a heavy sigh. The trees behind the motel swayed. Leaves swished and something groaned nearby. She ignored it all and went inside.

The door slammed shut behind her and the light came on. A voice that was both friendly and chilling spoke just behind her left ear.

"I've got some questions you need to answer."

CHAPTER THIRTY-FIVE

McNulty turned onto Cahuenga Boulevard from Odin Street and paralleled the Hollywood Freeway all the way to the Pilgrim Motel. He didn't have to cut through the Ford Theatre parking lot this time because the surface roads were all but empty. Traffic noise from the freeway drifted up the embankment but even that was lighter than usual. Taillights heading north. Headlights coming south.

He pulled into a parking space along the front of the motel and killed the engine. He didn't open the door, just sat back and took a deep breath. Giving death notices had been part of the job when he was in uniform, but he'd never had to break the news to a friend. More than a friend. Amy Moore could be the next big step in overcoming his past. He tried to formulate a plan, but nothing would come. The sky was beginning its move from black to dark blue. He checked the clock on the dash. It was five-thirty. Time to put up or shut up.

The climb to the upstairs balcony gave him time to gather his thoughts. The walk to the third room from the end settled his breathing. The light was on inside so that was a positive. He wouldn't have to wake Amy to break the bad news. He stood opposite the door and wondered whether to knock or use his key. Considering he hadn't phoned her all night, knocking felt like the way to go. He still didn't do anything, stepping back instead and leaning against the balcony rail. He turned his head up and looked at the stars. It was a clear night, but the glow of the city dimmed the star field. Faded glory, a bit like the Hollywood Walk Of Fame.

He closed his eyes and let out a sigh. After a few moments he stepped forward, raised his fist, and knocked gently on Amy's door. For the second time that night there was no reply. He knocked again, still gently. Not the copper's knock. Not loud enough to wake the dead. This was his girlfriend, not a police raid.

Girlfriend. He paused between knocks. He didn't think he'd ever used that description before, verbally or in his mind. It sounded good and bad at the same time. Good because it signified a giant step forward. Bad because the full Girlfriend Experience had been one of the things offered at the Northern X massage parlors. The term sullied the idea of having an actual girlfriend. He knocked again, a little louder this time.

Still no reply.

The curtains drapes were closed but he tried to peek through the small gap. He could only see a narrow space at the foot of the bed. Even changing the angle couldn't swing his view toward the bed to see if Amy was asleep. There was a screwed-up bathrobe on the floor. That was the first sign that something was wrong.

McNulty ran his fingers around the doorframe, checking for lever marks or indentations. The door hadn't been forced, unlike the door to the makeup trailer, so that eased his mind slightly. He pressed a hand against the door. It didn't swing open so he knew the lock was engaged. That eased his mind a bit more. No forced entry. He quickly checked the windows and found them to be locked as well. He was beginning to think Amy had simply fallen asleep after a long night's filming. He used his key and opened the door. As soon as he stepped inside, he knew he was mistaken. Amy Moore wasn't sleeping.

* * *

Half an hour later McNulty was on the phone to the 9-1-1 operator.

"What service do you require?"

"Police."

"And what is your emergency?"

McNulty leaned against the bathroom door and wondered how best to phrase it. He knew there were ways to explain the emergency that would prompt an immediate response and descriptions that would put you in a queue. Back in Yorkshire, calls were classified as Immediate, Planned 1, and Planned 2. Anything that didn't fall into those categories was deemed Non-Urgent and would be assigned to an inquiry officer three days down the line. This wasn't Non-Urgent, but as he stood in the bathroom doorway, he wondered, *what exactly is my emergency?*

Amy's room had been empty and the bed hadn't been slept in, but the coverlet had been dragged halfway off the bed and there was a bag of toiletries on the floor next to the bathrobe. McNulty stepped to one side and kicked the door shut, checking behind it for unwelcome intruders. He'd already been hit on the head once. He wasn't looking for a second helping.

Panic sucked the breath out of him, rooting him to the spot and refusing to let go. He couldn't move. His feet were planted, and his arms were locked. The only sound was a rhythmic pulse thudding in his ears. The motel was asleep, par for the course after a night shoot. There was a distant hum from an air conditioner and the occasional creak and groan from the water pipes in the building, but everything else was deathly silent.

Not quite everything.

He moved to his left and engaged the security bolt on the door. He didn't want any surprise visitors this time. No cops from an anonymous call, swooping down to find McNulty with a body in the bathtub. That thought sent a shiver down his spine because the not-quite-everything noise was coming from the bathroom. He stepped over the toiletries and bathrobe to get a better angle through the door but couldn't see past the bathroom cabinet. This was the same layout at J.B.'s room, but executive-suite luxurious. At the Pilgrim Motel luxurious meant a bathroom cabinet and a chrome-plated mixer tap. The noise wasn't coming from the bathroom cabinet. The tap was running.

"Amy?"

He tried not to sound panicky but couldn't keep the quiver out of his voice.

"You in there?"

He took another step toward the bathroom.

"Amy?"

He resisted the urge to raise his voice and took another step.

"It's me."

A stupid thing to say. People always say stupid things when tension robs them of common sense. When on the job, he'd always identified himself as a police officer in case anyone complained when they were arrested for hiding. Nobody was going to complain tonight. A final step brought him to the bathroom door. It opened inward, blocking the view to the right. He was looking at the floor, checking for signs of a disturbance but the floor was clear. The bathroom was tidy, nothing ransacked, and nothing strewn across the tiles.

The shower curtain was drawn across the bathtub.

He stood, angled into the bathroom with his back to the cabinet. Keeping his eyes on the shower curtain he reached for the faucet with one hand and turned it off. After a few last drips the silence was complete. He sidled across the floor and slowly raised his hand. The fingers touched the cheap vinyl curtain, but he couldn't bring himself to yank it open. He held his breath. His eyes bulged in his head. He took half a step forward and opened the curtain.

The bathtub was empty.

He let out a sigh and sat on the toilet lid. The strength drained out of him and it was all he could do to stop himself from sobbing. The relief was a physical thing. It emptied his chest and shook his shoulders. His hands trembled and he had to take short breaths to avoid hyperventilating. He leaned forward and rested his head in his hands.

Slowly the trembling stopped.

He gulped to moisten his lips and sat up straight. He scanned the bath panel and the ceiling tiles out of habit but there was no sign of tampering. Apart from the coverlet, the spilled toiletries and the running tap, the suite was as clean and tidy as when they'd left for the night shoot. He puffed out his cheeks and stood up. When he turned around, he saw what he'd missed by focusing on the shower curtain. The mirror wasn't broken this time, but the message was clear. Big red letters, using Amy's lipstick, shouted *WHERE?*

And underneath.

DON'T CALL THE POLICE
I WILL KNOW

The lipstick was in the washbasin where the intruder had washed his hands. McNulty leaned against the bathroom door and called the police.

CHAPTER THIRTY-SIX

"And what is your emergency?"

It was a perfectly reasonable question and the first thing any civilian operator would ask. Standing in the bathroom doorway it was obvious what his emergency was, but thinking back over the last few days it became clear he had a bigger problem. The intruder had access to information that only the police knew. The police and any civilian staff working frontline support services. Nine-one-one operators were frontline support services. along with filing clerks and typists and intelligence analysts.

McNulty felt a lifetime of bad decisions beckoning. Choices that stretched back to Crag View Children's Home and the Ecclesfield custody suite. A damaged headmaster and an injured pedophile. He could list a whole lot more, but the operator was asking if he was still there. He decided he wasn't and hung up.

The first thing he wanted to do was hit something. Express his rage by smashing some inanimate object. The obvious choice was to smash the telephone against the mirror, but he'd had enough bad luck without adding another seven years. At this time of night, he couldn't even scream without causing a stir and bringing unwanted questions. Instead, he put down the phone and sat on the edge of the bed. He let out a lung-emptying sigh and considered his options.

Option One.

The sensible choice. Phone the police and explain everything, including the missing girl, the attack in the compound and the real reason for the explosion during the night shoot. Also, the intruder at the makeup trailer, the message on the broken mirror, the fact that the girl had been staying with Kimberley Howe for safety, and that she had run away to Santa Clarita. And finally, that Amy Moore had been taken from her room and another message left on the mirror. Had he left anything out? He didn't think so.

Option Two.

What was Option Two? He sat on the bed and wracked his brain but couldn't come up with anything. Short of setting off in pursuit of an unknown assailant in an unknown direction, he was completely stumped. That left him considering the viability of Option One.

The problem with Option One was that he'd already lied to the police about the girl and the reason he'd gone to Montecito Heights. Factor in the probability that the intruder had information only the police could access—such as known associates of Amy Moore linking her to Kimberley Howe—and there was a compelling reason to not call the police. Add to that the coincidence of McNulty's being first on the scene of a brutal murder and now a kidnapping. Cops don't believe in coincidence so Option One would prevent McNulty from looking for Amy and the girl while they held him for questioning. So much for Option One. But what were the alternatives?

It all came down to who you could trust. He sat on the edge of the bed, nudging the spilled toiletries with his foot. The shampoos and body lotions had tumbled out of a bag that Amy had obviously packed for the girl. The bathrobe had come out of the bag as well. Something about the bathrobe caught his attention. He reached down and picked it up. It was a fluffy white bathrobe with Amy's initials on the breast pocket. The soft folds of fabric were stiff around the right-hand pocket. He reached into the pocket and pulled out a creased photograph. The photograph showed five children standing next to a dead tree with a shoulder of hillside in the background. He held the photo with gentle fingers as Option Two came into focus.

"Location managers keep a portfolio, don't they?"

"You know they do. It's no different here than in Boston."

"But Hollywood being the movie capital of the world, they'd have pictures of more locations than anyone else. Especially around L-A."

McNulty toyed with the battered Polaroid while he sat on the edge of the bed with the phone to his ear. Chuck Tanburro sounded less relaxed on the other end.

"And you need this at six in the morning, why?"

McNulty glanced through the bathroom door at the warning on the mirror. He thought about the last sentence of Amy's voicemail to Kimberley Howe.

"Because the bad shit just got worse and I need your help."

He put the photo down and considered the other reason he was ringing Tanburro. What he said in the next few minutes could change the course of the future and the course of the future could make amends for the course of his past. He chose his words carefully, then made his decision.

"How much do you trust Bob Snow?"

Tanburro didn't have to think about that.

"With my life."

McNulty had thought that would be the answer. He knew Bob Snow had been Tanburro's partner for six years until Tanburro retired and became a technical adviser on *CSI: New York*. Six years is a long time to be covering each other's backs. You literally trust your partner with your life. He had no doubt Snow felt the same way. McNulty was counting on it.

"I'm going to tell you something that, if it gets out, could get somebody killed."

Tanburro was quiet on the other end of the line. McNulty told him everything. Finding the girl at the Hollywood Collision Center. The compound, the explosion and the broken mirror. Moving the girl to Montecito Heights for safety, finding Kim's body, and discovering the impression of the note on the telephone pad. He finished with Amy's abduction and the second lipstick warning on the mirror, explaining why he didn't want the police involved. Tanburro interrupted.

"Bob Snow is the police."

McNulty nodded even though Tanburro couldn't see him.

"But this needs to stay off the system. Once it's on there, anyone with access can see it. I think this guy has access."

Tanburro kept his tone serious.

"And you're going to risk Amy Moore on that hunch?"

McNulty was equally serious.

"I've got Amy covered. I need you to find the girl."

He didn't give Tanburro time to interrupt again.

"I'm going to send you a photo. I think it's where the girl is heading. Where she came from. I'm hoping your location guy will recognize the place."

Tanburro reluctantly agreed. McNulty hung up and used the phone to photograph the Polaroid. He sent it to Tanburro and then sat looking at the shoulder of land and the dead tree in the background. He hoped he wasn't being too optimistic, saying he had Amy covered. He raised the phone again and dialed a second number. Despite the time Vincent D'Aquino answered after two rings. McNulty didn't have to introduce himself.

"Is it right what I hear? That career criminals hate pedophiles?"

CHAPTER THIRTY-SEVEN

McNulty ended the call and let out a huge sigh. Either he'd just done something extremely clever or made the biggest mistake of his life. He'd made a lot of mistakes so there were plenty to choose from. There was nothing more he could do for the next couple of hours, so once his hands stopped shaking, he went into the bathroom and cleaned the lipstick warning off the mirror. He straightened the bed and put the spilled toiletries and the bathrobe back into the bag. He paused for a moment while he considered keeping the battered Polaroid, but since he'd saved it on his phone he carefully put it in the bathrobe pocket. If all this went well, he'd be able to give the girl the bag and reunite her with her past. McNulty was still trying to disconnect from his.

It wasn't working.

Tidying the room took half an hour. Sitting around waiting for another message was going to take much longer, and sitting around wasn't McNulty's style. When instructions came it wouldn't be at the motel. He sat in the double seat and drummed his fingers on the armrest, wondering how to pass the time—sit here and wait or get up and do something? The trouble with doing nothing is that your mind fills in the blanks. His mind was in a place McNulty tried to avoid. Giving his mind time to mull over the past was a recipe for disaster and disaster pretty much summed up his past. Getting up and doing something depended on having something to get up and do. McNulty was struggling to find something to get up and do.

He stopped drumming his fingers and turned soft eyes on the room. Using soft eyes was a technique for scanning a crime scene without focusing on anything specific. It allowed you to see the bigger picture—the forest, not the trees—until a previously unseen piece of evidence leapt out at you. The previously unseen piece of evidence was in his pocket.

McNulty shifted in his seat and took out the note, the shaded piece of paper from Kimberley Howe's telephone notepad. The writing tried to look like a grownup's, but the phrasing was from a child's perspective. He turned the note over in his hands, checking the back and the front, and looking at it upside down. When he'd finished he again read it. Santa Clarita. How long would it have taken the girl to get there? When had she set off? What route had she taken? To whom would she show the note? The answers to those questions weren't at the motel. He stood up, checked his phone to see if it had enough charge, then swapped the note for his car keys.

Parking at Union Station was a nightmare, so McNulty left the car in the pickup and drop-off zone out front. Rows of tall, elegant palm trees and the red tiled roof made the station feel like it had been dropped into place from paradise. A blue sky and sunshine enhanced the effect. The clock tower watched over the area around the entrance like an amiable sentry. A Greyhound bus pulled in off of North Alameda and parked just beyond the pickup and drop-off zone. McNulty glanced at the bus, got out of the car, and entered the departures hall.

McNulty had only been to Union Station a couple of times. He was again amazed at how handsome it was with its heavy wooden beams supporting an ornate wood ceiling and its comfortable leather chairs lining the central walkway. He wondered what it must have looked like to an eight-year-old girl on her first visit. The arrivals and departures boards were on the far wall, arrivals on the left and departures on the right. A sign above the central plaza read, TO TRAINS & BUS PLAZA. There were listings for the Orange County Line, the Pacific Surfliner and Southwest Chief. McNulty ignored the departure board and went to search for the ticket information desk.

He walked through to the central hub. There was a Starbucks on the left and the restrooms and Trimana Fresh Foods Market on the right. The Amtrak ticket office was next to a window marked "Other Inquiries." McNulty went to Other Inquiries. The woman behind the ticket window looked bored and worn out. She didn't look up when McNulty stood in front of the window. He wanted to badge her and play the heavy cop card, but he didn't have police I.D. anymore. He used the English accent instead.

"Excuse me."

Even with a Yorkshire accent his voice did the trick. The woman perked up and looked at the man standing in front of her.

"Yes? Can I help you?"

McNulty could tell this woman had a limited attention span so he knew he'd have to work fast before she slumped back into bored and worn-out mode.

"Were you here yesterday?"

The woman's eyes took the first step toward the slump.

"I'm here every day."

McNulty gave a sad little smile.

"Slave drivers."

He took the note out of his pocket and slid it under the window.

"Have you seen this before?"

The woman glanced at the note but didn't touch it.

"A shaded copy letter?"

McNulty tapped the part he could reach with one finger.

"The original. The girl who wrote it is only eight."

"Really? She looked older."

McNulty really wanted to badge this woman.

"She didn't look eighteen. Which makes her a vulnerable minor."

"She didn't look vulnerable either."

McNulty forced himself to be civil. He didn't have the power to drag her out and slap the cuffs on. This was customer service, not a government agency. Maybe the transit authority. Either way, this woman's customer service face left a lot to be desired. McNulty needed to prod her while she was still marginally engaged.

"This is a young girl traveling alone."

He leaned closer to the window and softened his tone. The accent might still carry the day. The sad smile was more heartfelt this time, almost pleading. He let out a sigh to underline the above.

"If the wrong people find her, she's going to be way past vulnerable. Can you help?"

The sad smile, quiet tone and English accent got him over the line. The woman took the note, scrutinized it, then pushed it back through the slot. She looked more interested than she had probably looked for years. Ten minutes later McNulty was climbing the hill to Main and East Chavez. He was passing a statue of a Mexican on a horse when his phone started ringing. Without looking, he answered it, expecting Chuck Tanburro or Vincent D'Aquino. It was neither. The voice coming out of the device was cold and hard.

"Here's what you're going to do."

CHAPTER THIRTY-EIGHT

Chuck Tanburro met Bob Snow at the Wash & Fold Laundromat opposite Rampart Station on West 6th Street. Neither of them had any laundry but the strip mall had a coffee shop next door and no cop ever turns down free coffee. The coffee was as bad as Laundromat coffee always is. Tanburro screwed up his face after the first sip.

"I've tasted better washing powder."

Snow took a long drink of strong black coffee.

"I go along with the old adage." He put the cup down.

"Coffee is like sex. There's no such thing as bad coffee."

Tanburro looked at his ex-partner.

"That's pizza."

The detective looked back at him.

"Coffee is like pizza?"

Tanburro shook his head.

"There's no such thing as bad pizza."

Snow took another drink.

"They obviously never had sex with my wife."

Tanburro pushed his cup away and glanced around the outside seating. There were no other customers and rush hour had eased on West 6th Street. There was a trickle of traffic heading downtown and hardly anything coming out. The morning sun was still south and east, glinting off the police station across the street. Rampart Station was too dangerous for this conversation. The laundromat felt a lot safer.

"So, Bob. This other thing."

Tanburro laid it out pretty much the same way McNulty had. There was no attempt to play down how serious this was, a missing girl, an explosion, and two dead people, the Pink Poodle supplier and the woman at Montecito Heights. He finished with the kidnapping and the warning message, holding out his hands in a *that's it* motion. Snow ordered another coffee. When it arrived, he took a long, deep drink to help fire up his brain and give him time to formulate a response, which was from one friend to another.

"And you trust this guy?"

Tanburro rested both hands on the table.

"I trust what he says."

He shrugged.

"I'm not so sure about his judgment."

Snow put down the styrofoam cup.

"The insider-knowledge stuff you mean."

Tanburro gave a gentle shake of the head.

"The reason nobody believes conspiracy theorists is because they're usually full of shit."

Snow looked at his friend.

"Is McNulty full of shit?"

Tanburro considered that for a moment before letting out a sigh.

"I don't think so. Whoever the bad guy is, he knows stuff he shouldn't know."

Snow toyed with his cup but didn't drink.

"Doesn't mean L-A-P-D is feeding him information."

Tanburro nodded.

"That's the conspiracy-theory part."

Snow stopped toying with his cup.

"But somebody is."

Tanburro picked up his half-full cup, made sure the lid was securely attached and gave the cup a little shake. Cold coffee sloshed around inside. He swished it clockwise then counter-clockwise. When the sloshing stopped he drummed his fingers on the lid.

"We've all run a plate for a friendly P-I. Checked someone's record for a local employer. Maybe it's something like that."

Snow put his hand over Tanburro's to stop his friend's drumming fingers.

"This is dead people and kidnapping."

Tanburro didn't try to release his hand.

"The source might not know that."

Snow took his hand off and finished his second coffee.

"Think about this then. If I use my card in an A-T-M there's every chance someone in Moscow knows how much I withdrew."

Tanburro snorted a laugh.

"The Russians?"

Snow kept a straight face.

"They hacked Sony Pictures."

Tanburro shook his head.

"This is a California pedophile ring. Not the Russian Mob."

Snow leaned back in his chair.

"You don't think we've got hackers in California?"

He waved a hand to include everything around them.

"We practically invented hackers."

"We invented surfing as well. Doesn't mean the Beach Boys are hacking police headquarters."

Snow moved his hand in a *calm down* motion.

"I'm just saying. There's more than one explanation."

He went back to toying with his cup.

"It doesn't mean there's a mole in the L-A-P-D."

The pair sat in silence while they both digested that, Snow playing with his cup and Tanburro drumming his fingers. A helicopter drifted across North Hollywood and another echoed around the towers downtown. The sun was California hot, but the tables were in the shade. A marked police unit pulled out of Rampart Station and turned right on West 6th Street toward MacArthur Park. The world kept turning.

Snow stopped shifting his cup around the table and picked it up. Tanburro knew to stop drumming. When his partner stopped moving it was time to pay attention. The detective held the styrofoam cup in his hand.

"It's all academic anyway. We can't sit on this. We've got kidnapping, murder and child trafficking. Never mind the explosion and the Hollywood connection. F-B-I, A-T-F and D-E-A. They'll be falling over themselves, either passing the buck or claiming jurisdiction, depending on if we solve it."

He tightened his grip on the cup.

"Bottom line is, it's got to go on the system."

He crushed the cup and the lid popped off.

CHAPTER THIRTY-NINE

McNulty sat under the statue of Antonio Aguilar and ended the call. The Mexican was big, and his horse was bigger, but added together they weren't as heavy as the decision McNulty was about to make. Do as he was told, or call the police? Calling the police felt even more important now, but the stakes were so high that if he was wrong, he'd never be able to live with himself. He could barely live with himself now.

The sun had moved to high noon. The park opposite Union Station was beginning to fill up with lunch-break staff and picnickers. The air was alive with laughter and chit-chat. A taco truck risked a parking violation on Paseo De La Plaza around the back. A normal day in Downtown Los Angeles. The next few hours would be anything but normal. McNulty put the phone away and replayed the conversation in his head.

"Here's what you're going to do."

McNulty didn't need to ask who this was. There was only one thing he wanted to know.

"Where is she?"

The voice sounded almost amused.

"My question exactly."

McNulty's voice didn't.

"Where is Amy Moore?"

There was some intermittent background noise down the line that McNulty couldn't recognize. He glanced at the phone, expecting to see a blank screen, and was surprised to see a number with a Los Angeles area code. The caller obviously wasn't worried about McNulty's tracing the phone, so it was probably a burner that would be thrown away when it was no longer needed. The voice adopted a more conversational tone.

"We both want to get something back."

The background noise again. The man ignored it and carried on.

"I want the girl. You want your childhood."

McNulty moved into shade behind the statue.

"I want Amy Moore."

The man let out a sigh.

"You want to wipe the slate clean and think that saving the makeup lady will achieve that."

It sounded like he was enjoying this.

"You also think that giving the girl a childhood will assuage the guilt at throwing yours away with a broken nose and a Bible."

McNulty felt cold despite the midday heat. Goosebumps sprang up on his arms and neck. Information access and databases. McNulty's past was well documented, especially in the press after the Northern X fiasco—the hero ex-cop who helped bring down a child sex ring. His police career and subsequent move to America would be easy to find as well, if you had access to the right databases. This guy had access to the right databases. McNulty wasn't going to enter into a debate.

"How do I know she's okay?"

The voice was all business again.

"You found the woman at Montecito Heights?"

"Yes."

"Then you know what happens if you don't do what I want."

"I need to know Amy is okay. Otherwise go fuck yourself."

There was a scream on the caller's end, then it was muffled

to silence. McNulty almost crushed the phone in his hand. The voice returned, as calm as ever.

"There's no need to be rude. And no, she is not okay, but she is alive. That should be your main concern right now. Keeping her that way."

McNulty trembled against the side of the statue. He took shallow breaths to slow his heart rate. His usual response was to lose his temper and come out fighting, but he couldn't fight a voice down the phone, and losing his temper had pretty much lost him everything he'd ever held dear—his sister, his childhood and his job. Being a cop was all he had ever wanted to be, but losing his temper and slapping Daniel Roach, a kid who'd gotten away with molesting his baby sister back in West Yorkshire, had ended his career. Teaching an actor to walk like a cop was no substitute. Losing Amy Moore would be the last straw.

"What do you want?"

The voice was almost musical.

"That's better. You know what I want. I want Tilly Nutton."

Using the girl's name was a mistake. It stopped her from being that nameless "girl" and humanized her. It helped focus McNulty's purpose, slamming the door on his childhood. That was then and this was now. The only way forward was not to look back. McNulty ran some quick calculations in his mind while he decided how much he could say without giving up Tilly's location. The man already knew where she'd come from because that's how he'd traced her to the Hollywood Collision Center. North. That was a start. It might buy him some time.

"I don't know where she is."

Hard voice.

"Wrong answer."

McNulty spoke quickly to stop the caller from hurting Amy again.

"But I know where she's going."

He paused, then spoke slowly.

"She's heading north." He added weight to his tone. "Got a

bus at Union Station."

"Santa Clarita?"

McNulty was right. The caller did know where she'd come from. Good. That was a bargaining chip that wouldn't compromise the girl. The child traffickers would know where she'd escaped from, but McNulty didn't think that's where Tilly was headed. She was headed to a place with a dead tree and a shoulder of hillside. Back to the other kids who'd escaped with her and then been left behind.

"I think so."

McNulty could hear Amy whimpering in the background, but he tried to block it from his mind. He needed to stay focused.

"I'm still trying to find what bus she caught."

There was silence a moment then the voice was back to being cold and hard.

"Call me back when you find out."

McNulty couldn't leave without asking.

"Amy?"

The man threw McNulty a bone.

"When I have the girl, I'll tell you where to find her."

Then he hung up.

McNulty stood up and moved out from the shadow of Antonio Aguilar. The sun was warm but the beads of sweat on his forehead were from tension, not heat. He crossed the park and went back down the hill toward Union Station. He didn't need to see the bus stop anymore. The man had confirmed what he'd already known; the girl had gotten off at Santa Clarita. Where she had gone from there depended on two things, Chuck Tanburro finding the location in the photo and Vincent D'Aquino finding out where the girl had hopped a truck. That wasn't his priority at the moment though. He dialed the number and D'Aquino answered right away. McNulty didn't mince words.

"Tell me you've got something."

D'Aquino didn't mince words either.
"Yeah. Not over the phone."

CHAPTER FORTY

McNulty couldn't find a space at Jinky's Studio Café so he parked on Colfax Avenue just across the Los Angeles River. As usual the river was just a wide concrete storm drain missing the storm. There was a trickle of water along the central channel, but the rest was just a hot, dry riverbed. A news helicopter thudded overhead toward Studio City in the west, one of the few that wasn't covering the wildfires that had been raging out of control along the Pacific Coast Highway.

Something niggled in the back of his mind but wouldn't solidify as McNulty locked the car and walked back toward the café. He glanced up at the helicopter as it disappeared beyond the tall straight palms of Ventura Boulevard. He shook his head and continued along Colfax, but the niggle wouldn't be scratched.

If The Trails Café was a frontier-style snack bar, then Jinky's was more of a bar and restaurant with café styling. There was a snack menu for the lunch trade and a wine bar for the drinkers, as well as a full-service kitchen for serious diners. Outside seating ran along two sides next to Colfax Avenue and was shaded by red umbrellas. The main entrance was through the parking lot at the rear.

McNulty paused to get his bearings as the door closed behind him. A wooden sign read, WAIT HERE TO BE SEATED. McNulty scanned the interior while he waited. Restroom hallway to the left. Booths along both sides on the right. Bar straight ahead. The interior was adorned with classic movie posters. He noticed a framed sheet of *The Dirty Dozen* on the wall outside the gents' restroom, where it hung above a handful of empty beer barrels and gas canisters. There was a John Wayne wall leading to the outside seating, posters for *Big Jake*, *The Sons of Katie Elder* and *Rio Lobo* leading the way. Vincent D'Aquino was sitting under a red umbrella in the outside seating. He looked tougher than John Wayne.

McNulty didn't wait. He strode to the side door, trailed by a flustered waitress waving a menu. He spoke over his shoulder, pointing at D'Aquino.

"I'm with him."

The waitress stopped waving the menu and pulled out a chair at D'Aquino's table. McNulty sat as she pushed the chair under him. He didn't think he'd ever been ushered into a chair so elegantly. D'Aquino noticed McNulty's surprise.

"She thinks you're a big tipper."

He indicated the other customers.

"Lots of studio types."

McNulty glanced around the tables.

"She's going to be disappointed with an ex-cop and a car thief."

D'Aquino kept a straight face.

"Car mechanic. Others do the thieving."

McNulty checked to make sure there was nobody within hearing distance, then leaned forward, keeping his voice low so it mingled with the passing traffic on Colfax.

"Enough small talk. What have you got?"

D'Aquino understood the urgency so he gave the best first.

"I know where he's keeping the woman."

* * *

Amy Moore was groggy and in pain. She hadn't slept all night, her broken fingers throbbing relentlessly. Her hands were zip-tied in front so she could watch the man torture her, but her legs were free, so he wouldn't have to carry her. She didn't know where she was or how she'd gotten there, since she'd been sleeping off the chloroform he'd used to knock her out. What she did know was that she was in deep shit, and she wasn't one to use that kind of language lightly.

The drapes were closed, and the room was in darkness. She knew it was a house because of the furnishings and the layout. The ground-floor bedroom where she was now contained a king-sized bed and a bedside table. The door was closed but she remembered there being a kitchen to one side and a living room with a settee, a Laz-Z-Boy recliner and a big-screen TV. She cringed at the thought of the settee. That was where the man had broken the little and ring fingers of her left hand. He seemed satisfied with her answers because he hadn't broken anything else. It was as if he were stalling until time for the real reason she was here.

A truck rumbled past outside, the vibration rattling the window and shaking the drapes to let a sliver of light pop through. So, it was daytime. That meant she'd been here over-night. She tried to judge how long it had been since she'd been dumped in the bedroom and the lights turned off. Fear sent an electric shock down her spine as she heard movement in another part of the house. She let out a sigh and thought about the call she'd overheard.

The man had made a phone call earlier in the morning. She didn't know who he'd called or what was said, but he must have liked the outcome because he hadn't come in the bedroom to break more fingers. She was beginning to think she was bait in a bigger trap. She also knew she was expendable if the bait wasn't taken. She needed to get out of here or the next thing he'd break was her neck.

The movement in the house stopped. The truck faded into

the distance. The house fell silent, except for the pulse thumping in her ears. Amy swung her legs off the bed and sat up. The truck rattling the window had given her an idea.

"You sure about that?"

"I'm sure about everything."

McNulty craned his neck and looked down the street. A garbage truck rumbled past the café and turned right onto Ventura Boulevard. The houses along Colfax Avenue beyond the river and CBS Studio Center were dotted with shade trees. Beyond where McNulty had parked before walking to Jinky's.

"That's insane."

D'Aquino shrugged.

"Can you think of a safer place?"

McNulty remembered Bob Snow mentioning the address when they had met outside Hollywood Station. The niggle that had been in the back of his mind. *It wasn't the chef they found. It was the Pink Poodle guy. The dealer who was supplying the chef. Shot in his house on Colfax, over in Studio City.* The house had been a crime scene ever since, empty and sealed off with yellow police-line tape—the last place anyone was going to visit. The safest place to hide. McNulty still wasn't convinced.

"How d'you find him so quick?"

D'Aquino wasn't offended. He knew the technical adviser was dealing with all sorts of emotions, starting with concern for his girlfriend, as well as the missing girl. Even so, he wasn't going to tell McNulty everything.

"Cops have their ways. I have mine."

D'Aquino watched the garbage truck disappear then turned back to McNulty.

"When you don't rely on technology, grapevine gets you closer to the ground."

He kept still and remained impassive.

"The ground is where I live."

The two men sat looking at each other, mutual respect growing on both sides. While the other customers talked movie business, the ex-cop and the thief talked life and death. McNulty nodded his thanks but didn't speak. D'Aquino shifted in his seat and softened his tone.

"But this next bit."

He leaned forward.

"You're going to need the cops."

Chuck Tanburro said he'd get right on it and ended the call. He hadn't told McNulty that Bob Snow had started updating the system about the crimes already recorded. His only concession to his friendship with Snow had been not mentioning the missing girl yet. Calling in SWAT and the local police was going to warrant more information, starting with the name of the kidnapped woman and the location.

Tanburro called Snow. Amy Moore's name flashed all over the internal database. The detective got the ground troops moving, coordinating with SWAT and North Hollywood Police, who covered the Studio City section of L.A. Despite the urgency it still took forty-five minutes to set up the cordons and secure the scene. Forty-five minutes was too long.

CHAPTER FORTY-ONE

The Pink Poodle dealer's house was at the junction of Colfax Avenue and Valley Spring Lane, practically opposite Colfax Cove Apartments. There was no cove on Colfax and no valley, either, but there were plenty of escape routes. That's why the Pink Poodle dealer had chosen it and why the man in black was using it now. If you fled along Colfax, you'd get caught at either end, but if you cut across the back into Valley Spring, there was a maze of back streets taking you anywhere you wanted to go— north, south, east or west. Too many for the police to block. There were backyards and gardens hidden by hedgerows and trees. Plenty of hiding places. If you knew it was time to escape.

The man in black's phone pinged and he looked at the screen.

It was time to escape.

McNulty checked his watch. It had been almost half an hour since he'd called Chuck Tanburro and therefore almost as long since Tanburro had called Bob Snow. The detective would work fast, bypassing the need for a search warrant by asserting exigent circumstances. It was the police get-out-of-jail card, allowing an officer to force entry into any room in any building to save life or minimize harm. Bob Snow had enough just cause to set up an immediate operation. The wheels had been set into motion, they just weren't moving fast enough for McNulty.

The news helicopter drifted back across Ventura Boulevard and was quickly joined by another. The police chopper cut through the sky between them. The hostage situation had already made the news and the police were struggling to keep up. Ground units would take even longer to deploy. McNulty checked his watch again. D'Aquino laid a hand on McNulty's watch.

"Wait."

McNulty knew D'Aquino was right but couldn't get the image of Kimberley Howe's corpse out of his head. The twisted body and the broken fingers. He didn't think Amy could be a twisted body just yet, but he reckoned the broken fingers had already happened. Questioning under duress. She was safe as long as her abductor thought McNulty was looking for the girl and that the house on Colfax was still a secret. But if the news helicopters were showing up, it wasn't a secret anymore. The police operation had already leaked, and it was likely that the man in the house knew what the police knew. There was no time to wait. McNulty stood up and ducked under the umbrella. He was halfway through the café by the time D'Aquino decided to follow.

Amy heard the ping of the phone through the bedroom door, a deeper tone than the usual phone ping. There was immediate movement by the man and then the sound of footsteps approaching her room. The idea she'd had when the truck rattled the window became an urgent response. She didn't think the man was coming to ask her more questions. This was tying-up-loose-ends time, and Amy was a loose end.

Her plan was simple and stupid and had no right to work. She was handcuffed in front and up against a hardened killer who knew how to shoot and blow things up. He'd shown no emotion when breaking her fingers and likely wouldn't lose any sleep over killing her, either. She had zero chance of over-powering him and getting out. Stupid is as stupid does. She didn't understand what Forrest Gump had meant by that, but time and momentum worked in her favor—the short time before the police would arrive and his momentum when he burst into the room. Amy quickly moved to the window and pulled back the drapes with her good hand. She grabbed the bedside lamp and hurried to the door, where she pressed her body against the wall beside and behind it. Just as her captor turned the doorknob, she hurled the bedside lamp at the window.

McNulty was out of breath by the time he passed his car, which was parked at the side of the road facing Jinky's Studio Café. The muscles in his thighs screamed and hot air burned his lungs. He hadn't run this far and this fast in years. He was out of shape but not out for the count. He kept running and kept breathing but he couldn't help slowing down. The pounding footsteps behind him were fast and evenly balanced. Vincent D'Aquino was in better shape. He overtook McNulty, then cut right through an alley behind the gardens. McNulty agreed with the tactic and followed.

"You take the back."

He was struggling to get the words out.

"I'll take the front."

It was the only strategy that would work, since he was already three steps behind D'Aquino. It made sense to have the fitter man go for the obvious point of exit. With the police on their way the kidnapper would go out the back and disappear into the maze of gardens and backstreets. D'Aquino disappeared behind a hedgerow. McNulty kept going straight. He could see the Colfax Cove Apartments on the left just past the intersection with Valley Spring Lane. The yellow crime scene tape fluttered in the breeze at the Pink Poodle house. He found an extra burst of speed and headed straight for the house. Suddenly there was a crash and tinkle of broken glass as a lamp smashed through the window-pane and shattered on the sidewalk.

* * *

The man was on a tight schedule. He needed to finish the woman and get out before the police set up a cordon that was wider than the immediate area around the house. He knew the first cordon would be close, then they'd block the roads farther afield to stop anyone leaving the area. His car was parked outside the area that would comprise the initial cordon, but he needed to get to it quickly. He was thinking about that when he rushed into the bedroom.

The noise caught him by surprise, but his momentum carried him forward into the room. The window had smashed outward, suggesting that the makeup lady had dived through the window. In the split second it took him to realize what had really happened, the bedroom door slammed shut behind him.

Adrenaline kicked in and eradicated any leftover grogginess Amy had been feeling. A massive dose of the fight-or-flight drug had invaded her system, and she was moving faster than she'd ever moved before. She was through the living room and into the kitchen before the bedroom door burst open again. She kicked the kitchen door shut but there was nothing with which to block it, so she moved straight for the outside door, praying it wasn't locked.

With her hands zip-tied and two fingers on her left hand sticking out at an awkward angle she couldn't imagine how she'd turn the doorknob, but she noticed the splintered doorframe just in time. The cops had forced the door when they'd responded to the shooting of the drug dealer, and the door had been taped shut ever since. The crime scene tape had been cut when her abductor brought her in, and the door was still unlocked. She didn't know any of that. She just saw the splintered frame and shouldered the door open.

There was a short path to the gate and an alley ran between

the back gardens. The garden was unkempt and overgrown with trees and shrubs crowding the path. She ignored the trees and darted along the path. Vines and rose bushes tore at her legs but she made it to the gate before the kitchen door burst open behind her. For a brief moment she expected to be shot in the back, knowing how accurate the man had been when shooting up the catering trailer. She fought back the panic and kicked the gate open. The alley was long and straight to her right. The shortest stretch was on the left toward whatever street that was. She didn't look back and took the route of least resistance.

The muscles in her thighs screamed and hot air burned her lungs. She wasn't as out of shape as McNulty, but she was suffering the same effects, plus a pair of broken fingers and her hands being zip-tied. Being handcuffed made running difficult, the natural balance and flow thrown off. She came out of the alley and turned right, away from the house and the main road. Blood was pumping in her ears, sounding like racing footsteps chasing her. No matter how fast she ran the pulsing beat kept up with her.

She was three houses along the street when she realized the footsteps were real. She was on the verge of screaming when fright gave her an extra boost. The pain in her fingers dulled to a steady ache. The heavy thighs became sprinters' legs. Her breathing became even and purposeful. The pulse in her ears became life-giving speed.

The footsteps pounded concrete behind her.

She ran faster.

The footsteps kept up.

Amy was running out of gas. Her legs felt heavy but she forced them to keep going. Her abductor was shouting for her to stop. She ignored the voice. Did he think she was stupid? *Stupid is as stupid does.* The thought brought a smile to her lips. It might have been a smile of resignation, because the footsteps were closing in. She couldn't outrun him. She couldn't out fight him. This was the end. The voice called her name. She stumbled and fell, but strong arms caught her before she hit the ground.

"Amy. It's okay."

A man she'd never seen before lowered her to the ground and knelt beside her. He looked as hard as nails, his face etched with a lifetime of pain, but his expression was soft and caring. He gave her a gentle smile.

"You're okay."

Amy snorted a laugh as the world began to spin. She felt anything but okay. Her vision went in and out of focus. She waited for the hard man to finish what his partner hadn't, kill the woman who didn't have answers to his questions. She almost felt relieved that the fight was over. The man kept smiling, muttering kind words until his partner came up beside him. His partner looked more out of breath than Amy. His partner was Vince McNulty. Then the world went dark.

CHAPTER FORTY-TWO

This time there was no getting out of another detention at the police station. The house at Colfax and Valley Spring was a crime scene for the second time in three days, and Vince McNulty was once again found at the scene of a crime. Even for someone who believed in coincidence those numbers didn't add up. Especially when you factored in the third crime scene and the fact that McNulty had a key to Amy Moore's room at the Pilgrim Motel, the same motel where McNulty had been arrested in J.B.'s room. If all that wasn't damning enough, Bob Snow's update included McNulty's ambiguous version of events and omissions. One omission was his failure to disclose his discovery of the girl at Hollywood Collision Center. The latest omission resulted from the last thing Vincent D'Aquino had said before leaving Amy Moore in McNulty's arms: "I was never here." So, when asked who was involved, D'Aquino wasn't mentioned, leaving McNulty to explain how he'd managed to find out where the kidnapper was holding Amy.

"How is she?"

"Pretty banged up. In shock. Doctor says she'll be fine though."

McNulty was sitting with another detective in another interview room at the North Hollywood Police Station on Burbank Boulevard. Along with Hollenbeck Station and the Hollywood Division, this made three police stations at which McNulty had been detained in as many days. At least he wasn't under arrest. They knew he wasn't the one who had kidnapped Amy Moore because Amy Moore had told them so. She had given them a full account, as best she could remember, and a reasonable description of the kidnapper, but she hadn't yet been shown a photo array or talked to a sketch artist. She was still fragile from having her fingers splinted and the aftereffects of the chloroform.

"When can I see her?"

The North Hollywood detective pulled up a chair and sat opposite McNulty.

"Soon. We've got a few things to clear up first."

McNulty nodded. It was time to lay his cards on the table.

"Whatever you want to know."

What the detective wanted to know was, what the hell was going on? The kidnapping and hostage rescue was already linked to the killing of a drug dealer, the torture and murder of a woman in Montecito Heights, and the explosion of the catering trailer at The Trails Café. There was a tenuous link to the drugs trade and enough ambiguities to make McNulty a person of interest, if not an actual suspect.

McNulty laid his cards on the table.

Just not all of them.

"And you expect me to believe all that?"

"It's what happened. Supported by the evidence and not disputed by the witnesses."

"There aren't any witnesses."

"There's Amy Moore."

Here's how McNulty laid it out:

While filming a night sequence for Titanic Productions he found a runaway girl hiding under a tarpaulin at Hollywood

Collision Center. Together with Amy Moore he took her to the Pilgrim Motel, using the makeup trailer for transport, and kept her presence secret from the producer and crew.

"Why keep it a secret?"

"Because Larry Unger is all about the movie—not picking up waifs and strays."

That night, when McNulty was checking the production compound somebody who was skulking around between the makeup trailer and the catering trailer assaulted him. That prompted McNulty to move the girl in case the intruder had been looking for her. Amy Moore took her to a friend's, Kimberley Howe's, in Montecito Heights, again without telling anyone on the crew.

"Why not?"

"Because once you've told the lie you've got to stick with it."

"My point exactly."

McNulty ignored the implication and continued. The following night the location shoot moved to The Trails Café where shots were fired and the catering trailer was blown up. The chef, J.B. House, disappeared in the chaos, but the smoke from the fire had been heavy with marijuana. This had led McNulty to reconsider his idea of what the intruder—the one who had hit McNulty on the head the previous night in the motel parking compound—had been looking for. *(Omission: He didn't mention the producer's practically admitting that he sanctioned the drugs as corporate hospitality.)* Fearing for the chef's safety, McNulty checked J.B.'s motel room but J.B. wasn't there. What he found instead was a stash of Pink Poodle dealer bags and a bunch of armed police.

"They arrest you for supplying or possession?"

"It wasn't my supply."

After being released by the police, McNulty learned that the Pink Poodle supplier had been killed at his house on Colfax Avenue. When he got back to the motel, Amy Moore showed him the interior of the makeup trailer, which had been searched and trashed. There was a message on the broken mirror. WHERE? At that time, he was still uncertain whether that meant the girl or the drugs, but Amy called Kimberley Howe anyway to check on the girl. There was no answer so Amy left the "bad shit" message. They cleaned up the makeup trailer and prepared for the night shoot.

"And you still didn't tell the police about the girl."

"I still thought I could protect her."

"Better than the police?"

"She was institutionalized. Last thing she needed was another institution."

"But you knew her name by then?"

"Tilly Nutton. Yes."

By then it was time to resume the night shoot at The Trails Café. McNulty had prepped the actor, then left the shoot to check on Kimberley Howe and the girl. When he got to Montecito Heights the girl was gone and the woman was dead. Tortured first. McNulty had called the police. *(Omission. He didn't mention the forged note about the girl traveling alone to visit her aunt in Santa Clarita, which he'd found on the telephone pad.)*

"Why didn't you tell them about the girl?"

"This is where it's a bit of a grey area."

"Grey how?"

Waiting for the police to arrive at Kimberly Howe's had given McNulty time to wonder how the man had known that Amy had moved the girl to Kimberley Howe's and how he'd found her. Nobody on the film crew knew about Kimberly, Amy's only friend in Los Angeles. It wasn't on the movie database or any of the Hollywood trade websites. The only public connection between the two was that they'd once been arrested together during their troubled youth. Long time past. A distant memory. Not on anyone's radar unless you were searching the deep past. The only database of criminal history that the incident would show up on belonged to the police. If the man had access to that, McNulty didn't want the girl's name showing up anywhere on it.

"You think he's got a dirty cop?"

"I don't believe in dirty cops. But he's got access somehow."

"A bit far-fetched isn't it?"

"He knew SWAT were on the way today."

After being released McNulty had gone back to the motel. To Amy's room. Since they were in a relationship he'd had his own key. The room was empty, but there were signs of a disturbance and a warning message, written in lipstick, on the mirror. *WHERE? DON'T CALL THE POLICE. I WILL KNOW.* That seemed to confirm McNulty's suspicions about the culprit's access to inside information. He tidied the room and cleaned the mirror. He went to Union Station to see if the girl had caught a bus or a train. It was the obvious place for her to leave from. A Union Station employee remembered the girl asking about Santa Clarita and being directed to the bus stop. That's when the kidnapper had phoned McNulty and warned him to deliver the girl in exchange for Amy Moore.

"How did he get your number?"

"He broke Amy's fingers. Least she would give him is my number."

"But you still didn't call the police."

"Like I said. Grey area."

After numerous inquiries with people who did not want to be named, McNulty had learned that the man was holding Amy at the Pink Poodle supplier's house on Colfax Avenue. *(Omission: The person who did not want to be named was Vincent D'Aquino.)* He'd left Jinky's Studio Café to stake out the house and called Chuck Tanburro because the technical adviser had contacts in the LAPD. McNulty knew it would take a while to set up an operation. When the news helicopters showed up, he knew he couldn't wait any longer, so he'd run toward the house. When he got there, a lamp came flying out of a window, an obvious decoy, so he'd gone around to the back and caught up with Amy in the next street.

"And you expect me to believe all that?"

"It's what happened. Supported by the evidence and not disputed by the witnesses."

"There aren't any witnesses."

"There's Amy Moore."

They didn't have time to argue the case because there was a knock at the door. A man in a suit opened the door and asked the detective to step outside with him, leaving McNulty alone in the room. If there's a universal rule in law enforcement, it's that men in suits are bad news.

CHAPTER FORTY-THREE

"You've been a busy boy."

"And who the fuck are you?"

"I'm the man who's going to save the girl and cover your ass."

Men in suits aren't usually so forthright, so maybe this one wasn't going to be that bad. McNulty folded his arms, leaned back in his chair and decided to reserve judgment until he had more to work with. The man closed the interview room door and pulled a chair around the side of the table so there was no barrier between them. He sat down without straightening his trouser legs or worrying about wrinkling his suit. Another plus. McNulty didn't unfold his arms. The man kept steady eyes on the technical adviser and spoke in a calm and friendly voice.

"You've been through a lot. Let me explain."

Human trafficking is the fastest growing crime in America. Throw the net a little wider and it's high on the list of growth industries around the world and the biggest drain on law enforcement resources since terrorism leapfrogged drugs in government priorities. There was gang crime, drugs wars, and property crime, including car theft and burglary, both business and domestic. There was violence against the person, rape and sexual abuse.

Every major city has to deploy its police force to combat all of them, but the crime diverting personnel from everything except terrorism is human trafficking.

"Modern-day slavery?"

"Sex trade mainly."

McNulty felt the familiar chill down his spine.

"Yeah, Chuck mentioned that."

The man in the suit nodded.

"Tanburro? The technical adviser? He retired at the right time. It's easier filming cops than being a cop."

McNulty shrugged.

"Not as fulfilling though. Nobody wants to be an ex-anything."

"You speaking from personal experience?"

McNulty didn't answer. He didn't need to. He sighed but still didn't unfold his arms. There was a pause that should have been filled by both men taking a drink of coffee, but nobody had offered them coffee. It was usually shit coffee in police stations anyway. McNulty shifted in his seat. The man didn't let the pause become awkward. He still sounded calm and friendly.

"Anyway. Here's where we stand."

Bill Hedge introduced himself. He was the lead agent of the FBI Human Trafficking Task Force working out of the Los Angeles field office. He was responsible for the L.A. Anti-Trafficking Coordination Team and anything else relating to people smuggling. The ACT drew staff from the FBI, Homeland Security and the Department of Justice. Numbers were bolstered by stripping local DEA agents away from drug crime, a move that hadn't gone down well with the cops on the beat. For them drugs were still the main cause of street crime in Los Angeles. Hedge's current investigation involved a sex cartel moving children up from Mexico and distributing them across America. Starting with California.

"Like the drugs cartels?"

Hedge loosened his tie.

"They're branching out."

He undid the top button of his shirt.

"Still mainly drugs though."

McNulty responded to the loosening of the tie by unfolding his arms. The barriers were coming down. This was becoming more of a conversation than an interrogation. Hedge gave McNulty an understanding nod.

"I hear you had a little drugs trouble yourself."

McNulty shook his head.

"Not hard stuff. Just weed."

"Hard enough that they blew up your catering trailer."

"I don't think that was about weed."

Hedge moved his chair so he could rest one arm on the edge of the table and shifted his position. He tapped the table twice with one finger.

"I don't either."

He laid his hand flat on the table.

"Have you heard of Rodrigo Dominguez?"

McNulty sat up straight. He remembered Jim Grant telling him about his troubles with Rodrigo Dominguez, stretching all the way from Snake Pass in the U.K. to Montecito Heights in Los Angeles. Dominguez had been shot and killed by Grant in an underground garage during the bank robbery at Pershing Square.

"The Dominguez Cartel?"

Hedge watched McNulty's eyes.

"Moved on and diversified."

His tone became a little harder.

"Still working out of Mexico but Americanized for the U-S market. Antonio Rodriguez del Castillo runs the sex wing. He's on our records as Tony Castle. Castle is the one moving kids through California."

McNulty couldn't help hardening his eyes and setting his jaw. No matter how hard he tried, he could never escape the shadow of Crag View Children's Home. It would always be with him. Anyone trafficking kids for sex was right at the top of McNulty's shit list. Hedge noted the reaction and leaned forward.

"Which brings us to the girl you found at the Hollywood Collision Center."

The ACT and the Task Force had been trying to find the way station for the traffickers for the past six months—the first stop in America before spreading across the states like a virus. They'd been thinking about the industrial areas of Long Beach and South Los Angeles, mainly because of the port and the fact that nobody paid any attention to minorities in a place where everyone was a minority. In addition, coming up from the south, it made sense to have the halfway house as close to the entry point as possible. San Diego was too close to the border. South L.A. made perfect sense.

"Until you found the girl who'd hopped a truck just north of Santa Clarita."

That focused McNulty's attention. He was still keeping Vincent D'Aquino under wraps but remembered the other piece of information he had given McNulty at Jinky's Studio Café. The truck stop where the delivery driver had stopped for fuel and pizza. Hedge didn't have to refer to his notes.

"CCTV caught her climbing aboard at Sulphur Springs. Of course, we didn't think to look that far north until you discovered that she was heading back to Santa Clarita."

McNulty shifted in his chair.

"You heard about that, huh?"

"Once it's on the system, we hear about everything."

"That's what I'm worried about."

Hedge nodded.

"You mean the guy having access to the same information? Me too."

He tapped the table again.

"But back to the truck stop. They found a body in a dumpster there three days ago. Member of staff. Young kid. Every finger broken before he was killed."

McNulty felt that shiver again. Hedge noticed.

"Yes. That's how he tracked the girl to the Hollywood Collision Center."

He lowered his voice.

"And from there to you."

McNulty considered the chain of events that had led him into this. The truck stop, the girl, and Kimberley Howe. The trail of carnage that had followed an eight-year-old girl across Southern California. He let out a sigh. He felt guilty saying it, but he had to mention the obvious.

"Seems like a lot of effort for a single runaway."

Hedge didn't nod or blink or shake his head.

"It's not just one runaway. It's five or six. His entire stable."

McNulty looked at the FBI agent.

"Even so. He'd go on the rampage over six kids?"

It was Bill Hedge's turn to let out a sigh.

"It's more than just the kids. Tilly Nutton is Tony Castle's daughter."

CHAPTER FORTY-FOUR

Tilly Nutton crested the ridge and saw the valley stretch out ahead of her. Coming from the other direction she had done most of her traveling at night and hadn't paid much attention to just how big the distances were. Seeing it in the full glare of the afternoon sun made her feel tired before she'd really begun. She wondered if the others would be able to make the journey. She wondered if the others were even still there. That thought tired her more than looking at the vista so she sat in the shade of a dried-up tree and opened her backpack.

Setting off from Santa Clarita after a late breakfast Tilly had to decide whether to follow the same route as before or shave the corner by not heading north to Sulphur Springs. The truck stop had been a means to an end, it being the first sign of civilization heading east, apart from the manicured lawns of the Hillcrest housing development. It cut across the path of the I-5 and was the perfect staging area for transport south to Los Angeles.

Heading west was a different matter. She knew where she wanted to go but unlike the I-5, hitting the right spot would be easy to miss. She didn't have a map and a compass, so she was working off the angle of the sun and the time of day. At least she had a watch, so she knew it was just after two in the afternoon. The sun had moved past high noon and was heading west, the same as her, except she needed to be slightly north of west and across rugged terrain without a map.

She thought about the Polaroid. The shoulder of hillside and the hanging tree. She'd know it when she saw it, but there were a lot of hills between here and there. A sad little sigh trembled her lips as she remembered that she no longer had the photo. It was in the bathrobe pocket at the Pilgrim Motel. She felt guilty at leaving the woman who had been so kind to her, but living with guilt was becoming her default setting. The greater guilt was what she was trying to rectify by returning to Rancho Verde.

The cabin in the hills overlooking the lake wasn't really a ranch. The girls came up with the name because it was the only patch of green in a barren landscape and the green was what kept the horses happy, the rolling meadow on the western shore of the lake. Rancho Verde became synonymous with safety, but it didn't feel like a safe haven now. Not with the bad men trying to recapture them. Escaping was one thing. Having the people who were looking for her look the other way was a lot more important.

Six days ago the girl who went by the name of Tilly Nutton had come up with her master plan. The hacienda had a red-tiled roof and was surrounded by high adobe walls. The compound was dirt and gravel with a raised patio and barbecue pit. There was only one way in and one way out—the wooden gate under an imposing archway. You could drive in or drive out but there was no pedestrian access. The hacienda was so far from anywhere that nobody walked there anyway. It was about as secure a place as you could get without having sentries and guard towers.

The weak link was the bunkhouse.

The bunkhouse was where her father kept the girls.

And the bunkhouse was built into the west wall of the compound.

Six days ago, Tilly had forced open the bathroom window and squeezed between the bars on the outside. The bars had been there for years and were intended to keep people out, not little girls in. They obviously worked because the hacienda had never been burgled. Nobody had ever broken in. But burglars are usually adults. Eight-year-old girls are a lot smaller. The other kids were even younger. If you could get through the bars it was easy to escape from a place without sentries and guard towers.

In the pre-dawn light, she had broken several branches and scattered torn snatches of cloth, not enough to be obvious but enough to point the finger a certain direction. The finger pointed to the dry gulch that ran across the bottom of the hill, a boulder-strewn riverbed. No footprints in the sand. A couple of scuff marks on the stone. Heading south. The girls had gone north and then east, being careful not to leave a trail until they were far enough from the hacienda. South was the obvious direction. It had the nearest roads and the only public transport links, a bus into Ojala, then a Greyhound along the Pacific Coast Highway. To the north there was nothing. Nobody would make a break for it to the north.

Initial search parties went south. Nobody thought to look north then east.

Tilly leaned against the dried-up tree and ate the sandwich she'd made from the sliced meat and cheese. She also had an apple and one of the cans of soda, leaving the water until later, when she'd really need it. The rest she was saving for the others, if they were still there. There was no reason why they wouldn't be, since she'd told them she was going for help and it might take a few days. She didn't know why she'd lied to them, but she did know why she'd left.

The man who said he was her father was a very bad man. The things she had been forced to do left scars that were deeper than the cuts on her back, but what made it worse was that she felt responsible. This was her father, and he wasn't just doing it to her. The other girls weren't even eight yet. Helping them escape assuaged the guilt for a few days but then her mind turned in on itself. *This is my father. This is my fault.* So, she ran away for a second time, leaving the others behind.

The sandwich was dry without anything like mayo to add moisture. The apple made it more palatable and the soda helped swill it down, but it was still basically a dry meal. Sweat ran down her neck even in the shade. The tree had long since died and shrivelled up, but it was still a tree. The trunk was solid and the branches a tangled canopy. Sitting beside it gave some relief from the sun but not from the heat, which bounced back off the parched earth. Everything was bone-dry and miserable. It was a long way from the lush green meadow of Rancho Verde. The tree did remind her of the hanging tree at the Dough Flat Trailhead, but she missed the horses and the shoulder of hillside in the background.

She finished the soda and tilted the can until the drips ran dry. When she held it to one side the sun reflected off the base and formed a circle of light against the trunk. When she held her hand in front it felt like a magnifying glass burning her skin. She wondered if that was how it had started, the wildfire she'd seen on the news this morning at breakfast. She put the wrapping paper and the can back into the backpack and closed the top. When she looked up, she considered the landscape to the west, not searching for the shoulder of hillside but looking at the plumes of black smoke that were so big they looked like storm clouds on the horizon. They were farther away than she was going but closer than she'd like. After a few moments to gather herself she stood up, swung the backpack over her shoulder and set off in the direction of the fire.

CHAPTER FORTY-FIVE

A man in a suit carries more weight than frontline police, even if that man doesn't straighten his trouser legs or worry about wrinkling the suit. The FBI carries more weight than a single agent in a suit, and Bill Hedge had the backing of the FBI. It was the weight of that backing that got the LAPD to play ball. Playing ball meant releasing Vince McNulty without charge. He hadn't been arrested anyway, since he wasn't really a suspect, but he was a person of interest. The LAPD didn't like turning a person of interest loose without a full investigation. The full investigation turned out to be ninety minutes with the head of the Human Trafficking Task Force. Then they let him go.

Bill Hedge took McNulty back to his car. It was still parked on Colfax Avenue, halfway between the target house and Jinky's Studio Café. McNulty didn't think he'd ever been in a more impressive law enforcement ride. The Chevy Suburban was big and black and clean as a whistle. It was just like those blacked-out vehicles he'd seen in countless movies, with enough interior space that you could have played table tennis. The FBI agent went under the Hollywood Freeway and turned left onto Colfax. Like all American roads, Colfax ran for miles, north and south. The house number of the house on their right was 5503 and they weren't even halfway there. The Suburban headed south, toward the small numbers.

Neither man spoke. Hedge kept his eyes on the road and the Suburban at cruising altitude. McNulty turned his eyes inward as he replayed the last part of their conversation in the interview room.

"He turned out his own daughter?"

"Castle isn't much on family."

"I thought the cartels were all about family."

"Not when you sleep with the hired help."

McNulty leaned back in his seat and rubbed his eyes. He knew lots of kids who'd been born from the hired help, or at least born out of wedlock and often without fathers. Crag View was full of them. The great unwashed and unwanted. He felt even closer to Tilly Nutton and vowed to find her before any more harm could befall her.

"So why is he so keen to get her back?"

"Pride. Nobody gets out who he doesn't let out."

McNulty already disliked Antonio Rodriguez del Castillo. It didn't take much to get on McNulty's bad side, and Tony Castle already had a chapter all to himself.

"But he's not in South L-A?"

Hedge used the tabletop as a makeshift map. His hands moved across the surface to emphasize the relevant positions.

"Los Angeles."

He made a gesture lower down.

"South L-A and Long Beach."

Then he shaded in an area above Los Angeles.

"Santa Clarita and the Sulphur Springs Truck Stop."

He swept his hand all the way across the table.

"Using that as a starting point we've identified a place of interest over to the west. The local field office has known about it for months but had no reason to link it to Castle until now."

McNulty looked at the map.

"Over to the west where?"

Hedge tapped a spot to the left of the tabletop.

"Ojala. Over toward Santa Barbara."

McNulty vaguely knew that Santa Barbara was way past Ventura on the Pacific Coast Highway. He'd never heard of Ojala. Hedge tapped again.

"Hacienda El Condor."

"Is that the place in the photo?"

Hedge took his hands off the table and faced McNulty. They had both spent a lot of time looking at the picture on McNulty's phone.

"Ojala is in the hills but that's not the right background."

McNulty held his hands out, palms up. Almost pleading.

"But you can find it, right? You're the F-B-I."

Hedge shrugged.

"We're the F-B-I, not *National Geographic*."

McNulty pointed to the ceiling.

"I thought you had the world covered. Satellite photos."

Hedge indicated McNulty's phone.

"That's a Polaroid not a satellite. Things look different, top down."

He sat up straight and let out a sigh.

"And like you said. We're going to have to be careful what we put in the system. If this guy's got the access that he seems to have."

He tapped the table one last time.

"We don't want that photo going anywhere near the internet."

At about that time, somewhere between Bill Hedge giving the warning at North Hollywood Police Station and dropping McNulty off at his car, Chuck Tanburro was putting the Polaroid on the internet. Not the World Wide Web or the national police database but the closed-circuit system used by location managers to search for the specific needs of a movie production. Like tall buildings, small town main streets, trestle bridges or desert backdrops. Tanburro was looking for a hanging tree with a shoulder of hillside in the background.

"Does this ring any bells with you?"

He was meeting with Marc Chu at the Los Angeles Film School on Sunset Boulevard opposite the Cinerama Theatre. Chu was a location manager he'd worked with many times.

"No. Is this the only shot you've got?"

"Yes."

Chu examined the computer screen. The photo had been enhanced but you can only bring out detail that is already there. The creased Polaroid didn't have a lot of detail. He zoomed and panned and examined every inch of the image, then went back to full frame.

"And you reckon it's somewhere near Santa Clarita?"

"Ballpark. That's our starting point."

Chu was sitting at the computer. Tanburro was standing with his back against the door of the office they'd been allowed to use. The Film School enjoyed good links with the movie industry and had been happy to help. Tanburro didn't want this anywhere near the police system but thought the Location Database would be safe. Chu nodded and opened a search window on a separate screen.

"Okay. Let's tick off what we've got."

He pointed at the various parts of the image as he spoke.

"Plateau hilltop in the background. A fairly distinct dead tree that looks like a trident."

He leaned closer.

"Some kind of sign on the tree. Maybe a trailhead. Riding or hiking."

He moved his hand up the left of the screen.

"Way off to the side here. A sliver of something solid with a bit sticking out at the top. Might be a cabin with the eaves jutting out."

He indicated the lower right side of the photo.

"Deep background. Fairly green. Something that looks like a

horse."

He tapped a shadow on the green.

"So probably a riding trailhead."

He sat back and his fingers hovered over the keyboard.

"Up around that area it's all scorched earth and rubble so the green indicates a body of water. Not a river, they're all dried up. More likely a lake. So, let's start narrowing the search."

He typed in the things they knew and some things they could assume. Trailhead. Plateau. Trident tree. Cabin. Lake. Horses. He set the search parameter as Santa Clarita plus fifty miles all around, then pressed enter. The computer searched for matches and the Polaroid went into the system.

Bill Hedge pulled up behind McNulty's car but left the engine running. They'd passed the target house with its crime-scene tape and broken window and were facing Jinky's Studio Café. The crime scene tape had stuck in McNulty's mind more than the John Wayne posters. He unfastened his seatbelt but didn't get out. There was something he wanted to clarify before setting off for the hospital.

"So this guy is hired muscle. The one that got away."

Hedge turned sideways and leaned against his door.

"More of a tracker than muscle. He finds people. If he can't, he finds people who know where they are and asks questions."

McNulty thought about Amy.

"He does more than ask."

Hedge nodded.

"He can be very persuasive." He twirled a hand in the air. "And very evasive. Castle has been using him for years and we've never come close to a description until now."

"From Amy you mean?"

"Yes."

"So she's got protection at the hospital."

Hedge neither nodded nor shook his head.

"He's looking for the girl, not tying up loose ends. He'll be halfway to Santa Clarita by now."

McNulty rested a hand on the door handle.

"But you've got her covered, right?"

"She's covered."

McNulty puffed out his cheeks.

"Thanks."

He opened the passenger door and set one foot on the sidewalk before turning to the FBI agent.

"This guy got a name?"

Hedge shook his head.

"This guy's got nothing. He's chameleon. No face. No description."

"Until Amy."

Hedge put a hand on the steering wheel.

"She's covered."

McNulty looked at Hedge sitting sideway in his seat.

"What you got him filed under? Gecko?"

Hedge sat up and faced forward.

"His nickname is Blender."

McNulty got out of the Suburban.

"Because he blends in?"

Hedge glanced across at the passenger door.

"Because he once got answers by putting a kid's hand in a blender."

CHAPTER FORTY-SIX

Blender was currently blending at an undisclosed location in unrecognizable clothes. When he had questioned the employee at the truck stop, he'd been wearing dirty blue coveralls. When he'd visited Kimberley Howe, he'd worn the bright red trousers and yellow shirt of a man trying to sell you something. The real estate van he'd stolen had supported the anonymity, hiding in plain sight without a description from any of the neighbors. His night-time incursion at The Trails Café and later at the Pilgrim Motel was aided by his ninja outfit, all black and grey with non-reflective surfaces.

Now he was wearing what everyone else was wearing, not standing out and not drawing attention to himself. If anyone questioned his being there, he would feign urgency and move on fast. That's what people did at the undisclosed location. He paused with the clipboard and looked at the signs. When he saw the one he was looking for, he put the clipboard under one arm and headed for the stairs.

"That's it."

The computer had pulled up a list of possible locations. Chu and Tanburro scanned each one, checking the file pictures against their search criteria. It was Tanburro who spotted it first and pointed at the screen.

"Check the other views."

Chu clicked on each thumbnail image one at a time, checking all the views a location manager would need before visiting in person. Up the hillside. Across the valley. The cabin and the trailhead. The horse meadow. The lake. And the tree that looked like a trident. It turned out it was the tree that was most famous. Chu let out a reverential sigh.

"El Tenedor del Diablo."

He translated even though it was written under the image.

"The Devil's Fork."

Tanburro was looking at the background.

"Never mind the tree. The cabin."

He scanned the info sheet, trying to find the location.

"Where is this place?"

Chu clicked back to the home page with the thumbnail images then brought up Google Maps. Starting with Santa Clarita he zoomed and dragged until he found what he was looking for. Twelve miles north and west of the town. Right in the middle of nowhere.

"Western shore of Lake Piru."

He ran his finger over the map.

"Beginning of the Dough Flat Trailhead."

Chu clicked "Accept" in the search engine and the computer congratulated him and filed the search. He printed out the search result and the map.

"That's a long walk for short legs."

Tanburro took the pages from the printer and opened his phone.

"Even longer with bad men on your tail."

He opened recent calls and paused with his finger over the button. It was decision time. Bring in the police or call Vince McNulty? He only considered that for a moment, then made his choice. He pressed the call button and raised the phone to his ear.

* * *

Blender felt the phone vibrate in his pocket before he heard the ping of the incoming alert. Not a call but a message from his computer spotter. He paused in the hallway and checked the screen. A thin smile spread across his lips. The Devil's Fork? That seemed appropriate considering what the outcome would be once he caught up with the girl. He put the phone away. That was for later. The here and now was much more pressing. He straightened his medical smock, pulled the baseball cap down over his eyes and continued pushing the wheelchair. Nobody ever asked questions in a hospital when you were pushing a wheelchair. Not if you kept your head down and moved with purpose. He went straight past the room he wanted, angling around the cop sitting outside the door, and continued to the end of the hall. Nobody gave him a second glance.

Amy Moore was dozing in her hospital bed. Pain medication made her sleepy, but the dull ache kept her awake. Her fingers had been reset and splinted but most of the pain was psychological, knowing what might have happened if she hadn't thrown the bedside lamp through the window. She was also grieving. McNulty hadn't wanted to tell her about Kimberley Howe but Kim was the first thing she'd asked him about.

The room was quiet. There were no machines monitoring her vital signs and there was no traffic noise coming through the double-paned windows. She was swaddled in a cocoon of meds and bed sheets. Even the noise from the hallway was muffled and distant. Until she heard the ping of a phone alert. A deeper tone than the standard ping. She tried to sit up but was too weak to move.

CHAPTER FORTY-SEVEN

McNulty finally visited Amy Moore at the Kaiser Permanente Los Angeles Medical Center on Sunset Boulevard. Two miles east of the Los Angeles Film School and four hours after she'd collapsed into his arms on Valley Spring Lane. He left the car in the visitors' parking lot and went to the emergency entrance. Amy wasn't at the E.R.; she'd been moved to a private room to recover from the trauma of being kidnapped and tortured.

The woman at the reception desk told McNulty that Amy was on the sixth floor and directed him to a bank of elevators. The ascent was slow and smooth. It gave him time to consider the call he'd just received from Chuck Tanburro. The girl's Polaroid had been taken twelve miles from Santa Clarita at a cabin near Lake Piru and the Dough Flat Trailhead—somewhere in the wilderness between the Sulphur Springs Truck Stop and Hacienda El Condor. Tanburro had told Bob Snow, and since the kidnapper had been warned that the police were on their way to Colfax Avenue, they both agreed to keep it off the system.

That meant it was going to be difficult to get a police response team to the area without a few more phone calls and a lot more favors. Maybe they couldn't respond at all, since the police and fire departments up there were busy evacuating homes from the wildfires spreading from the west. McNulty didn't plan on waiting for the police response team, he was going to find the girl himself, but he couldn't do anything until he'd made his peace with Amy.

The elevator opened into a waiting area with a nurses' station and signs pointing to various wards and treatment areas. A hulking figure was sitting next to the water fountain and a much smaller man was looking out the window. Chuck Buchinsky stood up, but McNulty wasn't ready to talk. He held a hand up for the actor to stay where he was. Larry Unger didn't need the hand; guilt kept him standing by the window. McNulty moved to the nurses' station and asked which room Amy Moore was in.

"Are you Vince McNulty?"

"Yes."

The nurse gave him a stern look.

"She's been expecting you."

McNulty felt a sigh coming on but found himself holding his breath. He couldn't speak so he raised his eyebrows in a question and glanced both ways along the hallway. The nurse pointed to the left, away from the elevators.

"Six-eleven. The one with the cop sitting guard outside."

McNulty nodded his thanks and set off along the hallway. He could see the room with the chair outside, but the chair was empty. The door was closed and there was no cop sitting guard.

The cop was sitting but not in the chair outside Amy Moore's room. He was sitting in a wheelchair with his head twisted backward. Luring the cop into the storeroom had been easy. Everyone trusts a hospital orderly, especially one who's out of breath and panicky. The wheelchair helped sell the emergency, and the cop had been bored anyway. Hospital detail was a drag, even when it meant guarding a prisoner, but playing nursemaid to an injured witness was beyond slow. At least if it had been his case, he could have taken a statement or shown her photos of possible suspects, but just sitting—that was a drag.

Blender straightened the dead man's head but it lolled forward.

There was no blood and no vented fluids. The killer's smock was wrinkled, but not bloodstained. This was a recovery ward, not the E.R. He scoured the shelves and found a box of syringes and a plastic bottle of industrial-strength cleaner. The bottle was prominently labeled with a skull-and-crossbones poison warning. He opened one of the syringes, stabbed it into the side of the bottle, and drew back the plunger.

People die in hospitals all the time. Tucking the syringe up his sleeve, he eased his head into the hallway to survey the damage. There was none. The cop hadn't struggled; there hadn't been time. Blender parked the wheelchair next to the door and partially in the area behind it so that anyone entering would have to be all the way in to see it. Satisfied, he straightened his smock, tucked the clipboard under one arm, and went back out into the hallway. The rest was going to be easy.

McNulty opened his stride, walking like the cop he'd been teaching Buchinsky to be. Straight back, relaxed shoulders, balanced walk. Leaning a little bit forward. Eyes on the danger zone, the door with the number 611 in a slot above the door. The door was closed. That was a bad sign. If the cop had simply stepped inside, he would have left it partly open—unless the door was spring-loaded, which is what McNulty was hoping for.

He scanned the hallway as he closed the distance. Just the usual foot traffic. A nurse walking toward him. Two visitors going the other way. An orderly heading for the stairs. A doctor talking to an administrator beside an open door. No cop approaching the chair outside Amy's room, and nobody coming out.

"We've never come close to a description until now."

McNulty edged over to the opposite side of the hallway to give him a good run at the door if necessary.

"He's looking for the girl, not tying up loose ends."

He slowed down and tried for an angle through the hall window into to Amy's room, but the drapes were drawn for privacy. He tried to remember if they did that routinely in hospital—drew the blinds on a recovery ward. He shook his hands out to relax the fingers, then crossed the hallway to the door. He didn't want to barge in and get shot if the cop was inside the room, but he wasn't going to knock, either.

"She's covered."

It didn't feel like she was covered. He reached for the door handle and took a deep breath. How long had the cop been away from his post? Hoping he wasn't too late, he turned the handle, pushed the door open and went through, stepping immediately to one side. The door closed behind him. Spring-loaded. The cop wasn't there. Amy was slumped halfway out of the bed.

Blender dropped the syringe into a wastebasket on his way to the doors at the end of the hall. Away from the elevators. Toward the fire exit and stairs. His feet echoed on the concrete steps all the way down.

"Amy? What the fuck?"

McNulty dashed over and pushed her back onto the bed. Her head flopped from side to side, eyes glazed and unresponsive. McNulty pressed the emergency call button then rested her head against the pillows. Her neck stiffened and her eyes came into focus. She glanced around with a look of panic, hands flapping against the bed sheets. Words tumbled out of her mouth, garbled and in no particular order. Her breathing came in shallow gasps. She licked her lips and tried again but the words still wouldn't come.

Two nurses burst into the room and pushed McNulty aside. They went into emergency mode, checking Amy's vital signs and responses. This was a recovery room not the E.R. She wasn't hooked up to the usual machines because she hadn't needed them, so this was something else. After a few minutes they had her calmed down and sitting up. They gave her a drink of water to moisten her lips then turned to McNulty.

"Panic attack."

McNulty didn't understand.

"Like, breathe-into-a-paper-bag panic attack?"

The lead nurse shook her head.

"That's hyperventilating. No. Something panicked her."

Amy waved to get McNulty's attention. When he came closer, she gave him a hard clear stare.

"He was here. The guy from the house."

That got McNulty's attention.

"In the room?"

Amy pointed at the door.

"Outside. I heard his phone ping."

"He didn't come in?"

"He talked to the cop, then they left."

Sweat prickled the back of McNulty's neck. He looked at the door then turned to the head nurse.

"Call the police. I think they've got a man down."

He left the room and stood in the hallway. He looked right and left, trying to decide which way the killer had gone. To the right was the nurses' station and the waiting room. Too public. To the left were more recovery rooms and the fire exit. McNulty turned left. He ignored rooms 612 and 613, both of which had a green "Occupied" sign next to the room number. The stairs were too far; the cop wouldn't have left his post for that long. On the opposite side of the hallway was a medical office and a storeroom. Somebody was sitting at a desk in the office. The storeroom door was closed.

McNulty glanced back along the hall. Backup wouldn't be here for ages. The nurses were unarmed. *Of course they were unarmed; this was a hospital,* he reminded himself. He wished he'd asked them to call security because they'd be closer than the police. He didn't think they'd be armed either, but at least they'd have radios and restraints. There'd be no help for maybe twenty minutes. McNulty didn't have twenty minutes. He was on his own.

He reached for the doorknob to the storeroom, turned it slowly then quickly shoved it open. The door flew open and banged against something behind it, then tried to close again. McNulty stopped it with his foot. Nobody rushed out. Nobody shot, stabbed or spat at him. He scanned the shelves and the floor space. The room contained plenty of medical supplies but no people. It was empty. Until he stepped around the door and saw the wheelchair tucked against the wall.

Blender reached the bottom of the stairs and went out through the emergency fire exit. He was marginally annoyed but mainly disappointed. Everything had been going so smoothly when he'd tracked the girl from the truck stop to Los Angeles. It only started going wrong when the ex-cop and his girlfriend interfered, thinking they were saving an innocent runaway. Now the ex-cop had interfered again. Blender had seen McNulty approaching room 611 when he came out of the storeroom and had quickly aborted his plan. The woman was a lost cause now. He would have to take his chances that her description of him would be distorted. Judging from the mental state she was in, that was probably a safe bet. He preferred tracking instead of terminating anyway, and he actively disliked the interrogating.

As the sun warmed his face in the parking lot, he thought about retiring. The Castillo Cartel had paid him well over the years but their expanding into human trafficking and child sex left a bad taste. Hunting down El Jefe's daughter was the last straw, but you don't just walk away from the cartels, not without completing the job. So, yes, he would find the girl and the others she'd freed, then wipe his hands of this sordid business. Maybe he'd go into the movies. He headed right out of the parking lot on the way to his car. Next stop, Santa Clarita and El Tenedor del Diablo.

CHAPTER FORTY-EIGHT

There was so much to say and so little time to say it. Room 611 was quiet and empty apart from two people who had never felt so far apart. All the noise and commotion were farther down the hall where nurses attempted to treat a man who was beyond help and hospital staff cleared the area. The police were on their way. That's why McNulty didn't have much time. He didn't plan on being here this time when they asked for a statement and a description and everything else they would need for the homicide report. He'd be tied up for hours, even if they didn't arrest him for being first on the scene of yet another crime.

If what Amy had told him was correct, he didn't have hours. He needed to set off for the cabin by the lake and he needed to set off now. Talking to Chuck Tanburro had confirmed the urgency.

"You put the photo on the system?"

"Not the police database. Location manager stuff."

McNulty stood next to the nurse's station with his hand covering one ear while he held his phone to the other. He was working out the timeline before speaking again.

"And that was just before you called me?"

"Fifteen minutes, tops."

McNulty glanced at the door to Amy's room.

"When you uploaded it or when you got the hit?"

Tanburro sounded sheepish.

"The search result. Took a few minutes to confirm with reverse angles. Then I called you and Bob."

"He didn't use the police system?"

"Not after last time. He hasn't even started making calls yet."

McNulty watched two more nurses dash down the hall. He turned to see Chuck Buchinsky and Larry Unger, standing by the water fountain. He held up a finger for Buchinsky to wait then continued on the phone.

"That's about when this guy got another message alert. He's doesn't have a bent cop, he has a spotter with eyes on the net."

Tanburro didn't speak for a moment. McNulty could hear taps and clicks on the other end and some kind of news report playing in the background. When he spoke again his voice was heavy and sad. They both knew where McNulty was heading.

"You'd better watch out up there."

Tanburro spoke over the muffled sound of a news reporter's voice.

"The fires are spreading east."

McNulty looked at Buchinsky, the ex-firefighter trying to play a cop in a movie.

"I'll be careful."

He hung up.

Now that McNulty was in the room with Amy, he found he couldn't approach her. He knew he should offer support and comfort but couldn't bring himself to do it. He felt cursed. This woman had just had the scare of her life after already having been traumatized, and it was all McNulty's fault. That was how he looked at everything. Guilt followed him like a bad smell. Amy broke the spell.

"You going to stand there all day?"

McNulty raised his head.

"I haven't got all day."

Amy fluffed the pillows and sat up.

"You'd best say what you've got to say then."

McNulty wasn't sure what he wanted to say. He knew that *"I haven't got all day"* was a bad start. He crossed the room and stared out the window. Room 611 looked out the back of the hospital with a view of Hollyhock House in the Barnsdall Art Park. It was like a peaceful haven in a city of concrete and steel. Mirrored windows everywhere. The Hollywood sign way over to the right. It looked nothing like the view from Crag View Children's Home and yet it felt like he was right back there. A boy in a man's world who was about to become a man.

"I didn't know who she was when I broke the headmaster's nose."

His shoulders slumped.

"I should have known."

Amy shifted against the pillows.

"Your sister?"

McNulty turned sad eyes on the woman in the bed.

"It was more about who I was angry at than who I was protecting."

"And who were you angry with?"

The sad eyes hardened.

"Everyone."

He touched the tattoo that barely showed above his collar and thought about the journey from Crag View Children's Home to Titanic Productions. The tattoo had come after he'd left Crag View, the spindly dead branches of the tree a reminder that all life was fleeting and that there wasn't much hope in it anyway. His rage against the bullies and the poison within. He told himself it was all about helping the innocent, but even as a police officer it had been more about anger toward the wrongdoers. From Mr. Cruickshank to Daniel Roach and even the wife-beater in Savage, Maryland. Venting, not nurturing. Anger, not love. Even now he was more angry at the tracker than protective of the girl. What kind of rotgut shitbag did that make him?

"This is all my fault."

He leaned his back against the window.

"You. J.B. Kimberley."

He twirled a hand.

"Everything."

Amy took a sip of water to moisten her lips. She wanted her voice to be clear.

"If you hadn't found the girl, you mean?"

McNulty nodded.

"Domino theory. They all fell from there."

Amy put the plastic cup on the bedside table and sat up straight. She flexed her neck and braced her shoulders. When she spoke, there was no trace of the makeup lady who had spent her days making actors look good on camera.

"Bullshit."

Her jaw was firm, her eyes hard.

"The dominoes fell long before the Hollywood Collision Center."

She drew her legs up under the bed sheet and hugged her knees.

"Case in point. You're walking down the street with your friend and you find a puppy in the gutter. You take it home but you're no good at caring for puppies, so your friend takes over. Turns out your friend's a natural. The puppy blossoms. The puppy is real happy you found it. But then this other guy turns up, says the puppy is his, and he wants it back. Only he isn't asking. He's taking. He finds your friend and does bad things because your friend has the puppy. Not you."

She rested her chin on her knees.

"Is it your fault because you found the puppy?"

It was a rhetorical question. They both knew the answer, but McNulty couldn't shake the feeling he was responsible. It was that angry-man survivor guilt that had been dogging him all his life. He kept quiet. Amy didn't.

"Meantime the puppy's on the loose and gonna get hurt."

She jabbed a finger at McNulty.

"Unless you get out there and find it again."

She unfolded her arms and took another drink of water. Her hands were shaking until she forced them to stop. The intensity of the last few minutes had drained her, but she still looked strong. McNulty pushed off from the window and came over to the bed.

"When did you get so tough?"

Amy reached out and took his hand.

"When some fucker took my puppy and gave it a kicking."

McNulty squeezed her fingers.

"He hasn't kicked it yet."

She squeezed back.

"Then you'd better go find her before he does."

PART THREE
RECOVERED

"When the police come. We went that way."
—Vince McNulty

CHAPTER FORTY-NINE

The puppy was doing just fine on its own, thank you very much. Tilly Nutton was making better time on the return journey because she wasn't playing hide-and-seek anymore; she was going full steam ahead and devil take the hindmost. That was partly because she was taking the direct route instead of avoiding built-up areas, but mainly it was the urgency caused by the smoke clouds on the horizon.

She came down from the ridge to the south of Lake Piru, avoiding the treatment works behind the dam. It was late in the day now so the workers had left, but she still detoured around the fenced compound, just in case. The way her life had shaped up there'd been lots of just-in-cases to avoid. She paused at the bottom of the valley and looked up at the hills to the west. The sun had gone down hours ago, but the horizon was aglow with a sunset that had nothing to do with the sun. She could smell the smoke and feel the static in the air.

Hold off. Just a while longer. Please.

The self-named Rancho Verde was halfway up the western shore just beyond the Lake Piru Recreation Area and the Lake Store. The R.V. parking area was closed until the high season, but Piru Canyon Road was still the danger zone, the place where a passing motorist might wonder why an eight-year-old girl was hiking the trail alone. She scanned the road from the boundary fence then set off at a good pace. She only needed to get past the dam; then she could cut down to the lakeside footpath.

The red glow on the horizon was highlighted against a black sky that was all smoke, not night. Sparks and occasional glimmers of fire showed across the hilltops. Getting the girls away from the cabin was the only way they'd see another day. Tilly broke into a jog as she rounded the bend and the view of Lake Piru opened up before her.

"This is about the girl, isn't it?"

"You know about the girl?"

"Amy told me. Day after the makeup trailer got trashed."

That was the conversation in the waiting room just after McNulty came out from seeing Amy. Buchinsky knew about emergency action and it didn't take a genius to understand the cause and effect. Larry Unger kept quiet. This was a conversation between the alpha males in the room. Buchinsky showed his concern.

"Is she okay?"

McNulty separated the actor from his producer.

"She's a long way south of okay."

He glanced at the elevators then looked at the fire exit in the hall.

"I'll fill you in on the way."

He turned to Larry Unger and took a deep breath. The producer had taken a chance on him when McNulty had needed a break, employing the ex-cop when nobody else would. They'd been through a lot since then, but this was something Titanic Productions couldn't be involved in. There was a role for him to play though. McNulty nodded at the elevators.

"When the police come. We went that way."

Then he took Buchinsky in the opposite direction, explaining all the way down the fire exit stairs.

* * *

The lakeside path was quiet and peaceful, in complete contrast to the turmoil bubbling within. The dam disappeared behind the headland as Tilly followed the western shore, and the boat landing came into view. The floating jetty was almost empty with just a handful of pleasure boats moored at the tourist slips at one end. There were no tourists. Wrong time of year. There were no people at all. Wrong kind of weather. This was fire season. She glanced up the concrete slipway toward the Lake Store anyway, just to be on the safe side. The safe side felt a long way from where she was.

Once she was satisfied there was nobody around to spot her, she dashed across the slipway and disappeared behind the bushes that fringed the path. She rounded another headland, and all signs of humanity became a thing of the past. There was no sound apart from the distant rumble of helicopters dumping fire retardant across the hilltops. There was no birdsong. There was no wildlife. The horses were gone.

That was the first thing that gave her pause. She stopped halfway between the headland and the sloping meadow and scanned for signs that the horses had moved to the far end of the field, agitated perhaps by the proximity of the wildfire spreading from the west. The horses were allowed to roam free but only as far as the grass allowed. The meadow was fenced in at the top and enclosed by the lake on the right. It was still a compound, just a very big compound. The horses were no more free than the girls hiding in the cabin—if they were still hiding in the cabin. Whoever had come for the horses might have found the girls as well.

Tilly stood beside the lake, rooted to the spot. It was too late to go back and too frightening to go forward. The truth that the girls must have realized was too painful for Tilly to comprehend; that the girl who had helped them escape had abandoned them. She looked at the private jetty at the foot of the slope. The faded wooden dock was a crooked finger with a single mooring. The rowboat was tied bow and stern, the oars shipped across the four bench seats. When she'd arrived with the girls, she'd fantasised about rowing across a distant ocean but accepted now that they were as trapped here as they'd been at Hacienda El Condor.

She missed the horses.

Throwing one last glance across the meadow, she turned left onto the path from the jetty and began the climb toward the cabin.

McNulty had laid it all out for Buchinsky by the time they reached the parking lot. There was some back and forth as they left Kaiser Permanente behind, turning left onto Sunset Boulevard. There were arguments for and against McNulty's chosen course of action. In the end it came down to simple expediency. Avoiding time-consuming red tape and bureaucracy meant this was the fastest way to help the girl. Avoiding putting the location on the system was a moot point now, so that wasn't what stopped the police becoming involved, it was the pressing duties elsewhere in a region threatened by the biggest wildfire in L.A.'s history. So far, an area the size of Texas had been razed to the ground. Homes had been evacuated and people had died. The police and fire departments had enough on their plate without looking for a runaway girl—even if she was being pursued by a merciless killer.

They had run out of things to say by the time they reached the I-5 heading north. They were positively silent by the time McNulty swept between Santa Clarita on the right and Six Flags on the left, then took the 126 west at Castaic Junction. The Sulphur Springs truck stop was a mile farther north. They weren't going to the truck stop; McNulty was taking the fast road west along the Santa Clara Valley, looking for Piru Canyon Road, cutting the corner and making much better time across the hills than an eight-year-old girl on foot. He just hoped they were making better time than the man who was famous for putting a kid's fingers into a blender.

CHAPTER FIFTY

The walk up from the lake felt longer than Tilly remembered. She wasn't sure if that was because of the slope or the expectation. She let out a sigh halfway up. She knew it had nothing to do with the slope. The sky had darkened all along the ridgeline, clouds of smoke varying from angry grey to hellfire black, all laced with veins of fire that occasionally exploded with glittering sparks. It was like the world's deadliest fireworks display.

In the foreground, on a rise in the meadow, stood a dead tree shaped like a trident. El Tenedor del Diablo. Farther up the slope and to the left was the cabin, door closed and curtains drawn. There was no twinkle of light. There were no signs of life. It looked as empty as the field, now that the horses had gone. Tilly paused to catch her breath but mainly to scout the cabin one last time. She wished she still had the photo so she could see their faces again, because she didn't think she was going to find them at the end of the path.

She set off on the final stretch, the slope growing steeper with every step. The low, dull thud of helicopters sounded beyond the fire line. Tilly looked up but couldn't see them; no doubt they were taking a different flight path to avoid the smoke. She wondered which direction was best for putting out a fire, into the flames or from behind? Fire-retardant chemicals or water? She wasn't really interested, just trying to distract herself from the more pressing question. Had the girls waited or left?

The path levelled out as she reached the dusty turnaround in front of the porch steps. The cabin was sturdy frontier stock, built to last in a time when lasting meant having good defense and a solid roof. The logs looked like they'd been there forever, but the stone chimney built into the gable end was as crooked as the private jetty. There was no fire in the open hearth because there was no smoke coming from the chimney. She stood at the foot of the steps and scanned the cabin again. Delaying tactics. A sensible precaution. She knew from bitter experience the dangers of entering a strange place, the bitter part being that her own father had sent her into those places. She had the scars to prove it, both mental and physical.

The front door was still closed.

The curtains were still drawn.

Nobody looked out to see who was coming and nobody opened the door in greeting. The low rumble sounded like a growling animal getting ready to pounce. At first she thought it was her imagination but then she felt it vibrating through the ground, a dull roar that was getting louder by the second. Avalanche? Earthquake? Did wildfires have a knock-on effect with other natural disasters? She glanced at the shoulder of hillside behind the cabin, but the ground looked stable.

The roar grew louder.

Gravel shifted beneath her feet.

Then the sound acquired direction and it wasn't up ahead; it was behind her. She turned to see where it was coming from and saw the bright yellow shape come swooping in toward the dam. The seaplane flew low and straight, like a swan coming in to land, then splashed down as it refilled its water tanks before taking off again and banking toward the wildfire. More water to dump on the blaze, not fire-retardant chemicals.

The plane disappeared over the ridge and Tilly was left standing in relative silence. No horses. No traffic. Just the creek of a door. She snapped her head to the front and held her breath. The cabin door opened a few inches and stopped. It waited like that for a moment, then opened all the way.

McNulty followed Piru Canyon Road through the flatlands bordering the 126 and past the turnoff for Wes Thompson's Piru Rifle & Pistol Range. He found it strange that in a country full of guns and space to shoot them, anyone would need a designated shooting range. People had been shooting cans behind The Trails Café for years. The road ahead was still paved but the car was trailing a dust cloud you could see for miles. If anyone was looking for a dust cloud coming toward them.

He kept his eyes on the road as it twisted and turned. The sweeping left-hand bend opened up a view of the broad white expanse of Lake Piru Dam. The treatment works looked abandoned, the gate in the chain-link fence closed and padlocked. There were no vehicles in the compound. There were no workers milling around. Part of that was the time of day, long past closing time, but he reckoned most of it was the sign of impending doom.

That sign was the thick black smoke and tongues of flame licking along the hilltops to the west. The sky was turning to night long before it was night. The fire was taking everything before it. Occasionally a tree along the ridgeline would go up like a roman candle, sending sparks into the air. A bright yellow seaplane scooped water from the lake then banked west over the hills. The dam grew closer, the lake a long flat teardrop in the valley. McNulty focused on his driving. Buchinsky scanned the wooded hillside on the left.

"The minute it hits those trees."

He jerked a thumb over his shoulder.

"We'd best hit the escape pod because it'll be down here in a rush."

McNulty passed the treatment works and headed toward the dam.

"After we check the cabin."

Buchinsky tore his eyes away from the hellfire smoke.
"If it comes down here there won't be a cabin."

The cabin door opened but nobody came out. Tilly looked at the darkness inside and couldn't see anything. She climbed the first two steps, checking the windows on either side of the door. The curtains didn't twitch. Nobody looked out. She went up the last two steps and stood on the porch, the backpack suddenly heavy on her shoulder. The weight crushing her chest was heavier. She took a deep breath and let it out slowly. She wanted to call out, see if there was a response, but her mouth was dry, and her nerves wound tight. One step at a time. That's what she told herself. It worked for that Chinaman and his journey of a thousand miles.

First step.

The windows separated, drawing the door closer.

Second step.

The curtains were only in her peripheral vision now.

Third step.

The tall dark rectangle was all she could see.

Final step.

Tilly stood on the threshold between her future and the past. Stepping through the door would bring them both together, the thing she had run away from and the girls she had come back to save. She had no illusions about her motives. What she was really trying to save was herself, and the only way to do that was to help the other girls. That was the only way to assuage the guilt. She let out one last sigh then went through the door.

It didn't close behind her. There was no sudden movement or threat. As her eyes adjusted to the gloom, she saw faces looking at her from the shadows. Pale frightened faces with staring eyes. She recognized them one by one but couldn't bring herself to go to them. She stood in the doorway, gripping the shoulder strap for support. The bag of food was her only offering and she couldn't even bring herself to offer that. She swallowed to moisten her mouth but still didn't trust her voice. She supposed this was what facing your demons must feel like, not being able to hug the people you needed to hug.

Her eyes didn't blink.

The faces stared back at her.

Then the girls surged forward in one collective movement and four sets of arms embraced her. There was endless chatter and nervous laughter and Tilly spoke gibberish in response to the outpouring of love. Her cheeks were damp with tears, but it didn't feel like she was crying, she was smiling. There was no need to explain why she'd taken so long coming back. Nobody questioned her loyalty. This was what friends did for each other. It was never, "Where have you been?" it was always, "Nice to see you." And it was. It was great to see the girls again.

Tilly swung the backpack off her shoulder and started handing out the food. The chatter slowed and Tilly opened the curtains. The cabin brightened and she could see their faces properly for the first time. She soaked up their enthusiasm and couldn't help laughing. Just a gentle chuckle; not a belly laugh. She scanned the happy faces then the smile froze on her lips.

"Where's Lucy?"

The girls fell silent until Sasha spoke.

"She went for help."

She lowered her eyes then looked at Tilly.

"When you didn't come back, we thought something had happened to you."

Tilly thought about all the things that *had* happened since she'd left for the Sulphur Springs Truck Stop. Jumping a truck to Los Angeles. Being found hiding at Hollywood Collision Center. Staying at the Pilgrim Motel and then being moved to the house at Montecito Heights. The explosion that signalled the bad men had found her, then forging a letter so she could make her way back to Santa Clarita. Yes, a lot had happened since she'd abandoned the girls she was meant to protect, but going for help around here?

"Help from who?"

Sasha waved toward the hills behind the cabin.

"The firefighters."

"Firefighters? Where?"

"Over the hill."

Tilly was aghast. She glanced toward the back of the cabin where the hillside wore a crown of smoke and fire.

"She went toward the fire?"

CHAPTER FIFTY-ONE

McNulty saw the entrance almost too late and had to slam on the brakes. There was no skidding or sliding or screeching of tires; he hadn't been going fast enough for a dramatic stop. After the recreation area, Piru Canyon Road became a snake that wriggled between the hillside on the left and the lake on the right, cutting back on itself every other turn, becoming more of a dirt road with each succeeding bend. There weren't enough straight stretches to pick up speed and there was no incentive anyway when you were looking for the turnoff to El Tenedor del Diablo.

He noticed the tree before he saw the entrance. He backed up, pulled into the driveway and parked in front of the gate. The meadow was fenced in, but it was only a token fence. It wasn't to keep people out or hold people in. It was for the horses, which don't jump fences unless they need to and never leave the green, green grass of home.

But there were no horses.

The dust settled as McNulty got out. The gate wasn't padlocked but he didn't want to frighten the girl, if the girl was here. He glanced at the hanging tree and understood why it was a desired location. Looking at it from this side, it looked more like a devil's pitchfork, standing on a grassy knoll overlooking the lake. The dead branches stuck up like a witch's fingers and he couldn't help touching the tattoo on the side of his own neck, a dead tree with branches that stuck up like a witch's fingers. It never ceased to amaze him how his life kept circling back to those formative years—the gothic children's home of Crag View, a troubled girl, and a broken nose.

"Do you want to go on your own?"

Buchinsky had gotten out too but hadn't approached the gate. The actor showed more intuition than McNulty had given him credit for. Buchinsky seemed to sense McNulty's reluctance and stepped back to give him the time and room he needed. Or maybe it was just plain common sense. He stood beside the car and spoke across the roof.

"She doesn't know me."

McNulty nodded and tossed him the keys.

"I doubt she'll be glad to see me, either, but…"

He shrugged then, indicating the wooded hillside behind them.

"Keep an eye on the fire. You're better at that than me."

They both glanced up at the glowing ridge. Hell was coming; it was only a matter of when. McNulty had been carrying his personal hell far too long. This was his chance to help balance the books. Buchinsky tapped the car roof, leaving a handprint in the dust.

"Make it quick. Those trees are tinder-dry."

Tilly heard the car and wondered if the fire department had already arrived. Then she realized it was a car, not a firetruck, and replayed her reaction to news of the explosion at the movie location. *They've found me.*

"You four. Hide in the bedroom."

The girls didn't move.

"Now."

Anita and Maxine went through the kitchen and into the bedroom, the only other room in the cabin. The kitchen and living room were open to each other, and the bathroom was a lean-to shed out back. Maria looked at Sasha and then Tilly but didn't move. After a few moments she lost her nerve and joined the others in the bedroom. Sasha had taken charge while Tilly was away. She wasn't ready to run and hide again just yet.

"You don't think it's Lucy bringing help?"

Tilly looked at the girl who'd stepped up after Tilly had abandoned them.

"I don't think it's worth taking the risk."

They could hear the gate open and close, but the footsteps were drowned by another seaplane drawing water from the lake. It swept down then roared off to help douse the fires. Fires that would torch the valley for sure.

"They're not taking us back."

A shiver ran down Sasha's spine. All the girls knew what going back would mean, but except for Tilly, Sasha understood more than the rest. She nodded and her eyes hardened.

"It's here or nowhere then."

Tilly scanned the interior, reacquainting herself with the layout. The open-plan living room and kitchenette with its stove powered by gas bottles through a line from the back wall. The stone fireplace. The countertops and cabinets with cups and plates and eating utensils. And matches.

"Remember the Alamo."

They all remembered the John Wayne movie because it was one of Antonio Rodriguez del Castillo's favorites, him being a Mexican and the Mexicans winning over John Wayne. Sasha gave Tilly a sideways look.

"You know they all died at The Alamo, right?"

Tilly smiled.

"Took a few Mexicans with them though."

She nodded toward back window.

"They think this place is getting hot? Let's give them hot."

Then she waved at the stove.

"Turn the gas on."

* * *

McNulty crossed the dirt and gravel turnaround slowly and carefully. He was trying for nonthreatening but looked like a man walking a tightrope, small mincing steps and swaying shoulders that reminded him of the John Wayne poster at Jinky's Studio Café, the one where the Duke was framed by an open door as he went inside. *Rio Lobo*, he thought. Without the cowboy hat and the rifle. The cabin looked like it was from a western, but the blazing ridgeline was all disaster movie. The sky was dark and brooding above the trees, not much different from McNulty's mood down here.

He paused at the foot of the porch steps and scanned the front aspect, unintentionally mimicking the eight-year-old girl who had done exactly the same thing fewer than twenty minutes ago. The curtains were open on either side of the front door but nobody was looking out. The curtains being open gave him hope. If the cabin had been abandoned due to the wildfires it was unlikely anyone would have left them open.

He wished he still had the Polaroid so he could hold it up like a peace offering, or his police badge, giving him license to go wherever he pleased. He didn't have a warrant and he wasn't a cop anymore, but he invoked the common-law right of access if he feared for someone's life. The way the hilltop was looking right now, that fear was very real.

He climbed the steps, one step at a time, pausing on each one to cycle through his assessment scan. Left-hand window, door, right-hand window.

First step. Left middle and right.

Second step. Left middle and right.

Third step. He changed the cycle. Right middle and left.

Fourth step. Left middle and right again.

Now that he was on the porch he stopped to listen as well. He cycled left to right. He cocked an ear to listen for any sound coming from inside. He concentrated on the door. If Tilly Nutton was hiding in the cabin, he didn't want to scare her by knocking on the door, and he surely didn't want to kick it open like a police raid. He wanted to be the kindly uncle come to take her home. Except home was the last place she'd want to go. He knew, because Crag View was the last place he wanted to go. So a place of safety was the preferred option. At the moment, that place was anywhere away from the wildfires raging across the ridgeline.

He walked toward the door and paused.

Should he call out to let her know who was here? Would she recognize his voice? And even if she did, would that assuage her fears? After all, he hadn't done anything except pull her out from beneath a tarpaulin, move her to a motel where the Blender had tracked her and then to the house in Montecito Heights, where she'd run away again. That was without the night-shoot explosion and the murder of Kimberley Howe. Why would hearing his voice give her any confidence at all?

In the end he didn't knock, and he didn't call out. He simply turned the handle and opened the door, slowly and easily and unthreateningly. He let it swing open and stepped through the gap, little steps and swaying shoulders. Just like John Wayne in *Rio Lobo*, except for the smell of gas and the eyes staring out of the gloom. The girl raised her hands, one holding a matchbox and the other a match. McNulty held his hands up in surrender. Neither of them spoke a word; they just stood there staring at each other.

CHAPTER FIFTY-TWO

Buchinsky felt the static before he heard the crackle and snap of brittle timber. The hairs stood up on the back of his neck. He'd been on site at countless fires in his previous career, and this was the part he hadn't missed—the part where he sensed the fire coming alive and getting ready to move. You could call it flashpoint or crossover, the point where the temperature reaches critical mass and flashes over, burning everything; but what it really was, was trouble.

He turned from resting his arms across the roof of the car and looked at the hillside behind him. The sky was completely dark overhead now, but it wasn't the sky he was worried about. The ridgeline was a jagged sawtooth silhouette against the smoke, bejewelled with sparks and licks of flame. The trees on the hillside were touched with glimmers of light from the fire atop the ridge. They swayed in a heat rush like the blast wave that pushes ahead of a nuclear detonation, then they stopped and stood upright. Still and silent.

The crackle grew louder. The hairs on his forearms copied the hairs on the back of his neck, then the trees nearest the ridge exploded like roman candles and the crackling became a roar.

"You came all this way just to find me?"

That's where they ended up, but it wasn't where they'd started. They looked at each other for what seemed like an age, then McNulty slowly lowered his hands. The girl didn't lower hers, keeping the match held against the scratch pad on the side of the matchbox. McNulty put a hand across his mouth and nose and waved the other at the stove.

"Can we turn the gas off now?"

He uncovered his mouth to speak more clearly.

"I'm obviously not who you were expecting."

Tilly's hands wavered and she glanced at the stove before turning steady eyes back to the man in the doorway.

"Just because you're not who I'm expecting doesn't mean you're who I want to see."

McNulty stepped outside to take a breath of air and stayed on the porch.

"It *does* mean I'm not here to take you back to your father."

Tilly's blinked then stared harder.

"Nobody's taking me back to my father."

Her eyes were watering because of the gas.

"Taking me back's not what he wants."

McNulty saw the pain in her eyes.

"Blowing up the others isn't what *you* want. So please? The gas?"

Tilly looked at John Wayne standing in the door of The Alamo and wondered what it would be like if the Mexicans didn't win. Her hands felt heavy and they drifted apart. She glanced at the bedroom door then back at the man who'd found her among the auto parts at Hollywood Collision Center. She put the match back into the box and turned the gas off. McNulty opened the front windows and Tilly opened the back. The gas cleared only to be replaced by the smell of burning wood and smoke—but it was better than the gas.

The bedroom door opened and four more pairs of eyes stared out. McNulty saw them and let out a sigh. He'd seen worried eyes before, always kids and always frightened. He touched the tattoo on the side of his neck and knew what he'd have to say to win their trust. It wasn't something he liked talking about.

"She was about your age when it happened. My sister. Back at Crag View Children's Home where I grew up. The headmaster was going to…"

He shrugged.

"I don't know what made me do it. But it wasn't good. I broke his nose with a Bible."

He split his attention between the four girls in the bedroom doorway and the one who had risked everything to get them away from her father.

"Never saw her again. As a child."

He swallowed to stop his mouth from becoming too dry to speak.

"I was thirteen."

He shrugged again.

"And now I'm not."

Tilly knew all about hard-luck stories and understood how difficult it was to talk about them. She had seen something in his eyes when he'd first found her, and she saw it again now, multiplied by ten. A sadness that hid behind the show of strength and confidence. People stand up straight because it's what they're supposed to do. When life shits on them they either buckle or stand up straighter. Standing straighter camouflages the pain but it's always there, behind the eyes.

"You came all this way just to find me."

They looked at each and both knew the truth. McNulty wasn't here to find the girl; he was here to find himself. That was something an eight-year-old girl shouldn't have to understand, but Tilly Nutton was eight going on eighty. McNulty saw it in her eyes and felt embarrassed that she'd seen through him. It made him sad to think she'd seen enough in her short life to understand. He stood up straighter…

"We can exchange stories later."

…and nodded toward the back window.

"But we need to get you girls out of here before the fire spreads."

The other four came out to join Tilly, but none moved forward. Five girls standing in a group— just like the Polaroid— beside El Tenedor del Diablo. Again, McNulty wished he still had the photo, the photo that Tilly must have taken because she wasn't in it, to give back to them. McNulty scanned the group again and did the math. Five girls in the picture plus a sixth behind the camera. Five girls in the cabin, *including* the one who had been behind the camera. He pointed at the bedroom.

"Is the other girl in there?"

The group huddled together. McNulty felt the dynamic change as Tilly's shoulders sagged and a different girl stepped forward.

"Lucy went to get help."

She jerked a thumb toward the back of the cabin.

"From the firefighters. Up the hill."

Footsteps sounded on the dirt and gravel turnaround. Moving fast. Running. The big man took the stairs two at a time and pounded across the porch. The girls backed off at the sight of him and McNulty waved a placating hand.

"He's with me."

The man had obviously overheard what the girl said.

"The fire's not up the hill anymore. It's halfway down and moving fast."

CHAPTER FIFTY-THREE

The rock-strewn hillside was a tinderbox of dead wood and live trees that barely clung to life in a landscape parched from relentless sun and lack of rain. Flames crackled and snapped as row after row of spruce and pine caught fire. The dead trees simply burned but the living pines exploded in a *whoosh* of sparks and flame. Some leaned and fell immediately. Others died on their feet, tall and straight like candles in the night.

The heat was like a furnace. The flames were like hell itself. The fire swept down the hill, moving erratically in a jagged line, engulfing everything in its path. Above the cabin it was still halfway up the hill; to the south it was already down to the recreation area and the Lake Store. Gas bottles exploded and trees fell alongside Piru Canyon Road. The Smokey Bear sign, which warned that the risk of fire was high, disappeared in a cloud of sparks and smoke.

"We're not leaving without her."

It was Tilly who stepped up again, shoulders back and confidence returned. The others closed ranks behind her and didn't see the shadow that flickered in her eyes.

"I left them once. I'm not doing it again."

McNulty stood in the doorway. He knew this wasn't going

to be easy so he slowed things down, despite feeling Buchinsky's impatience behind him on the porch. He looked at Tilly and softened his expression.

"There was this movie I watched growing up. I caught it at an exhibition with my friend Donkey Flowers. Frank Sinatra wants to get everyone out of this prisoner of war camp at the same time, but Trevor Howard prefers getting them out one at a time."

McNulty took a step into the cabin.

"At the time, I was trying to save this girl from a sex ring, and Donkey was always telling me, 'You can't save everyone.' I guess it all came down to my failure to save my sister."

He let out a sigh and made eye contact with the other girls, then again with Tilly.

"At the end of the movie, Trevor Howard says, as a voice voice-over, 'I once told you, Von Ryan. If only one gets out, it's a victory.'"

Tilly looked at the man who'd come to get her out of the prisoner of war camp.

"Why did he say it as a voice-over?"

McNulty shrugged. That was the part he didn't want to tell, but Tilly wanted to know.

"Did he get them all out?"

McNulty nodded.

"Pretty much."

The girl tilted her head.

"But he didn't make it. At the end. That's why the voice-over."

McNulty didn't nod or shake his head or make any movement at all.

"Getting one out isn't a victory if it means leaving one behind."

He lowered his voice.

"But risking five to save one isn't good math."

Tilly jerked upright.

"I'm not leaving her."

McNulty held up a placating hand, then nodded toward

Buchinsky. There was only one way he was getting these girls out of here.

"My friend here used to be a firefighter."

Tilly craned her neck to see past McNulty.

"That's Donkey Flowers?"

McNulty shook his head.

"Chuck Buchinsky. Donk was…"

He waved the question aside and indicated the group of girls.

"Anyway. Chuck's going to drive you five down the hill."

He tapped his chest then pointed toward the fire.

"I'll go find Lucy."

Buchinsky started to protest but McNulty held up a hand. He looked Tilly in the eye and they both understood the truth of the situation: The other girls wouldn't leave without Tilly, and Tilly couldn't leave without looking for Lucy. Impasse. The only way to break the deadlock was for somebody to go look for the missing girl while the ex-firefighter saved the others.

"You promise?"

"Cross my heart."

Nobody moved. The girls stood behind Tilly. McNulty stood near the doorway. Buchinsky waited on the porch. It was a frozen tableau of the point at which indecision turns into decisive action. Tilly looked at the man she'd first seen through a gap in a tarpaulin at Hollywood Collision Center. They both knew that Von Ryan wasn't going to make it, but at least he would have found himself in the end.

"Okay."

Then everyone moved at once.

CHAPTER FIFTY-FOUR

The heat surprised McNulty as he led the girls across the driveway in front of the cabin. The fire was still a long way up the hillside, but he could feel its presence all the way across Piru Canyon Road. He stepped to one side and let Buchinsky take the lead, a hulking Pied Piper using the car keys instead of a flute to signal for the children to follow him.

The girl who was second-in-command went first, followed by the three younger girls and Tilly, who was bringing up the rear. They all filed past McNulty until Tilly broke off from the line. She stood beside McNulty and watched the girls cross the turnaround and head up the slope toward the gate. She turned to look at the view where she had taken a photo with a borrowed Polaroid camera, the hanging tree and the lake and the field where horses used to graze. There were no horses grazing today. In a few short hours there'd be no grass for them to graze on. She turned back to the man she would never see again.

"You want to know which way she went?"

McNulty didn't need to know which way she'd gone because whichever way it was, he wasn't going to find her. The fire was two-thirds of the way down the hill above the cabin and fringing Piru Canyon Road to the north and south. If Lucy had gone up the hill looking for a firefighter, she wasn't going to be one of the ones Von Ryan got out. He couldn't tell the girl that though. It was no coincidence he'd started thinking of her as "The Girl" again. It made the lie feel less personal.

"Which way?"

Tilly scanned the hillside as if recalling the missing girl's route but what she was really doing was avoiding looking at the man who was about to sacrifice himself so she could save the other four. The other girls wouldn't leave without Tilly and Tilly couldn't leave without offering a grain of hope about Lucy. McNulty was that grain of hope. She couldn't bring herself to say the words, so she simply looked into the distance until that was too hard as well. She looked at McNulty and McNulty looked at her.

Tilly let out a sigh.

McNulty nodded.

Buchinsky and the other girls were almost at the gate. The view across the lake was clear and peaceful, the smoke not having spread that far yet. The cabin was in the foreground from this angle and El Tenedor del Diablo wasn't so much a Devil's Fork as just another dead tree in the middle distance. Horses would have been a nice touch but today wasn't a day for nice touches. McNulty looked at the view then smiled at the girl who was going to prove Trevor Howard right when he said, *If only one gets out, it's a victory.* Tilly didn't smile back. This wasn't a smiling day, either. She turned away and followed the others.

McNulty gave her a head start then set off for a low section of fence to the right of the gate. He wasn't going to climb the fence, but he needed to make it look good until Buchinsky drove the girls away. He wasn't going to use the gate, either. When all was said and done the cabin seemed as good a place as any to wait for the inevitable. Part of him had already accepted his fate but the Yorkshireman in him wouldn't give up without a fight. He glanced at the lake and the boat moored at the crooked jetty and wondered how far he'd have to row to avoid being toasted on the surface. He didn't really consider that an option. People got toasted all the time in wildfires, hiding in their swimming pools.

He slowed down so he wouldn't outpace Buchinsky and the girls. The road was just ahead, a manmade leveling of the hillside to allow passing traffic. On a day like today the only traffic was McNulty's car parked in the mouth of the driveway. He stopped to watch Buchinsky open the gate and usher the girls through. As before, Tilly brought up the rear. She paused at the gate and looked over her shoulder. It took a moment to find McNulty but then their eyes met one last time. He wasn't sure but he thought she gave him a little nod and he did the same. The weight lifted from his chest. Maybe Trevor Howard was right.

The girl turned away and went through the gate. McNulty continued his slow walk to nowhere. Buchinsky clicked the key fob and the car beeped as the doors unlocked, then McNulty saw Buchinsky stop and look at the bend in the road. He couldn't see what Buchinsky was seeing, but he heard it, an engine that sounded bigger than a car but smaller than a firetruck.

In the end it was somewhere between. A big square SUV with a light bar on the roof came around the corner and pulled into the drive. It was bright red with a fancy badge on the side and Fire Chief written on the door. It crunched gravel and stopped next to McNulty's car, faster than McNulty had stopped, tires spitting dust. When the cloud settled a man with a smoke-stained face and a heavy coat got out. The coat was open and swinging free. Standing beside him was a little girl who looked more bedraggled than the firefighter.

Buchinsky watched the Fire Chief skid to a stop and get out. The girl looked like she'd been through a war but was otherwise okay. There was no blood or broken bones. Even more important, there was no singed hair or melted skin. Before he could stop her, Tilly Nutton dashed between the parked vehicles and hugged the girl. That answered one question—where the girl had gone when she went looking for help. It answered another, too—whether she had found help or not.

The ex-firefighter-turned-actor looked at the man who was still doing the job he'd loved and thought about a third question. Why did the Fire Chief have a smoke-stained face but a clean turnout coat?

CHAPTER FIFTY-FIVE

The real reason Blender was nicknamed Blender was because he could blend in anywhere. The best way to blend in at a wildfire was to dress like a firefighter. He knew the nickname had been given added weight by all those stories about putting a kid's fingers in a blender, but that had been taken out of context and was completely exaggerated. He would never put a kid's fingers in a blender and the only pain he'd ever caused a child was the loss of a parent. Hurting kids wasn't his purview. That was one of the things that made this assignment harder to swallow and pushed him closer to retirement. Seeing how dangerous firefighting was only reinforced the thought that Hollywood was a better option. After all, he'd been playing one part or another anyway since he'd started working for Antonio Rodriguez del Castillo.

Stealing the Forward Command Vehicle had been almost as easy as getting the uniform. The Santa Clarita fire chief wasn't using it because he was one of those, get-stuck-in-with-the-guys kind of fire chiefs. He was at the front line with the rest of his crew and didn't want the SUV getting caught up in the firebreaks and evacuations that were keeping his department busy across the Dough Flat Trailhead. L.A. County Fire Station 126 in Santa Clarita was practically deserted, the Battalion 6 HQ having been stripped of its personnel to help cut firebreaks and evacuate civilians across the ridgeline. Blender's detouring to get outfitted had given the technical adviser and his ex-firefighter friend the lead in the race to find the girl, but being first wasn't as important as being there at the end.

He'd intended to be there at the end.

From Santa Clarita he'd followed the same route that McNulty had taken, the 126 then Piru Canyon Road, but being half an hour behind the movie men meant that once he was past Wes Thompson's Piru Rifle & Pistol Range and the Lake Piru Dam, the fire was dangerously close to blocking the road. The Recreation Area and Lake Store had already been engulfed, so it wouldn't be long before the trees falling alongside the road would be falling across it. Once that happened there'd be no going back; it would be forge ahead or die.

Then one of those little miracles happened that can change everything. Coming around a bend after the Lake Store he'd seen a girl scramble down the hill and sit beside the road. At first, he thought he'd found Tilly Nutton—without having to kill the ex-cop and the actor—but he soon learned it was even better than that, because returning Tilly Nutton was pointless if the other girls were still on the loose. Playing the returning firefighter who rescued the girl would be a great way of completing his assignment with minimal fuss. He'd helped the girl into the SUV and continued along Piru Canyon Road. After one more bend he'd seen the car parked in front of the ranch-style gate and the other girls coming toward him like lambs to the slaughter.

"Road's gonna be cut off pretty soon. You'd better get them in the truck real quick, then follow me."

Blender stepped aside and waved the girls toward the open door. There was enough room in the SUV to fit a battalion of firefighters, so five girls would be no problem. Six girls if he included the one who'd started all the trouble. He fully intended to include Tilly Nutton, who had finished hugging the bedraggled girl and was shepherding her flock toward the SUV. The fire-fighter-turned-actor looked less convinced.

"How come you're using the fire chief's truck? You're no fire chief."

Blender wiped a hand across his forehead. Maybe smudging dirt on his face had been a step too far. He noticed the actor looking at his turnout coat. No, it wasn't the dirty face, it was the clean turnout coat. None of that mattered because the actor had worked in the fire department. He knew the insignia and rank structure. Blender had stolen the fire chief's truck, but the uniform was from the locker room. It could be anybody's.

"Checking for stragglers."

He waved toward the fire.

"Chief's leading from the front. You remember how that works, right?"

The actor shrugged, his brow creasing with a frown.

"Actually, no."

He kept steady eyes on the intruder.

"My chief never left his office unless it was to polish his firetruck."

Blender kept his tone light.

"He polished it himself?"

The actor shook his head.

"Figure of speech."

He pointed at Blender's open turnout coat.

"But he'd never let his guys near a fire with an open coat."

Blender nodded his understanding. The actor's chief probably wouldn't let a firefighter near a fire without his helmet, either, but that wasn't the problem. Blender reckoned he could talk his way around an ex-firefighter, but there was a reason people always said, "Once a cop, always a cop." It was the technical adviser coming through the gate that concerned him.

McNulty's relief at not having to sacrifice himself was negated by the fact that somebody else had saved the girls from the jaws of death. Jaws of death might be an extreme view but with the fire creeping down the hillside, it wasn't much of an exaggeration. He felt jealous at letting the firefighter save the day and guilty about feeling jealous. Guilt always played a big part in his makeup. He wondered when he was going to grow out of that.

He watched the emotional reunion as he moved from the low fence to the gate but couldn't hear what Buchinsky and the firefighter were saying. He could sense it though. If there was one thing cops were good at, it was recognizing a frosty atmosphere, and despite the heat, the atmosphere here was positively icy. He saw the firefighter wipe a hand across his forehead, then fidget with his open turnout coat. It was the smoke-stained face that got his attention. He'd seen that face before.

"Checking for stragglers," the face said.

McNulty approached the opening and leaned on the gatepost. There was some more back and forth between the actor and the firefighter, but McNulty was concentrating on the face, trying to picture it without the camouflage—without the uniform that helped him blend in at a wildfire. Where else had McNulty been where somebody had disguised himself to blend in?

"But he'd never let his guys near a fire with an open coat."

McNulty heard the words and realized he wasn't the only one who was suspicious. Maybe all that cop training was beginning to pay off with the ex-firefighter. More likely it was because Buchinsky actually *was* an ex-firefighter. An open coat at a wildfire was as out of place as a baseball cap in a hospital. McNulty remembered seeing the man in the medical smock turn around outside room 611, but he hadn't realized the significance until now. The face had been cleaner then and McNulty only gotten only a fleeting look, but the man wiping his brow had the same demeanor and shifty eyes.

The girls were halfway to the SUV. Buchinsky took half a step toward the firefighter. The firefighter glanced at McNulty coming through the gate. In a situation like this, the person who wins is the one who acts first. Blender took a gun out of his coat pocket and shot Buchinsky in the chest.

CHAPTER FIFTY-SIX

In moments of crisis the way to cope is to compartmentalize, prioritize and take decisive action. Medical emergencies call it triage, treating patients with the most serious injuries first. Yorkshiremen call it "time to shit or get off the pot." McNulty was ready to shit.

The crisis on Piru Canyon Road was threefold. There was the rescue operation to save six girls. There was the fire raging just across the road and coming closer every second. And there was the man with the gun. All of those were sufficiently serious to be a priority in their own right, but there was a fourth that was more urgent—the man who had been shot in the chest. McNulty dashed to Buchinsky as he sagged to the ground. For a big man he went down gracefully. McNulty took his coat off and folded it into a makeshift pad, shoving it under Buchinsky's shirt and pressing the actor's hand against it.

"Keep the pressure on."

Buchinsky looked at McNulty with slow eyes.

"You think we didn't do first aid?"

The ex-firefighter did his own first aid, holding the pad against the entry wound and taking shallow breaths to check if he'd been shot in the lung. No blood came out of his mouth. The lung was fine. None of the vital organs had been hit, just the meaty part of the chest below the right shoulder. McNulty watched Buchinsky do the relevant checks and was even more impressed with the actor he was teaching to walk like a cop. McNulty nodded and Buchinsky nodded back. The man standing over them spoke calmly but firmly.

"Did I get your attention?"

The man with the gun had gotten McNulty's attention but not all of it. The other parts of the crisis still needed triage—the girls and the fire and the man with the chest wound. One of those had the power to trump all the rest. McNulty glanced up the hillside then focused on the man they called Blender.

"It's not me you should be worried about."

The man's eyes didn't flicker. He wasn't going to be fooled by that old, "Look out behind you," trick. McNulty met his gaze with steady eyes.

"Do you know what Fahrenheit four-fifty-one is?"

Buchinsky didn't think McNulty was talking about the Ray Bradbury novel where a firefighter burns books or the fabled temperature when paper spontaneously ignites, but he knew where McNulty was going with this. Flashover. Firefighters had been battling it for years. Cops knew about it, too. It's when the temperature a room gets so hot that everything in it catches fire—curtains, wallpaper, bedding. It wasn't four hundred and fifty-one degrees Fahrenheit, but it was very hot. The hillside overlooking Piru Canyon Road was getting very hot. Holding the pad firmly against his chest, Buchinsky forced himself to his feet and stood beside McNulty.

"He's not a firefighter but he was a cop. You should listen to him."

McNulty saw Blender's eyes flick to the actor then back to him. He glanced at Buchinsky, who was looking stronger by the minute, then looked at the gun in Blender's hand. It was a hitman's gun, maybe a .22. Small caliber, intended for close-quarter headshots. The bullet wasn't big enough to smash its way out through the skull and simply rattled around inside mushing the brain. No stopping power for someone as big as the ex-firefighter. Blender kept the gun pointed at the space between the two men. McNulty took half a step to one side, opening the gap.

"Before you get both of us."

He waved a hand toward the hillside.

"It's gonna hit Fahrenheit four-fifty-one."

The shrug and the sigh suggested resignation as he glanced at the girls.

"And that's going to do your job for you."

The gunman snorted a laugh.

"I'm not here to kill them. I'm here to take them back."

McNulty snorted a laugh in return.

"Yeah, like that makes a difference."

He leaned to one side, widening the gap some more.

"I suppose you're going to say you don't hurt kids."

"I don't."

"What about the fingers in the blender?"

"I didn't do that, either."

Blender shrugged.

"It does add weight when people hire me."

His face became serious.

"The thing is, when somebody pays me, I always finish the job."

McNulty smiled at a childhood memory. A movie, but not *Von Ryan's Express*. He looked the gunman in the eye.

"Lee Van Cleef. In that spaghetti western with Clint Eastwood."

Blender proved he really did like movies.

"The second one. With Eli Wallach. I could never figure out if he was the Bad or the Ugly."

McNulty relaxed his arms and shifted balance to both legs.

"But you always finish the job?"

Blender nodded.

"I do."

McNulty ran a few variables through his mind as he saw a possible delaying tactic. Maybe even a way of cancelling the contract altogether. He made a sweeping gesture to include the girls.

"The job in this case being to take the runaways back to Hacienda El Condor."

He indicated the smoke-obscured horizon to the west.

"Over there in Ojala."

Blender nodded again but spoke cautiously.

"Yes."

McNulty put on his most trustworthy cop face.

"You haven't been keeping up with the news, have you?" A frown creased his brow as he got serious.

"Ojala was evacuated two hours ago. Never made it to the hacienda. They don't have exact numbers yet, but they reckon..." He shrugged.

"I don't know. Half a dozen dead, at least."

CHAPTER FIFTY-SEVEN

The thing about lying is, if you're going to lie, lie big. Don't say, "They stole three hundred dollars," say, "The gang got away with fifteen million dollars." Most people will believe fifteen million. They don't care about three hundred. McNulty had no idea what areas had been evacuated, but he knew Ojala was west of Piru Canyon Road and the wildfires had been eating everything to the west. Hitmen and trackers aren't the same as most people, but you mention fifteen million and you'll get their attention. McNulty got Blender's attention.

"So, really. You don't have a job anymore."

The gunman didn't lower his guard.

"And you know this, how?"

McNulty jerked a thumb at Buchinsky.

"I'm heading into wildfire territory with an ex-firefighter. You don't think he's keeping up to date?"

The gunman looked at McNulty and Buchinsky, the gun trained loosely on the gap between them. The girls huddled together, crouched beside McNulty's car. The actor adjusted the wadded coat against the gunshot wound. The ex-cop did the ex-cop thing, staying loose in case he had to act fast. They all waited to hear what the gunman would say next.

"You don't think I've been keeping up to date myself?"

He waved the gun toward the technical adviser's car.

"Check the radio."

Blender hadn't been keeping up to date any more than the ex-cop
he was confronting, but the suggestion that Antonio Rodriguez
del Castillo might have perished along with his hateful child sex
ring could provide a convenient way out for the man considering
a career in Hollywood. During his time working for the cartel the
gang had swung from supplying drugs to smuggling children.
Blender had few scruples, but there was a reason that pedophiles
had it rough in prison. Hardened criminals don't like people who
mess around with kids. That stance was only slightly mitigated
when the kiddy fiddling was a business model.

He doubted he'd be so lucky, having Ojala burn to the
ground, taking Hacienda El Condor with it, but he was open to
the possibility. He supposed there were plenty of jobs that left a
bad taste in the mouth when you got home, but working for
Castillo was a whole lot worse than repossessing homes or being
a slaughterman. Being a hitman and a torturer was bad enough,
but look what working for the cartel had done for him: He was
more famous for putting a kid's fingers in a blender than for
finding people and getting them to talk, and the blender story
wasn't even something he'd done. No, getting out from under
that was an appealing prospect, so he told the ex-cop to check
the car radio.

"Local news should be covering the fire zones."

The ex-cop went to his car and opened the driver's door. He
was about to lean through the opening when another thought
struck the hitman. He pointed the gun at McNulty.

"Stop."

The ex-cop had seemed too eager to get into his car. Blender
knew that English cops weren't routinely armed but that didn't
mean McNulty hadn't picked up a few bad habits since he'd
moved to America. Like having a concealed carry permit to
keep a gun in the glove box. Blender jerked the .22 toward the

forward-command vehicle.

"Use mine. Keys are in the ignition."

The girls were still huddled together. The actor finished adjusting the wadded coat against the gunshot wound. The ex-cop stopped doing the ex-cop thing and looked tense as he closed the car door and crossed the gap to the SUV. His eyes darted from the gun to the girls to the ex-firefighter then he opened the passenger door. He couldn't reach the radio, so he had to climb in to turn the engine on. The exhaust rumbled and the radio started spouting news.

Blender took a step closer to the open door to hear the radio. The SUV door had opened away from him so he couldn't see the hillside reflected in the window. The first sign that something was wrong was the look on the ex-cop's face.

McNulty saw it in the rear-view mirror. The point when time was up, and triage was a moot point. Fahrenheit 451. Shit-or-get-off-the-pot time. The trees bordering Piru Canyon Road seemed to shimmer in the mirror, wavering like a heat haze on a distant road or trees swaying in the breeze. Sparks developed on the extremities like fireflies on your fingertips. They stood out from the smoke and flames in the background. Static crackled and raised the hairs on McNulty's forearms. He felt them bristle up the back of his neck.

The crackling grew louder.

The sparks multiplied.

There was a whooshing sound as the heat rushed forward, igniting trees from halfway up the hill all the way to the roadside. Row after row of pine and fir exploded in showers of sparks. The wave of fire rushed toward the parked cars at the gate, six feet off the ground and all the way to the treetops. The sparks became burning debris, dancing in the breeze. Branches and pinecones and stripped bark became burning shrapnel as flashover engulfed the trees.

Buchinsky dropped to the ground, sheltering the girls under broad shoulders and outstretched arms. Tilly Nutton looked at McNulty with terrified eyes. McNulty didn't have time to look at her. He put the SUV into reverse and slammed the gunman with the open door.

CHAPTER FIFTY-EIGHT

Piru Canyon Road became a river of fire. Exploding trees fell across the road, blocking it in both directions and setting fire to the boundary fence and the scrub and brush bordering the meadow. The roof of the cabin began to smoulder. The paint on McNulty's car began to bubble and melt. McNulty wasn't in McNulty's car; he was driving backward in the fire chief's SUV, dragging Blender into the road. Into the river of fire. McNulty gave it a final burst of speed then dived out of the driver's door. The SUV crashed into a tangle of fallen trees, lifting the rear wheels off the ground and ripping the turnout coat off the gunman's back. He was still alive when his hair caught fire and a sliver from a snapped tree branch pierced his lung. The blood coming out of his mouth bubbled in the heat.

McNulty tumbled and rolled but he didn't stop moving. Using forward momentum, he was up on his feet, keeping low as he dashed to where Buchinsky was sheltering the girls. Melted paint caught fire on the car and the side windows popped with the heat. There was no need to say anything. Everyone knew it was time to get off the pot; they just didn't know where to go. Tilly tried the obvious.

"The cabin?"

McNulty helped Buchinsky to his knees and split the girls into two groups of three. They all got ready to run. McNulty glanced at the log cabin then looked at Tilly.

"Gas bottles and wood? No."

He nodded down the slope where the grass was already turning brown.

"The lake."

Row or swim? Boat or water? McNulty turned the choices over in his head as he urged his three girls toward the lake. Speed was of the essence, but he didn't know what he was going to do when he reached the water. Behind him, in the burning gateway, the car reached its own Fahrenheit 451 and exploded when the gas tank caught fire. Denuded tree trunks tumbled down the slope, spreading fire across the grass. The roof of the cabin went from smouldering to blazing in a matter of seconds.

Buchinsky stayed behind the other three girls, arms wide as if herding sheep. McNulty did the same, only faster, and reached the jetty first. Being first is only good if you know what to do next. McNulty didn't know what to do next. His mind raced, trying to ignore the stories of families being cooked in their swimming pools while sheltering from the fire. He told himself the lake was bigger than a swimming pool but that meant it was farther to swim across.

The gas bottles behind the cabin exploded, ripping the back wall apart and dropping the roof into the cavity. Pieces of splintered wood flew through the air. A blazing log bounced and rolled down the path toward the jetty. It hit another log coming from the side and the two locked horns, forming a deadfall that the other trees got caught behind. The heat was incredible and made McNulty's decision for him.

"Into the water."

Two girls waded into the shallows, but Tilly stood with her toes at the shoreline. She looked at the fire then the lake and finally at McNulty. The fear in her eyes said she was caught between a rock and a hard place.

"I can't swim."

Buchinsky's three girls stood beside Tilly. The second-in-command spoke.

"We can't either."

McNulty felt his hair begin to singe. Time was up. It was either death by fire or drowning. At least with drowning there were two adults who could try and keep the girls afloat. A bigger tree crashed into the deadfall and broke the logjam, sending the blazing wreckage hurtling toward the jetty. McNulty was about to push the girls into the water when Buchinsky picked two of them up and lifted them over the side of the rowboat.

The logs came crashing down the path as McNulty untied the mooring rope. Buchinsky threw the other two girls into the boat and pushed with all his strength. McNulty jumped in and reached for the two girls who were swimming. They held onto the side of the boat as Buchinsky jumped in. The logs hit the wooden jetty, splintering the walkway and breaking the supports. The dried planks caught fire immediately. The boat slid past the end of the dock into dark, clear water that reflected the inferno behind.

The heat was too intense. The swimming pool wasn't going to save them. The girls cowered in the bottom of the boat. The entire shoreline was ablaze, the crooked jetty bringing the fire out onto the lake like a flaming pointer. McNulty knew, even if they all grabbed an oar, they couldn't row fast enough or far enough to beat the fire. This was going to be their swimming pool and it wasn't going to save them.

He glanced at Tilly. Why did it always come down to this? Whenever he tried to save anybody he ended up making things worse. The broken nose and the Bible had only succeeded in getting his sister exported from Crag View. Saving Tilly Nutton at Hollywood Collision Center had only swapped life on the streets for death in the water. Why couldn't he just leave well enough alone?

He felt the boat jerk sideways and the motion caught him by

surprise. A slap on the shoulder turned him toward Buchinsky and the ex-firefighter made a twirling motion with one hand then rocked the boat. McNulty didn't understand so Buchinsky rocked the boat again, cupped one hand palm upwards then turned it over.

"Turtle."

McNulty got it.

"Submarine."

The two men worked together, rocking the boat one way and then the other. On the third attempt the boat turned turtle, dumping the girls into the water, then covering them with the shell. McNulty took a deep breath and pulled the girls into the air pocket under the boat. They all found something to hold on to, the bench seats mostly and the oarlocks. Buchinsky settled at the bow and McNulty at the stern, and everyone kicked their legs in unison. The turtle began to swim away from the fire, steam rising off the hull.

The submarine glided farther into the lake.

The water helped cool the burns on their skins and the swimming motion helped settled their nerves. It was relaxing and smooth and lifesaving, and the farther they went the cooler the water became. Instead of gasping for breath the girls settled into a rhythm. Instead of facing imminent death, they all believed they were going to make it. Then something grabbed McNulty's leg and dragged him from under the boat.

CHAPTER FIFTY-NINE

Blender had felt pain before, but nothing compared to being burned alive. The heat was all-encompassing, but it was the cooked-pork smell that made him feel sick. His mind still had enough control to be surprised that cooked human actually did smell like roast pork; then the pain kicked in and all restraint went out the window. He remembered hitting his thumb with a hammer once when he was putting up some bookshelves in his apartment. His first reaction was to snarl and shout and smash three holes in the wall. Now he was going to do so much more than smash three holes in this wall.

Thankfully he couldn't see how bad he looked as he crossed the road and ran down the hill. He was too busy watching the two men and the six girls flee toward the lake. He saw the boat capsize and glide away from the jetty, then he dived into the water and felt the pain all over again.

McNulty was dragged down and sideways from under the boat. The surprise forced him to take a breath and taking a breath sucked water into his lungs. Panic kicked in and he thrashed his arms and legs to get free from whatever had grabbed him. He felt something jar against his foot then he broke the surface gasping for air. Water belched out of his mouth and he coughed and spluttered as he blinked the water out of his eyes.

The overturned boat had moved a long way from the shore-line, the wooden hull steaming but not catching fire. The wildfire had turned the meadow into scorched earth, the fallen trees still burning along with the log cabin and the burned-out cars. The heat was still there but not as intense as it had been on the race for the jetty. Maybe the swimming pool would save them after all.

That thought was stillborn as something grabbed his leg again and tried to pull him under. He was ready this time and thrashed his legs until he broke free again. His mind raced. He knew there was fishing on the lake but surely nothing big enough to drag him down. This wasn't Moby Dick or that giant octopus grabbing Kirk Douglas. This was something else.

The something else broke the surface six feet from McNulty and the ex-cop was almost sick. The face that swam toward him was a horror mask of melted skin and burned hair. One ear was gone, and the eyes were permanently open, their lids having been burned away. Blender's top lip had melted off, leaving a grinning nightmare of blood and teeth. Pieces of skin floated off around the man who had killed Kimberley Howe and kidnapped Amy Moore. The face mouthed words that were just guttural sounds in the water.

Then a hand reached out and snagged McNulty's arm, making him scream in disgust. He grabbed Blender's arm and the skin slid off like a sleeve. Blood seeped out of the wound, staining the water around them. The other hand came up holding a knife, but the hitman couldn't swim and stab at the same time. McNulty kicked the melting man and backstroked away from him. Panic gave him strength. He swam faster than he'd ever swum before. The roar in his ears felt like his head would explode.

Blender kept his head above water and came after McNulty.

McNulty kicked harder and flexed his arms.

The pulsing roar wasn't in McNulty's head. It was all around him. He glanced toward the shore in case a firetruck had made it through the flames but all he could see was smoke and fire. He turned over in case a motorboat was coming to the rescue, but the lake was empty apart from the overturned boat that was still protecting six girls and an ex-firefighter.

Blender took advantage of McNulty's pausing and closed the distance between them. McNulty saw him and backpedalled again. The roar grew louder, the noise familiar. He felt the surge of air as the seaplane skimmed the lake, sucking water into its empty tanks. The bow wave forced him to one side, but Blender was directly in its path. The front of the plane hit him in the face and the weight dragged him under. When the plane took off and banked toward the fire, the hitman was gone. A few minutes later the plane used the water—not fire retardant— and a little something else. McNulty swam back toward the boat. It was time to turn turtle again and prove that Von Ryan had been right: getting them all out was the real victory.

CHAPTER SIXTY

"Do you think they suffered?"

"Do you care?"

They were standing on a section of scorched earth just north of Ojala. The landscape had been dry and barren even before the wildfire but now it looked like hell had come and swallowed it whole. Tilly looked at the remains of Hacienda El Condor and let out a sigh.

"I shouldn't. But I do."

McNulty scuffed a dry patch of dirt with the toe of his shoe and looked at the girl who by rights should have never wanted to see this place again but had insisted on taking a look after the police and the hospital had finished with her. It had been almost a week since the rescue at Lake Piru but the fire and the over-turned boat felt like a lifetime ago. McNulty could empathize. He hadn't had the pleasure of seeing Crag View burned to the ground, but he had visited years after it closed when it was just a shell of its former self, full of memories and ghosts. Tilly Nutton's ghosts were fresher. McNulty kicked more dirt.

"When I think about growing up. Back in *my* dark place..."

He drew a line in the sand, then scrubbed it out.

"...I'm not sure how I'd feel if I saw it burned to the ground. Whether I'd care whether Mister Cruckshank suffered."

He looked at the girl he'd first seen through a gap in the

tarpaulin at Hollywood Collision Center.

"The main thing I remember is this: The dinner lady was nice. And I always try to remember the nice."

Tilly turned steady eyes on the Hollywood man who couldn't have been further from a Hollywood man.

"Does it work?"

McNulty shook his head.

"Hardly ever."

He raised his eyebrows.

"But the food was good."

Tilly looked at the still-smouldering ruins of the place that held nothing but bad memories. Most of the walls were still upright, but the roof tiles and ceiling joists had collapsed into the cavity that had been the main house and the dormitory. The courtyard walls and entrance had been bulldozed during the rescue attempt but like the buildings themselves, there had been nothing to save. Tilly spoke in a voice that sounded far beyond her years.

"I don't remember the food."

The reason they were staring at the ruins of Hacienda El Condor was because McNulty had been amazingly prescient when he'd told Blender that the hacienda had been destroyed by the wildfire that had cut a swathe through Ojala and the hills west of Lake Piru. He'd even been close with the number of dead, five, not six, the bodies still to be identified but unlikely to include Antonio Rodriguez del Castillo. Cartel bosses don't get caught in wildfires; the authorities are never that lucky.

McNulty learned about his prescience while being treated for cuts and burns at the Henry Mayo Memorial Hospital in Santa Clarita. Another hospital. Another waiting room. Buchinsky reckoned McNulty should buy a lottery ticket. Larry Unger thought he'd hit the jackpot with another marketable hero starring in his latest movie. Until Buchinsky closed him down.

"What do you mean, we can't use it for publicity?"

This was while they waited for the girls to be checked over.

"People died in the fires. You're not using that to promote the movie."

Larry never gave up without a fight.

"It's in times of hardship people need a ray of light."

Buchinsky gave the producer a steely glare but didn't speak. Amy Moore stood at the window overlooking the parking lot and stayed out of the conversation. She'd worked for Titanic Productions long enough to know how much Unger liked free publicity, although the cost of this was anything but free. McNulty stepped between the two men, nursing his freshly bandaged arms.

"He's a firefighter."

Buchinsky stood like an immovable rock.

"Retired."

McNulty gave a half smile.

"But not ex."

Buchinsky didn't speak. McNulty said it for him.

"You can take the man out of the firefighter but not the firefighter out of the man."

The two exes-who-would-never-be-ex looked at each other. It was Buchinsky's turn to give a half smile.

"Once a cop always a cop."

Larry Unger listened to the macho backslapping and shook his head.

"I'm going to be sick."

Buchinsky saw the look on Unger's face and couldn't resist twisting the knife.

"I've been thinking about that whole name thing. You know, how it looks on the poster. I think I'm going to change it."

Unger looked suspicious. McNulty and Amy just listened. Buchinsky waited a beat then dropped his bombshell.

"Charles Bronson."

Unger snorted a laugh.

"You're kidding, right?"

Buchinsky shrugged.

"It's plain and strong."

Unger puffed out his cheeks.

"It's also fifty years too late. Biggest star of the seventies already took it."

Buchinsky's face turned blank then he went through a range of expressions as he showed the producer he was considering his options. His eyes widened.

"I guess you're stuck with Chuck Buchinsky then."

McNulty put an arm around Amy's waist as the producer stormed off toward the water fountain. McNulty nodded. He understood the importance of humor to deal with traumatic incidents. Cops had been using it for years. The door to the treatment room opened and a doctor in scrubs came over.

"Are you McNulty?"

"Yes."

The doctor nodded back toward the door.

"She wants to talk to you."

They had talked a lot but didn't go deep, mainly about the other girls and what would happen next. There were no parents, at least none they knew about, and McNulty didn't want them going into the system. He'd grown up in the system and knew how that would work out. There was plenty to decide and a lot of people to be consulted but McNulty thought there was room to maneuver. Back in his Crag View days he hadn't had a Hollywood producer and an outpouring of goodwill to help him. Tilly Nutton would be a different story.

So, almost a week later, McNulty had driven her across the 126 to Ventura then up the 33 to Ojala, Buchinsky beside him in the front and Amy with Tilly in the back. There wasn't much conversation—driving through Ojala was a sobering experience. Hacienda El Condor wasn't the only place that had burned to the ground and the five bad men weren't the only people who had died. Some of them might even have been dinner ladies.

"I don't remember the food."

McNulty finished kicking dirt and turned his face to the sky. He took a deep breath of clear mountain air and let it out slowly. There was still a hint of burned wood and scorched earth, but the air was surprisingly sweet. Fresh shoots of growth wouldn't spring up until the first rain, but if one thing was certain it was that after fire cleared the dead wood regrowth would follow. Sometimes you have to clear your past to follow your future. That all sounded a bit pretentious, so he simplified it for the girl.

"Then remember today."

He nodded toward Amy who was standing beside the car.

"And look at tomorrow."

A gust of wind kicked up a twister in the dirt. It swirled around the girl, obscuring her view. The ruins disappeared and the car was hidden behind a veil of dust. Tilly closed her eyes and covered her mouth, holding her breath until the twister subsided. It drifted off toward the hacienda as if trying to carry it away and left the car in a clear patch of bright afternoon sunlight. The blue sky was warm and clear, suggesting a future that was finished with darkness and pain. She glanced at the woman who had been so kind then looked at McNulty.

"You said that didn't work."

McNulty brushed the dust from his face.

"Not always."

He waved a hand at the hacienda.

"You can leave it behind, but you'll never forget."

His voice sounded wistful.

"Somebody once told me, it's not the shit that happens but how you get over it."

He looked at Tilly.

"The past is the past. It's tomorrow that counts."

He nodded toward Amy again.

"And tomorrow starts today."

Tilly looked deeply into McNulty's eyes as if trying to see if that were true. Her expression made her look eight going on eighty. She tilted her head and kept looking at him.

"Did you read that on a greeting card?"

McNulty smiled.

"It does sound a bit cheesy doesn't it?"

Tilly didn't nod or shake her head, just kept staring at him.

"But do you believe it?"

He looked at Amy and the firefighter then back at the girl. The swirl of dust disappeared, and the day became bright and clear. The sun warmed his back and glinted of the windshield. He held his breath for a moment, then nodded.

"Yes, I do."

ACKNOWLEDGMENTS

At the risk of repeating myself, I am going to repeat myself. Because the acknowledgements will always be the same. Here comes the repeat:

As readers, I'm sure you already know that books don't simply pop out of the author's brain and into the bookstore. It takes a lot of work by a lot of people to put this book in your hands. Once again, it's time to thank the people who helped make this happen, in no particular order. Eric Campbell and Lance Wright at Down & Out Books for continuing to have faith in me. Donna Bagdasarian for being my agent in the early days and suggesting that I set my books in America. Good call, Donna. And to the growing list of authors who have supported me along the way, including Lee Child, Reed Farrel Coleman, Nick Petrie, Chris Mooney, Matt Hilton, Andrew Grant, Bruce Coffin and Ace Atkins. Oh and one more person, who deserves her name carved in stone. My editor, who spilled more red ink and blood than anyone should have to. Cynthia Bushmann, Cynthia Bushmann, Cynthia Bushmann. Consider it carved. As always, I've saved the most important for last, you, the reader. This book didn't simply pop into your hands, you made the effort to seek it out. I appreciate your support. Happy reading.

Ex-army, retired cop and former scenes-of-crime officer, **COLIN CAMPBELL** served with the West Yorkshire police for thirty years. He is the author of the UK crime novels *Blue Knight White Cross* and *Northern Ex*, and the U.S. thrillers featuring rogue Yorkshire Cop Jim Grant and Vince McNulty.

CampbellFiction.com

On the following pages are a few
more great titles from the
Down & Out Books publishing family.

For a complete list of books and to
sign up for our newsletter,
go to DownAndOutBooks.com.

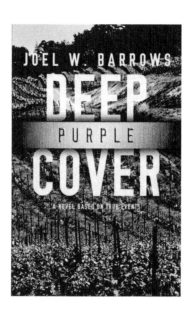

Deep Purple Cover
The Deep Cover Series
Joel W. Barrows

Down & Out Books
May 2022
978-1-64396-263-4

Things in Napa Valley are not as they seem. Everyone wants to get into the wine business, but at what cost?

When the co-owner of Pavesi Vineyards goes missing there are few clues to his disappearance. When his remains unexpectedly turn up, dark forces loom large.

FBI Special Agent Rowan Parks is assigned to the case and quickly realizes that the Bureau needs someone on the inside. There is only one person to call, her former lover, and ATF's greatest undercover operative, David Ward.

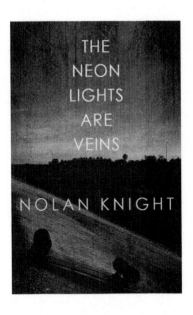

The Neon Lights Are Veins
Nolan Knight

Down & Out Books
May 2022
978-1-64396-265-8

The underbelly of Los Angeles, 2008; a place where hard-lucks scrounge for hope in gutters.

Alvi Drake is an aged pro skateboarder whose lone thrill is a pill-fueled escape from the terror of past ghosts. When news hits of the disappearance of an old flame, he sets out to find her— the biggest mistake in his track ridden life.

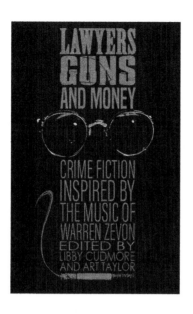

Lawyers, Guns, and Money
Crime Fiction Inspired by the Music of Warren Zevon
Edited by Libby Cudmore and Art Taylor

Down & Out Books
June 2022
978-1-64396-266-5

The songs of Warren Zevon are rich with crime and intrigue and suspense—guns and gunners, assassins and drug dealers, a supernatural serial killer, and a heap of hapless losers along the way too. And Zevon himself was a fan of crime fiction.

15 fantastic writers offer fresh spins on his discography with tales that span the mystery genre: caper, espionage, noir, paranormal, private eye, and more. Contributors include Gray Basnight, William Boyle, Dana Cameron, Libby Cudmore, Hilary Davidson, Steve Liskow, Nick Mamatas, Paul D. Marks, matthew quinn martin, Josh Pachter, Charles Salzberg, Laura Ellen Scott, Alex Segura, Kevin Burton Smith, and Brian Thornton.

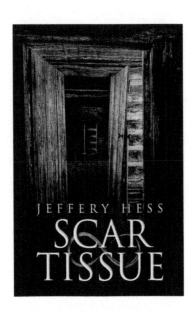

Scar Tissue
Jeffery Hess

Down & Out Books
June 2022
978-1-64396-267-2

A forty-year-old self-cutting workaholic abandons everything she knows for a stripper with a death wish. Both lives change, only one ends.

Scar Tissue is a psychological noir novel that stunningly brings to life a world others dare not dream of. This is a vivid and memorable portrayal of desire as seen through the eyes of two women with dark hearts and very different goals who cross paths at critical moments in their lives. The power of their hopes and despair, their weaknesses and strengths is a testament to the yearning that resides inside all of us.

Printed in Great Britain
by Amazon

82369859R00174